The Wideness of the Sea

By Katie Cu

D1506379

Published by Piscataqua Press
An imprint of RiverRun Bookstore, Inc.
142 Fleet Street Portsmouth, NH 03801
www.riverrunbookstore.com
www.piscataquapress.com

ISBN: 978-1-944393-40-3

Printed in the United States of America

To Rob, RJ, Sophie, Lucy, and Andrew, who lived through
the making of this book with grace, cheer, and love.

On The Sea
by John Keats

It keeps eternal whisperings around
Desolate shores, and with its mighty swell
Gluts twice ten thousand Caverns, till the spell
Of Hecate leaves them their old shadowy sound.
Often 'tis in such gentle temper found,
That scarcely will the very smallest shell
Be moved for days from where it sometime fell.
When last the winds of Heaven were unbound.
Oh, ye! who have your eyeballs vexed and tired,
Feast them upon the wideness of the Sea;
Oh ye! whose ears are dinned with uproar rude,
Or fed too much with cloying melody---
Sit ye near some old Cavern's Mouth and brood,
Until ye start, as if the sea nymphs quired!

Beauty is ever to the lonely mind a shadow fleeting; she is never plain.
She is a visitor who leaves behind the gift of grief, the souvenir of pain.

- Christopher Morley

Chapter 1

Anna had just finished the 10th grade the summer she first saw a blue lobster.

Her mother strolled out from the kitchen, wiping her hands on a towel, and walked over to where Anna was sitting in a crab apple tree with her sister, Marie, who was back home in New Harbor, Maine from college for summer break. "They've found a blue lobster down at the harbor," she called.

A moment later, Anna and Marie were riding their bikes the mile and a half to the harbor co-op, where the lobster boats unloaded their daily catch. The morning summer sun made the water so bright you could hardly see past the harbor bell, the horizon line a blinding flash of white. She squinted her eyes as she eased her bike down in the parking lot and ran toward the wall of traps that were lined up along the edge of the dock. There was a crowd already gathered; the lobsterman who had caught the rare lobster held it in a white plastic bucket, allowing all the people – kids mostly, idle in summer break – to see the azure blue creature up close. Anna pushed aside shoulders and elbows and knees until she stood behind a boy she didn't know hunched over the bucket. She stood on her tiptoes over his shoulder, balancing her palms on his back, straining to catch a view. When some kids pushed her from behind she was thrust into him until he fell over, catching himself on the sides of the bucket. "Hey, watch it…" he said, turning toward her.

His eyes met hers, and a flash of recognition followed. He was friends with her brother, two years older than her. He stared back at her, the length of his gaze starting to make her feel uncomfortable, like she had vertigo, or had been staring at the sun too long. She tried to say "sorry" but no words could come out of her mouth. The strands of her dark hair that stuck to beads of sweat on her forehead blocked her vision, and she pushed them out of her eyes.

"Here, do you want to take a look?" he asked, moving to the side. She stepped forward because she didn't know what else to do. She peered down and saw the blue lobster, looking like a glass version of itself, with lighter blue around the claws, and a more concentrated pigment in its body, sitting in a few inches of water. She knew from living in a harbor town how rare this was – only one in two million lobsters were born with this genetic anomaly. But the lobster also triggered something else in her. She knew that color.

"Ultramarine," she said.

"Huh?" Said the boy whose name she didn't know, but whose eyes she did.

"The color blue…of the lobster," she stammered. "It is just like the paint color named 'ultramarine'. I use it – I mean, my mom uses it all the time". She closed her eyes and could picture a painting of the lobster in her mind. She would mix in white to get the color of the claws, some black to get the shading around the legs. She was aware of the boy standing staring at her as she closed her eyes. She opened them and looked across the bucket at him. Just then, other viewers jostled her from her spot and swallowed her up. She strained to see the boy again, but he was gone.

That afternoon, she went into the barn and set to work putting the image in her head on a canvas. Her mother decided to join her and paint a blue lobster as well. As she worked, she kept thinking about those eyes. They were almost the same color blue. Andrew's eyes. She had asked her brother what his name was.

Anna Goodrich was pulled out of her memory by the voice of the man in front of her. He was tall, heavy set, and wore an expensive looking trench coat. He stood in the gallery where Anna worked in Mid-town, New York City, on a rainy Friday afternoon in April, weighing his decision between two paintings. One was an oil painting of a river in Upstate New York. The other was a painting of a lobster boat, the water a shade of ultramarine that looked electric, like a blue lobster, set off by the red and white of the boat.

"I think I just feel this one more," he said, gesturing to the lobster boat painting. "And I have loved the other works by this artist," he added. "I think it is a better investment overall." She knew he loved the painting; talking about the investment value was like giving the mind permission to fall in love, because it made sense. She had seen it happen before, and it was one of the reasons she loved working in the gallery when she wasn't painting. She would have told the man she was the artist if she wasn't so distracted by her daydream.

"I'll take it," he said. "Can you have it delivered to my wife on Third Avenue?" he asked as he wrote down the address.

"Of course," Anna said. "My pleasure."

"Be careful with ultramarine, it dominates so easily, it must be balanced by the other elements," her mother had said when she painted the blue lobster painting with Anna. By the time she had painted this picture of the boat, Anna had mastered this lesson.

Later that afternoon after she had closed the gallery, the spring air was so fresh and fragrant it beckoned her to walk home instead of taking the subway. The rain had given way to a warm sun that felt almost tropical to the New Yorkers walking around in their boots and duffle coats. Everything with roots started exploding; you could almost see leaves and blossoms unfurl before your eyes. The tree-tops were a lacy green against the blue sky and the pink blossoms on the redwood trees looked like cotton candy. A group of teenagers walked past Anna with all their sweaters and long sleeve shirts tied around their waists, punch drunk on shedding their layers. Rows of giggling preschoolers passed holding hands, like a chain of cut out paper dolls.

Anna skipped up the steps of her building, and made her way upstairs to the apartment she shared with her best friend, Georgia, a successful freelance photographer. The old floorboards creaked as she walked into her apartment, and as she set down her purse and coat, she saw that Georgia had dropped a stack of mail on the coffee table. It had been eight years since Anna had answered her room-mate ad when she moved to New York, and in that time, she had never been able to put it in the basket Anna had set out in the kitch-en specifically for mail. What she lacked in organization, though, she more than made up for in loyalty and spontaneous fun, which Anna considered a fair trade.

She set the mail in the basket then made her way to her clos-et to get dressed for the rooftop party they were all invited to that evening. As she looked through her closet to pick out something to wear, the end of the week fatigue crept over her and she almost con-sidered begging off the plans. She looked at the canvas in the corner of her room, an acrylic painting she was working on of couple at a table outside at a restaurant, and thought about how nice it would be to put on her most comfortable clothes, have a glass of wine and work on it. But she had barely seen her boyfriend, Raphael, at all that week, and he worked with the guys throwing the party. Georgia was also coming with her boyfriend Jake, so there was no way she could back out. Anna pulled out a black cowl-neck dress and resigned her-self to a Friday night out.

A few hours later, Anna stood with her long arm raised, black heels in an oily puddle, trying to hail a cab on Second Ave. As soon as she found one, she eased into the black pleather, staring out the window and letting the magic of the city lights lull her. As the cab stopped at a red light, she suddenly thought back to her day dream about the blue lobster. She closed her eyes and could picture painting with her mother in the barn, and could practically smell the mildew and cedar from the old abandoned stalls mingling with the smell of the paints. She loved having memories of painting with her mom, of learning from her. As she pressed her back into the seat, letting it hold up her fatigue, she held the whole lovely memory for a moment. When her phone rang, it popped like a bubble. It was Miranda, one of her favorite students at the Boys and Girls club, where she taught on Tuesday afternoons.

"Hey Anna, are we still on for the Met tomorrow?
  "You bet. 10:30 sound ok?"
    "Sure, I'll meet you by the front desk. Also, I wanted to ask you a favor – could you write my recommendation for the New School?"
    "Yes, of course," Anna practically squealed. She had been hoping Miranda could talk her mother into letting her apply. A single mother, Maria Rivera was raising Miranda, who was 14 and her sister, Gabriella, who was 12, alone on a hotel housekeeper's salary after their father died shortly after they had immigrated to the US from Mexico when the girls were little. Miranda had been taking classes with Anna since she was in third grade, and was a gifted artist. Anna tried to encourage her, and unofficially became a big sister to her. She loved her round face, infectious smile and shining dark eyes, and her big heart was always enthusiastic about something, whether it was a new paint brush or discovering a new artist.

"Anna, have you ever seen a Caravaggio? He is amazing!" she would exclaim, tossing her long, dark hair over her shoulder. The next week, she would greet Anna with her eyes wide. "Did you know that Frida Kalho once lived in New York!" she gushed as she set up her paint and canvas for the lesson.

Last month, Anna had gone to Miranda's apartment in the Bronx, which was small and clean, with plastic flowers on the kitchen table, though the building had broken windows, and the sound of shouting from various directions made Anna feel uneasy. She sat down with her mom, Maria, to talk about the New School, an art high school for gifted students near Central Park and Anna's gallery. Her mom wasn't excited about the studio hours the students were expected to put in on nights and weekends. She was eager for her to pick up some shifts doing laundry at the hotel once she was in high school.

"I don't see how art fairs and rich friends are going to help Miranda get a good job," she had said, her hair combed back into a pony tail, wearing the same red zip up hoodie that she had on every time Anna had met her. She was petite and curvy, and had a pretty face even without makeup. "I want her to get a good education, but the kind that gets you into a good college, not the kind that distracts you and helps you sell paintings in Central Park," her mother had said, her expression firm, her hand gently sliding a medallion of Our Lady of Guadalupe back and forth on a chain around her neck.

"She is so talented, though. This will get her into a good school, I promise," Anna pleaded.

"Let me think about it," Maria had said.

"How did you convince her?" Anna asked Miranda.

"I begged her. And I promised her I would clean apartments with my aunt all summer and save for the school year."

"I'm so glad, Miranda. Let's talk about the essay tomorrow at lunch after the Met, ok?"

"Ok, Anna. Thank you!" her enthusiasm contagious.

Anna smiled as she hung up her phone, and seconds later it buzzed again. She answered to the velvety sound of Raphael's voice.

"Hey hon, where are you?" he asked. "I just got here."

"I'm three blocks away, be there in a minute. By the way, I'm meeting Miranda at the Met tomorrow morning, so if you want to do brunch we have to go early. Did you still want to go with Georgia and everyone to dinner tomorrow night?"

"As long as I get to see you at all of it, it sounds good to me. And I'm glad you're going to see Miranda. You're pretty great with her, you know," he said, the sound of jazz music from the party seeping through the phone.

"She's a great girl. It's easy," Anna said. "Ok, I'm jumping out now, love you."

"Ok, see you in a second. Love you too," said Raphael.

Anna paid for the cab and threw her phone in her purse, and headed into the building.

She left it there, stashed next to the toaster in the minimalist white kitchen while she mingled with Raphael and friends on the gorgeous rooftop, the jazz somehow a perfect complement to the incredible views of the city. She always had fun with Raphael at parties – he made everyone laugh, his charm and his ability to make people feel good on full display. It wasn't until she saw the line for the bathroom and grabbed her phone for a distraction while she waited that she saw the messages; three from her sister, Marie, and one from her aunt. She set down her sweaty glass of Sauvignon Blanc in an empty space of the bookshelf and went back outside to call her sister. The air was pleasantly cool, and lights on the topiaries mingled with the lights of the skyline as she waited for her sister to answer. She glanced over at Raphael on the couch, laughing with friends, his brown hair slightly overgrown, making him look like a teenager. She wondered where her best friend Georgia was. She should have been here by now.

"Hello?" her sister answered in a muffled voice.

"Marie, what's going on? I have three messages from you," Anna asked.

"It's Uncle Charlie," said Marie. Her voice faltered and sounded like she had swallowed syrup. "He had a heart attack, Anna. He didn't make it."

The news hit hard, then slowly spread through her nervous system. The lights from the trees on the patio and the skyline blurred and she felt dizzy. She focused on the window in the building across the street, where an Indian couple stood in their kitchen making dinner, the woman's red sari standing out among a sea of gray brick.

"Oh God." She let out the breath she had been holding. "Oh my God. How's Aunt Catherine? How's Dad?" She thought of her aunt, Uncle Charlie's devoted sister, and her father, and how the three of them were always so close, their own unit with their own understanding of each other, how she had sensed this even when she was little. She cupped her forehead in her hand and then started to massage the muscles there.

"Aunt Catherine's in shock. Dad's broken up, but still . . . Dad." Anna watched the Indian couple, the woman gesturing at the stove as her much taller husband stirred what was in the pan. She seemed annoyed at whatever he had done to the dish. Anna had the sudden urge to check her phone for Uncle Charlie's number, to call him up and hear his voice, just to prove that her sister's words couldn't possibly be true.

"Should I come up there tonight? Or wait a few days? Do you know when they're going to have the funeral yet?" Anna's mind welcomed the switch from an unpleasant reality to simple, practical logistics. She started to think about her schedule, what she would have to cancel and switch around to make the trip. She worked at the Genevieve Keller Gallery in Midtown, just a few blocks from where they were tonight, and hoped that her boss would cover for her. She would have to cancel her plans with Raphael next week, dinner with friends and an art show. She looked over at him, his arm across the back of the couch, his other hand holding a Scotch, his face lit up from laughing. The discordant feelings of joy at seeing him and the devastating sadness seemed to crash together in her head, and it started pounding.

"Aunt Catherine already talked to the priest at St. Pat's. Monday or Tuesday would be best, considering the weekend mass schedule." Anna could hear her sister gently shooing away her two-and-a-half-year-old. Anna adored her nephew Henry, and smiled at the thought of him. Marie succeeded in bribing him with a lollipop. "Think you'll bring Raphael?" she asked.

"Not sure yet, I'll talk it over with him. He's with some friends at the moment so I'll wait till we head home. I'll call tomorrow, let you know our plans. Hey Marie, where'd it happen? The heart attack, I mean," Anna suddenly thought to ask.

"You know where they unload the lobster traps at the co-op? He was out there watching the boats coming in." Anna knew that spot. It was right where they had seen the blue lobster. How strange that she should think of that memory today.

Georgia came rushing up to Anna just as she put her phone down, her boyfriend Jake headed over to where Raphael sat. "You are not going to believe what is happening over there at that table," she said, kissing Anna's cheeks. "Cronuts. Cronuts are happening," Georgia gushed.

Anna sat stone-faced, not saying anything. "What's wrong with you? I say Cronuts and you say nothing? Did someone die or something? Oh my gosh, someone did, didn't they?"

Anna nodded, her chest and her throat tight. Finally she pointed to the bathroom, which mercifully had no line. She was so glad her friend was there in the safety of the tiny, warm bathroom.

"My uncle died. My sweet, sweet uncle. He was three years younger than my dad! He lived a mile down the road from us my whole life." Saying it out loud helped make it real. Her uncle had died. Vibrant, hilarious, bigger-than-life Uncle Charlie was gone.

"Oh, sweetie, I'm so sorry." She hugged her friend, and suddenly the balloon in Anna's chest burst, and tears started to overflow. Georgia pulled out a handful of tissues and put them up next to her cheeks, catching them as they fell.

A little later, after waving goodbye to everyone, Anna pulled her camel coat tighter around herself to ward off the spring evening and took hold of Raphael's arm as they walked to find a cab. His wide muscles felt nice under his white shirt, no doubt the same one he wore to work as a trader earlier that day, since it was Friday and they always went straight out for drinks after work. She waited until they were riding in the cab, the lights of the city hitting Raphael's face, illuminating his impossibly long eyelashes, to tell him.

"My sister called while we were there. My uncle Charlie passed away," Anna said. Her mind went back to his cozy white cottage on the ocean, where she had spent so much time growing up. For some reason she thought of the funny-shaped ice cubes his ancient freezer made that he always put in her soda. She could hear his strong voice laughing in her ear. She could see his brown eyes, so like her father's, always asking questions, and she could see the cigar in his hand that was practically an appendage. She loved the smell of his cigar. Her chest twisted as she thought of him, her mind trying to evade the painful information that he was gone.

"Was he the one we stayed wit' a few summers ago?" Raphael asked. "The one wit' the house on the harbor?" His very slight Argentinean accent came out sometimes after a few drinks. He reached out his hand to embrace hers, his nails too short from chewing on them, his skin perpetually tan. Anna thought back. They had been dating for almost four years, so it would be when they had just started dating that she had brought him home. The idea of staying with her father was out, since at that time she and her dad had barely spoken in almost three years, so they stayed with Uncle Charlie. Anna put her hand in his.

"Yeah," she said. She stared at Uncle Charlie's number on her phone. She longed to call him, to hear his voice again on the other line. "That's the one."

"I'm sorry, hon. He was an amazing guy. And one hell of a poker player."

Anna smiled at the memory of Raphael losing to her uncle that weekend. Nothing won respect for Raphael faster than bragging rights. "He was an amazing guy," she said nodding, the city lights blurred by her tears.

Chapter 2

"Raphael's not coming," Anna said to her sister the next morning. "He can't leave work at the moment. Something to do with China and U.S. treasuries, not sure what it's all about but he can't get away. I'm flying up tonight. Can I stay with you?" She tossed some socks and sweaters into a red suitcase as she spoke. She hoped her sister didn't catch the strain in her voice, giving away the disappointment she felt that Raphael couldn't come.

"I'll clean up the spare bedroom," Marie said, "but what about staying with Dad?"

Anna's brain cramped at the thought of entering her father's house, bags hanging at her side.

"Thanks, I'll take the spare room. Don't worry about the mess," Anna said. She heard Marie's muffled voice over the phone say to Henry, "No, honey, no cookies before breakfast, I said." Despite the cloud of grief she was in, she was excited to see her nephew. "So I'm flying into Portland at six forty-five. Sorry, I know that's right in the middle of dinner, but you'll be there, right?"

"I'll be there. Mike is home tonight, and actually, it will be nice to process everything," Marie said. "It is so hard to remember Uncle Charlie just died while I am chasing after Henry. Want to grab dinner in Portland on the way back?" she asked. The artsy port town was about an hour and a half south of her sister's house in Damariscotta, and Anna welcomed the idea of a night with her sister in such a cozy city.

"Sounds perfect," Anna said as she threw her makeup bag into her luggage. "See you soon."

Anna quickly called Genevieve's cell. Her boss picked up right away. "Why aren't you sleeping in like all the other twenty-some-things in this city?" she said with her typical sarcasm. Anna had learned long ago that this was just a cover for her vulnerable core. She also knew that Genevieve was already dressed, had walked her Corgi, and was seated at the café right across from her apartment like she was every Saturday morning at 8 am.

"Hey Genevieve. I'm actually heading to Maine for a funeral - my uncle just passed away suddenly. I'm not sure when I'll be back, probably next week." Anna stood staring at her reflection in the window of her living room, her long dark wet hair and white robe making her look even younger than her twenty-eight years.

"Oh, darling, I'm sorry to hear that. Take whatever time you need, of course. Sarah and I can fill in at the gallery on your days. Though I am dying to see what you are working on right now."

Anna glanced over at the large canvas in her living room. She liked the start of it, the older couple sat leaning into each other in a sweet way at the table outside a restaurant, her brush strokes bold though the scene came off as soft, but she was stuck on the woman's face.

"It can wait, of course. Call me as soon as you know when you're coming back. Big hugs, dear," Genevieve said. Anna knew she could count on Genevieve to be supportive. She was the closest thing Anna had to family in the city, beside Raphael and Georgia. Though she was fiercely competitive and had a sophisticated, cynical New Yorker attitude, she was quite maternal to Anna. They were lucky to have found each other years ago.

She put the phone down and tossed it into her bag with its charger. She glanced at the painting. It could wait. The city would barely notice she was gone. *Except for Miranda*, she quickly remembered. She pulled out her phone to text her.

Sorry, M. I have to go up to Maine for a funeral. My uncle just passed away suddenly.

In seconds, three little dots appeared.

Oh no, Anna. So sorry to hear it. My mom and I will pray for your family.

Thanks, love. Will get in touch when I am back in town and we'll reschedule, ok? And I will work on your essay while I'm in Maine, I promise.

Ok! Thank you! Anna laughed at the string of hearts and smiles the young girl sent back as a reply.

Anna also realized she should give Georgia a call – she had to leave early this morning for a photography job. "Hey Georgia, it's me, just wanted to let you know I'm headed to Maine for the funeral and everything, and I am probably going to stay with my family for a little while," she said. "Can you pile up my mail on my dresser? Thanks, Peaches, give me a call when you can." Anna shook the towel through her wet hair, and stared at the painting. She walked over, and realized exactly what the woman should look like. She picked up a brush, and suddenly filled in her face, the blush in her cheeks a cheerful red that matched the tulips in the window box behind her. She wasn't finished, but it was an improvement.

A few hours later, she sat at the airport with Raphael, the table littered with coffee stirrers and the detritus of their lunch. She was glad he came to see her off, a last deposit of moral support before the storm.

"I wish you could come with me," she said.

"I wish I could too, it's just the hardest time to get away. I'll call you every day, I promise. Please, try to take this time for you and your family. You'll be back before you know it," he said, his eyes smiling, his hands reassuring her.

"I know. It's just you're such a great distraction around my dad. Without you there I might actually have to talk to him."

"Look, as Uncle Charlie would tell you from his perch on a cloud, there might not be that much time left with your dad. Maybe you should go and try to smooth things over. As my grandfather from

Argentina used to say, find some *buena onda* with him. Good vibrations," he said. Something about the way he crooked his head and the earnest way he was trying to help Anna get along with her father made him look like a little boy, and she laughed out loud.

"Ok, Raph, I will go try to find some *bueno onda* with him."

At her gate, which felt unusually quiet for a Saturday afternoon, Anna bought every tabloid magazine in the bookstore. She looked over at the novels along the wall and sighed. There wasn't a brain cell left that could concentrate tonight. She just felt tremendously sad. That Charlie was gone. That she was traveling to his funeral alone. She dreaded the funeral. Her legs turned to live wires just as her feet turned to cinderblocks when she imagined the funeral home, the wake, the cemetery. She thought of all the time her family had spent at Uncle Charlie's house. His view of the ocean was so special, they just naturally gathered there for weekend meals and holidays. When her mother was still alive she used his boathouse for painting. Uncle Charlie always encouraged them to come over, especially after her mom passed away. She wished she could just walk into his house like she used to, grab a drink, look at the view, and listen to him crack jokes with everyone. She remembered how competitive he was, how he always wanted them to play poker so he could beat them and gloat. She thought she had more time to see him, to have another visit and play one more game of poker.

But most of all she was tired. Grief had curled through her body like a whisper of smoke and sedated every muscle. She wanted to lie down and never get up. But they were calling to board her plane, so she pulled herself up from the sticky leather seat and got in line.

She made her way to her seat and buckled in, and before they had lifted off the ground, she was asleep.

Anna woke to a soft dinging sound, a flush of the toilet, and someone coughing. A cold stream of air was coming at her from somewhere, and she pulled her cashmere cardigan closer around her shoulders. Her hair had fallen out of her ponytail holder, and she looked out the window with her blurry eyes as she fixed it. She could see her reflection in the window, and her blue eyes and rosy complexion stared back at her, though she could see dark circles under her eyes. There was a runway beneath them, and the sun was setting in the western sky, making for a dramatic horizon. She felt her stomach lurch as they descended, and she pushed the back of the seat in front of her to steady herself.

The owner of the cough glanced over at her, his blue oxford neatly pressed and his glasses making him look intelligent. "Looks like you don't enjoy this part," he said. He had the fingers of one hand inside a thick book while the other hand rested on his thigh. "What brings you to Maine?" he asked, his interest hard to ignore.

"A funeral," Anna said. Her throat was dry and her head hurt. The man stiffened and he crossed his arms.

"Sorry to hear that," he said.

"Thanks," she said. She wasn't feeling the least bit chatty, so she pulled out one of her magazines and feigned intense interest at the divorce of two movie stars. Thankfully, her neighbor followed suit and opened his book. They stayed that way until they felt the jolt of the wheels hitting the ground. Anna looked out her window, and a small pocket of her heart expanded as her eyes took in the landscape. It was filled with tall pine trees, not Christmas-tree shaped, but Northern white pine trees that had wide middle branches and narrow upper and lower branches. These were Maine pine trees. When she saw them, Anna knew she was home.

She checked her messages as she waited to get off the plane, and there was already one from Raphael. *Goodnight Anna. I love you. I'll call you tomorrow.*

She texted him back the same, then let Marie know she was there, and headed to baggage claim. Her phone dinged, *I'm outside,* just as her bag came around the carousel. She grabbed it and headed out to the sidewalk where her sister's silver minivan was waiting.

Anna was so happy to see her sister's dimpled smile and chestnut brown eyes. Her sandy blond hair was pulled back, and the bangs she had cut since Anna had last seen her were overgrown and resting in her eyelashes. They made her look youthful, and instantly transported Anna back to their childhood, when she wore bangs and ponytails every day.

"Hey there," her sister said, hugging her hard. "Feels like ages since I've seen you. You look great. Very sophisticated."

Anna glanced down at her leather jacket over her cardigan, and realized that her everyday dress in the city was considered dressed up in Maine. "Thanks. I think I just put on something that felt like armor to deal with all the heartache. Love the bangs. How's everyone doing?"

"Ok. They're in planning mode. But no one has made it to his house yet. I think Dad is planning on stopping there. To get his suit."

They both fell quiet as her sister made her way out of the airport. The reality kept hitting Anna anew, like a wave that kept crashing on the rock of her consciousness.

As the minivan settled onto the highway, Marie sighed. "Let's go get a drink in Portland," she said.

"Sounds perfect," Anna said.

As they drove she took in the roads that were so familiar to her but she had not laid eyes on in a long time. Their names and landmarks seemed to trigger her memory, like the negative of a photo. Portland had been one of her favorite towns ever since her mom used to bring them along to her art shows. They had rented a house one summer on Peak Island, a few miles out in Casco Bay, just a short ferry ride away from Portland. Her mom had spent the early mornings painting scenes from the island, and they bought ice cream from the tiny store, and picked wild blueberries in the bushes, and swam for hours in the chilly ocean waters, watching the ferry come and go.

They parked near the ferry landing, and walked around the cobblestone streets in Old Port. They picked a quiet bistro and settled into plates of comfort food. Immediately, their senses were ambushed with pleasure, from the glow of candles and the warmth of the fire, the smells of garlic and roasted meat. They settled into plush chairs under glowing sconces, and happily ordered a bottle of red from the cheerful server that moved with such grace, her smile permanently fixed. She returned with the wine and took their order, and as it breathed, so did they.

"I can't believe he's gone," Marie finally said.

"I can't either. Did he, you know, have any pain? Did he say anything when it was happening?" Anna asked, heartbroken to picture her uncle's last moments. "No, they said it was massive, he died very quickly."

"Do you think it's easier? To have it happen quickly? Or to have time, like we did with mom?"

"I don't know," Marie answered. "They are both so hard, but I guess to have time, to know, is easier on us. To have them feel no pain, though. That's easier on them."

Anna nodded and stared out the window. "Do you think he knew?"

Marie looked at her. "Aunt Catherine said he had stopped by her house that morning, just to say hi. It wasn't something he normally did. He brought over some coffee he thought she would like, gave her a hug, and shook hands with Uncle Joe. Isn't that weird?"

Anna thought of her daydream yesterday at the time her Uncle died. "I don't think it's weird. I think that sounds about right."

"I'm just relieved he didn't suffer."

Anna nodded. "How's Dad doing?"

"He's just really quiet. He hasn't talked about it much, other than logistics."

"Well that is hard to picture. Dad quiet?"

"He's taken it hard, Anna. Go easy on him this week, ok?"

The waiter reappeared and set down plates with glowing piles of meat and pasta.

"I wasn't going to go on him at all, Marie. If you recall he usually has a go on me," Anna said, diving into the pappardelle with a highly polished fork. "Anyway, I have a new motto I am trying out. *Bueno onda*. It means good vibrations in Spanish."

"Well, this food is giving me *bueno onda*," Marie said laughing. "This place is amazing. My short ribs are literally melting in my mouth. Hey, have you eaten at Stephen's restaurant yet?"

"No, I have been meaning to but Providence is three hours north of me. I haven't had that big of a window to trek up there," Anna said.

"Maybe after all this settles we can try to make it down there."

Anna agreed. "Or if he has pasta like this, even sooner." They ate until their stomachs were full and happy, even if their hearts were still heavy.

They got in the car and drove home, past Booth Bay, through Wiscasset, past Bath Iron works, through Damariscotta, the lights of the little town twinkling over the Damariscotta River, through Bristol, until they wound their way down the road to Pemaquid. This was where Anna had grown up - a small quiet town nestled out on a peninsula in mid-coast Maine. It was where all her childhood memories could be summoned, where despite its peace and tranquility, held the kind of power over her that a place called home seems to have.

When they got out at Marie's house, a cozy white colonial nestled into a wooded lot that had the ocean a hundred yards across the street, Anna looked up. How could she forget how brilliant the stars were here? It was like staring into a sea of diamonds, while being wrapped in navy blue velvet. In the distance, through the dark, she heard the ocean roaring and then ceasing, the rhythm echoing off the rocky coast, instantly matching some ancient rhythm deep in her veins. She turned around and followed her sister into the house, ready to face the hard week ahead together.

Chapter 3

When she had picked out the black wool Marni dress at a sample sale that winter, she'd had no idea she would be wearing it to her uncle's funeral. But she felt somehow stronger, ready to handle the tidal emotions of the day when the neat, fitted dress was zipped up, and she blessed the impulse that steered her to buy it. She brushed her hair and twisted it up loosely. She put on a touch of makeup and a strand of pearls, and sighed as she looked at her reflection. Raphael always told her that her beautiful eyes were her best accessory. *If he could see them now, he wouldn't say that,* Anna thought, touching the puff circles that had formed underneath.

The wake had been the night before, and they had been up late with their cousins, Sarah and Phillip and a few of their close friends. Aunt Catherine's kids were constantly trying to one up each other on their comedic timing, and they were such a breath of fresh air to be around. They had grown up with Anna and were a few years younger, and were now working nearby, Sarah teaching at the grade school in Damariscotta and Phillip a budding engineer at Bath Iron Works, designing ships. They had brought their well-honed drinking skills to their mom's kitchen and Anna drank beer and wine with them until one o'clock in the morning, telling stories about Uncle Charlie, and eating quiche and lasagna that friends and neighbors had dropped off. Aunt Catherine and Uncle Joe always joked that they couldn't wait until they moved out, but Anna thought they secretly loved still having twenty-somethings in the house. It made them feel young and needed.

Uncle Charlie never had any children. Somehow that was a comfort to her now; she didn't have to console his children. He had spoiled his nieces and nephews, giving each of them so much that his death had been a shock to them all. In the aftermath of such a hard night, the alcohol softened the leaden emotion that had settled down around their hearts. The result had been a rough night of sleep, and she sighed at the dark circles still under her eyes before patting her concealer on.

When she headed downstairs for breakfast, she greeted her brother-in-law, drinking coffee with the paper spread out in front of him at the farmer's table. His white T-shirt and stubble face were somehow endearing to Anna.

"Morning, Mike," Anna said. She heard a two-year-old shriek at her, then dodge under Mike's legs. "Morning, Henry!" She filled her coffee cup.

"Boo!" A very pleased, blond boy popped up, fire truck in one hand. "Boo, Auntie!" he said again as he struggled away from his father, coming close to bumping his head on the table as he made his way out from under it. Anna could see bits of Stephen and her dad in him, but he also looked a lot like Mike with his blond hair and Nordic genes. Mike liked to joke that he descended from Vikings, and offered as proof that his last name, Hansen, was really Hanssen a few generations back. With his fair coloring and stocky build and broad shoulders, it was easy to believe him, and friends and relatives had gifted his offspring with more than one Viking helmet when he was born.

"Whoa there, killer," Mike said as he reached for Henry. "Gonna hit your head." He picked up the child and placed him on the seat next to him. "Morning, Anna." He pulled out a chair for Anna next to Henry. "Auntie will be here for a few days, bud. You'll have lots of time with her." Anna sat down and sipped her coffee, smiling. She was unprepared for how much her nephew had grown since her last visit. His unconditional love surprised her most of all. Last time she had seen him, he was more concerned with the nearest cracker or toy, but now he was a little man with a sense of humor and big imagination.

"He's such a big boy now," she said, picking up his toy car that fell. "How are you doing, Mike? Are they treating you well at the hospital?"

"Things are good. Busy." Mike wiped up the coffee ring underneath his cup with a paper napkin. He was in Internal Medicine, and Anna loved to ask him about his most difficult cases, but before she could, Maria breezed in holding an outfit for Henry in her hands, her hair in wet strands around her face.

"Mike, can you put this on him after he eats some cereal? I am going to go finish getting ready. Hey, Anna," she said, kissing her quickly on the cheek. "If you're hungry, there are some bagels in the fridge or some cereal in the pantry." She poured herself coffee. "Have you talked to Stephen?" she asked, stirring in cream while pushing toys under the cabinets with her feet, out of the path of travel.

"Yes, he said he'll meet us at the church," Anna said. "The restaurant closed late last night and he had to drive up this morning. He said they're doing really well, considering they've only been open for a few months."

"That's great," Mike said as he poured cereal into a plastic bowl for Henry. "Gotta give it to your brother—it takes guts to open a restaurant in this economy."

Anna thought briefly of her brother. She had missed him terribly last night. His drive up from Rhode Island would normally be five hours, but with Boston traffic, he had to leave at four a.m. to make it to the funeral by 10. He would no doubt be exhausted when he got here. Anna felt another pang of guilt that she hadn't been there yet, and promised herself she would soon.

A light drizzle started as they ducked into the minivan to head over to St. Patrick's. The funeral was being held at the same Catholic Church they went to growing up, and where her mother was buried. She had been a devout Catholic, and they held her funeral there eight years earlier. It was fitting that they were going to say goodbye to Charlie there.

They made their way from Pemaquid through Damariscotta, which was a quintessential New England town, surrounded by inlets and estuaries, with picturesque views everywhere your eye landed. During the summer, people flocked here to drink in its coastal beauty, and the sidewalks that ran outside Main Street's shops and galleries and book stores would be completely full once the busy season started in June. Her mother had kept a gallery here in downtown Damariscotta. She had built up a name for herself when she had spent summers working with the artists on Mohegan Island, and was considered part of a group that was in high demand. The gallery held art from many different artists, but a lot of them were her mom's. She sold her beautiful coastal paintings to tourists all summer long. Anna had spent hours exploring the cafes, bookshops, and gift stores here on days when she joined her mother in the shop. When she died, they closed it, and put most of the paintings at Uncle Charlie's. Her father couldn't bear to be near them, and he couldn't bear to sell them.

The thought of seeing her father shortly made her stiffen. She had spoken to him last night only briefly. He had been a mascot for his extended family, greeting older relatives and friends, some of whom Anna didn't even know. She let him handle the mourners while she engaged with her cousins, and the night had slipped by without actually having to face him.

Now in the light of day, she realized she was avoiding him. As if he was reading her mind, Mike looked back to Anna as he stopped to let tourists cross the narrow street.

"When was the last time you saw your dad, Anna? Was it last Christmas?"

"Oh, you mean the time when he had too many Scotches before dinner and went off on me for working at someone else's gallery. How I was wasting my talent, my life. Yes, that's the last time I saw him," she said, her pulse racing at the memory, which she tried to calm by smiling at her nephew.

Marie put on her lipstick in the mirror on the visor.

"Hasn't he been like that ever since your mom passed away?" Mike asked.

"To put it mildly," Marie answered, flicking up the visor. "Ever since she died, he's just been really crazy about her pursuing her art. It's the reason Anna moved to New York. That and he was hounding her to work at The Foundation."

Anna rolled her eyes at the mention of the organization that was essentially their dad's fourth child. It was easier to just forget it existed.

"Your dad demanded that you work at The Foundation?" Mike asked Anna.

"Oh, he wanted me to start it with him. He had grand plans for us," Anna said. "Why shouldn't I want to devote my summers to helping budding artists find their way, especially since it was in my mother's name, and she had done the very same thing for me. No pressure there at all."

"He was a bit unfair about that," Marie agreed.

As if Anna's head didn't already hurt, from the wine and general sadness of the day, remembering how her father had built a flourishing summer enrichment program and was the toast of Anna's alma mater, the University of Maine's Orono campus in the summer time, not to mention the magazine features, newspaper articles, and a reoccurring spot on Maine's Public Radio that followed. It all just made her want to go home and put the covers over her head. She could see the headlines before her eyes: "Grieving Widower Gives Back" and "Art Professor Creates Legacy in Wife's Memory." Once, a reporter had called her at the Gallery to interview her for a piece.

"Can you tell me about how you must feel towards your father in creating the Therese Goodrich Foundation for Artistic Youth?" they asked.

"No comment," she had said right before hanging up.

How could she comment that her dad just wanted to control her life? The Christmas outburst was just another in a long line of arguments since her mother died, when his attitude toward her painting became an obsessive focus. Her talent had become apparent at a young age, and her parents had celebrated it. It was a source of closeness for her mother and her. Before he had just been support-ive, leaving the tending and nurturing to her mother. But since her death, his constant pressure that she must use her talent, must foster it and grow was so hard to bear in the wake of losing her mother.

When she graduated from college, she was exhausted from finish-ing school and her mother's death. She wanted to take a break from painting. She couldn't make her brush do what it used to, couldn't make the canvas look like what her mind saw. But no matter how she pleaded with him, he would not stop pushing her toward some serious next step. He couldn't hear that she needed time to grieve. She had to get away from the pressure.

After she left Maine and moved to New York, they didn't speak for three years. It took a long time for Anna to stop being angry. And since she was so angry, he barely acknowledged her at family gatherings. It was impossible to have a relationship with him. Anna felt frustration at the pressure, for sure, but the deeper wound was the complete lack of empathy, of support. Especially while trying to cope with the hardest thing she had ever gone through—her moth-er's death. It felt like she had lost both parents at the same time.

"I think I recently started to find some empathy for what he must have been going through at that time," Anna said, watching the windshield wipers pulse. "But it's eight years later, and he is still treating me like a failure. Even if I wanted a prodigal homecoming, it would require him to have some open arms, which doesn't seem likely."

Marie handed Anna some tissues. "I had hoped you guys had finally moved forward—or at least started to talk civilly to each oth-er—at Henry's christening two years ago. Remember when I pulled you aside and begged you to be a family again for Henry's sake? You both looked at each other, and then he'd shrugged and said, 'A family for Henry it is'?"

"Yes, that weekend we tried to make small talk and we were cor-dial. But by the end of the weekend, in place of cold shouldering me and freezing me out, he picked up where he left off, trying to steer my choices toward his idea of a successful art career, doing grad school at RISD or NYU, working at the Foundation in the summer, helping him keep our mother's memory alive."

"Sounds like you all got lost in the woods when you lost her," Mike said. "You need a compass to find your way." Marie nodded and squeezed Mike's shoulder.

"It seems like the only person John Goodrich ever took directions from was our mom," Anna said. "So I don't see us finding our way back anytime soon."

As they pulled into the churchyard, Anna took in St. Patrick's. At the front, it was an old brick church built in the 1700s. Behind it, a larger wooden church had been erected, and Anna had always admired the different shades of tan and cream they had used to paint the exterior and interior of this church. The neutral background set off the colorful stained-glass windows in a dramatic fashion, and the whole effect was so beautiful, she found she couldn't take her eyes off it as they got out of the car. She held Henry's hand as they walked across the gravel parking lot. As she took in the scene she felt an immediate desire to come back here and paint it. She hadn't brought any of her supplies, but she mentally noted that a visit to the art-supply store would suffice.

As they walked inside the vestibule, she spotted Aunt Catherine with her arm on her husband, Uncle Joe. Phillip and Sarah stood behind her, talking to the priest. She walked over to give her a hug, making sure that Marie still held on to Henry's other hand. "How are you holding up today?" Anna asked her when she reached her side. She saw her aunt's watery, puffy eyes, and though she knew she had taken great care at her appearance—she always did—she could see the physical toll of losing her brother roll across her features.

"I'm all right, damn it," she said. Her eyes began to fill as she spoke. "I'll be all right. How are you dear?" she asked as she pushed a tissue in the corner of her eye.

"The wine helped." Anna shrugged. "So does seeing your children. It's great to have all the cousins together again. If there's anything good in this situation, it's being together as a family." Anna was so distressed at seeing her usually solid, jovial aunt cry that tears sprang to her eyes. This wasn't their first time comforting each other.

"Come on, let's go sit down," Aunt Catherine said as she reached her ample arm around her. "You look beautiful, dear."

As they made their way toward the pews, Anna saw her brother, Stephen, entering the church. She made her way toward him, where they quietly hugged each other. "Where's Raphael?" he asked.

Anna's heart tugged at the topic of Raphael. "He couldn't leave work—the markets were going to be choppy today and there was a lot at stake. He had to be there." She found herself apologizing for him, wishing her strong, sweet boyfriend was right next to her instead of hundreds of miles away at his desk. She wasn't in the mood to examine it now, and she switched gears quickly.

"How was your ride up? You must be exhausted," she said.

Stephen nodded his head. Anna noticed that exhausted barely covered how tired her brother looked.

"It's crazy, but I couldn't have missed this. They'll have to survive one night without me." He grinned broadly, his wavy brown hair shorter than the last time she had seen him, and with more gray hairs filling his temple. Stephen always made you feel like you were the most important thing to him at the moment, like her mother always did, and Anna was basking in the feeling.

Marie joined them and leaned in for a hug, Henry at her heels. "Hey, little man," Stephen gushed, quickly squatting down to give Henry a high five. Henry didn't even pretend to be shy; he just went in for the kill. "Uncle Stevie!" he squealed as he hugged his uncle. "D'you have a 'prise for me?" Stephen had conditioned him for this question. He always showed up with a little gift for his nephew. "Well, let's see. I think I might." And he pulled out a Matchbox car from his suit jacket.

Just at that moment—Anna could almost feel him coming—John Goodrich strolled into the church, his tall presence commanding, an effect that was amplified by his distinguished appearance. White hair and mustache, well-tailored charcoal gray wool suit. Marie had inherited his olive skin and round dark eyes, one of the only gifts his Italian father had given him. Both Anna and Stephen had fair skin, dark hair, and blue eyes like their Irish mother. His posture gave strangers the impression he was the head of a business or perhaps a politician, but in reality he was a retired art history professor who had spent his career at Bowdoin college in nearby Brunswick, Maine. Anna noticed that he had more wrinkles around his eyes, and his stomach had started to put on the suggestion of a pouch, though he had always been slim like Stephen. *He is getting older*, Anna thought.

"Stephen," he said. He put his hand on his son's shoulder. They shook hands, then hugged quickly. His eyes displayed a warmth, though either the sad occasion or his stoicism eclipsed the sentiment from becoming a full smile.

"Hey, Dad," Stephen said. "I'm so sorry about Uncle Charlie." He let the words out raw and strong.

"The bastard beat me to it. Sixty-six years old, and here I am pushing seventy. It was that damn board of directors of the bank that killed him, obviously." He spoke loudly, and a few heads from the other side of the church turned in his direction.

Just then a man came to tap him and he then turned to Stephen. "The hearse is here. Will you help carry the casket?" At the word *hearse*, Anna was snapped back into the reality of the day. It hit her hard. A bagpiper began to play. She looked over at her aunt and sister crying, and her eyes welled with tears. She sat down next to Henry, and was so grateful to have the little boy's hand to hold as the casket entered the church.

As she stared at the dark brown casket, she tried to remember Uncle Charlie. His habit of telling bad jokes. His love of Johnny Walker, lobster, and watching *Charlie Rose*, the PBS talk show. He was a funny guy, and though his zest diminished a little with age, he still loved to have everyone gathered in his backyard, facing the water, a big cocktail in his hand, smoking cigars with her father under the stars.

"*Grant them eternal rest, O Lord*," the priest said.

Anna remembered one Christmas when she was probably six. She had gotten a new bike, her first, and had brought it to Uncle Charlie's when they went over for Christmas dinner. While the women made dinner, and her dad helped Stephen assemble a model airplane, he went out with her to practice riding the big bike for almost an hour until she got it. She remembered his cheeks rosy with cold, his brown corduroy pants dirty from kneeling down and adjusting the seat height. He cheered her on like a high school football coach. Of course, she had loved him fiercely ever since. Her chest ached at the memory, and tears fell onto her dress.

"*And may perpetual light shine upon them,*" the priest continued, sprinkling holy water on the casket.

Anna suddenly realized a huge part of the hurt of losing Uncle Charlie was losing her history. He was part of the memories of her life before her mom died. Before she had moved away. She wanted every part of that life to stay here, preserved, up in Maine, so when she was ready she could come back to it. But now, he was gone. She suddenly realized with a sharp sting of regret that the people who know you well, that have known you for your whole life, are irreplaceable. No new addition in your life can ever have what you shared with them. Your past is gone, except for the people who carry it with you. But they take that part of you with them when they go.

Anna believed perpetual light would shine on her uncle. She just wished she could feel some of it on her right now too.

After the Mass, the family went to the cemetery, and the cold, steel-gray sky cooperated in echoing the feelings of everyone there. Though Anna's mother had been buried at St. Patrick's, Uncle Charlie was being buried down the road. The service was mercifully short. Anna felt numb. She couldn't help but notice a dandelion growing right next to the hole they had dug for Uncle Charlie. It felt mocking; a sign of spring next to cold emptiness. She couldn't believe he was going to stay there, in the ground, the mocking dandelion his only companion. A wind was coming in strong from the ocean, whipping every lose strand of hair into a frenzy. A light rain started to fall as the ceremony finished, and they walked away from the cemetery holding their hands or purses or coats over their heads.

Marie put her hand on her sister's arm as they were walking. "Hey, Annie," she whispered, "don't you think you should ride over with

Dad, you know, so he's not all alone?" She nudged her sister's arm as she spoke. Anna wanted to ride in her sister's minivan, distracted by the musings of her nephew, but she knew her sister was right. She could only ignore her father for so long. She stepped carefully across the gravel onto the wet grass, her patent-leather heel getting caught a few times on her way over to her father's black sedan.

"Hey, Dad. Mind if I ride with you?" she asked, though she opened the door and climbed inside before he could answer.

The ride to the restaurant was not long, but within the first few miles Anna found herself glancing at the clock on the dashboard. "So how are you feeling?" she asked, knowing that a direct emotional assault was the least successful way to get her father to talk, but she couldn't seem to muster the energy for idle banter. She looked over at his thick white hair, his gray mustache that was tinged with brown around his mouth from his cigars. She even noted how handsome he looked in his suit.

"As well as can be expected, I guess," he answered. Anna nodded and stared out the window, glancing at the Maine pine trees, the stone walls, the wet muddy roads, mentally taking in the tragic beauty of the wet spring day. Life and death and new life seemed intertwined with each other, giving her vertigo.

"So how is the big city?" her father managed after the silence had become thick.

"Fine, I guess. Busy." She was stealing Mike's line.

"Have you looked into any art programs lately?" he asked.

The muscles in Anna's shoulders tightened, and she reminded herself to breathe in slowly. "No, actually, I haven't. I'm happy at the gallery."

"Glad you can be happy selling other artists' work," he said. His tone was casual, but Anna knew behind this statement was the minefield she discreetly tried to sidestep every time she came home.

"It's a living," Anna said, trying to smile.

"But it's not a life," her father replied, turning into the parking lot of the Irish pub.

Anna was relieved, since she suddenly craved a good strong drink.

That afternoon, after saying goodbye to family and friends, Anna, Marie, Stephen and their cousins, Sarah and Phillip, decided to head over to one of their favorite hangouts, Shaw's Wharf, a local seafood restaurant and bar on the harbor. They had asked their dad to join them, but he begged off, saying he was too tired, much to Anna's relief. Aunt Catherine and Uncle Joe were still hosting some out of town family at their house and told the kids to go have fun. Anna was so glad that Mike offered to take Henry home for a nap and told Marie to join them.

They sat looking out at New Harbor, a busy working harbor scattered with buoys and lobster boats and skiffs. The bar was open to the elements, with no doors, just a wooden beamed ceiling overhead and a dock below, though plastic barriers managed to ward off some of the chill. They arrived around four o'clock, just as the lobster boats were rolling in with the day's catch, which was mostly cod at this time of year. They had changed into jeans and sweaters, and despite the tense muscles and ever-present fatigue Anna had felt since her sister's phone call last Saturday night, it felt cozy and comforting to be at a favorite spot with such beloved company on a Tuesday night. Her uncle's funeral had temporarily hijacked their lives, and Anna was discovering that it was a much-needed break. She felt something in her soften and relax, some part of her she had forgotten. She had missed her family connections. She had missed home, missed Maine, more than she had realized.

It wasn't that she was miserable in New York. It was exciting and fun living in the city. But there were these moments – when she was day dreaming, or riding the subway, that she felt disconnected from parts of herself. When she was doing her art, she forgot about it and was able to be in touch with something real. But when she was alone, she could feel something was off. And then oddly, when she was around other people, at a dinner party or sitting on the couch next to Raphael reading the paper, she sometimes suddenly felt very alone. She chalked this up to losing her mom, perhaps. Or just being an artist. Besides, she knew she could call Marie or Georgia, and she wouldn't feel this way with them. Most of the time she pushed away the feeling, telling herself not to feel too sorry for herself.

She reached for her plastic cup, filled with the local microbrew, the coldness of the beer mixing with her chilly fingers, when she looked up and saw a face she recognized. He was making his way over to where Anna sat at the bar, with his thick, sandy-blond hair going in a million directions, his weathered face, and his blue eyes the color of her favorite blue paint - ultramarine. He had on bright orange overalls and rubber boots. She was staring at Andrew Toomey.

It was such a surprise, though it shouldn't have been. Anna had sat at this bar many times with Andrew, when his day on the boat was done and she had missed him enough to wait for his return. He started out working with his father, but toward the end of the time they were together, his dad's MS had progressed, and he started taking over more and more of his dad's territory. Anna knew he had been working toward his own boat when they finished college.

"Hey, Anna, if you needed another emotional highlight of the day, how about running into your old boyfriend?" Marie said under her breath.

"Where?" Stephen asked, turning around conspicuously. He had been friends with Andrew first, after all.

"Could you be any louder?" Anna whispered. She froze a bit, though she wasn't sure why. She had nothing to be afraid of, yet she felt her legs shaking under her jeans, and she couldn't seem to take a deep breath.

He walked right next to where the three of them were seated, an arm's length away. If Andrew had spotted her yet, he didn't look like he cared one bit. She heard him talking to the bartender over the low music playing. "Two Pemaquid Ales," he ordered. Anna looked up again and realized his friend Chris was standing right beside him, tall and stout-chested with a thick dark beard. He had often helped Andrew out as sternman. He turned to Chris in his orange overalls and handed him a beer.

It was Stephen who broke the ice. "Hey, Andrew, haven't seen you in ages," he said, his tone friendly as he reached out his hand.

Anyone would be happy to see Stephen.

Andrew slowly turned around. "Oh my Lord, Stephen? Stephen Goodrich?" And just like that, Anna saw his eyes flick toward her. The expression on his face was a mix of shock and something like fear. "Anna?" he said, his voice barely a whisper.

Anna had regained herself slightly, enough to slide off the barstool and come around for a hug. "Hi there, Andrew. It's really nice to see you." She hugged him quickly, and then sat down again facing him. She was surprised at the truth of that statement. She could feel the shock subside and a swell of joy rise up in her, childlike, pure happiness in being near him.

"What are you all doin' here?" Andrew asked. Anna still registered shock in his tone, but something else made her a bit guarded, like she had trespassed on someone's lawn.

"Our Uncle Charlie passed away," she said. Anna remembered all the times Andrew had joined them for a holiday or a Friday night fish & chips feast at her uncle's house. He no doubt remembered him well. "We had the wake last night and the funeral today." Keeping to specific facts helped her avoid the tide of her thoughts.

Andrew finally broke out of his stupor and sat down towards them, gesturing to Chris to do the same. He reached for his beer and took a large sip. "That's right, I think I heard the news but didn't connect . . . I didn't realize you'd all be here. I'm so sorry to hear it. Your Uncle Charlie was one of a kind, and we will all miss him." He took a sip of his beer and looked up, and Anna could feel the weight of his eyes on her, in her chest and hands and legs. It took her by complete surprise that her ex-boyfriend from high school and college, whom she hadn't seen in more than seven years, would have this effect on her. She hadn't even had a passing thought about him in months, besides the day in the gallery when she remembered the blue lobster. She struggled to speak, but Stephen again stepped in.

"We're just here for a couple days. How are you? Still fishing, I see." Stephen gestured toward the harbor.

Andrew nodded his assent. "Carrying on the family business." The change in conversation was a relief, and Andrew seemed to snap into a more personable version of himself, the kind you'd meet at the gas station or a wedding. "Except for a few spots, lobster fishing starts May 1st and ends December 1st, but there are a lot of limits on when you can pull up traps during that period, to help keep overfishing in check. The summer months are the easiest time to work since the lobsters come to shallower waters when the temperatures rise. Right now, we've been fishing for cod mainly this weekend, testing out a new engine and gear. Sort of a spring break to get ready. Chris has been helping me out." He looked like he had more to add but took a sip of beer instead.

"He pays me in beer," Chris said. He looked just as Anna remembered him from high school, and was built like a bear, with chocolate colored hair and eyes, and a sense of humor that charmed everyone around him. He must have stayed in Pemaquid, helping Andrew.

Anna listened, remembering the hoarse, strong voice, no trace of a Maine accent, just a clear intelligent softness mixed with a confidence that always seemed to help him to use fewer words to get his point across. She found she was very curious which boat was his and looked out over the names painted in the back left side of the boats in the harbor. Her eyes landed on a white boat with green and black paint and the words *Christina Therese* across the back. That must be it, she thought, since Christina was his mom's name. She hadn't known her middle name, but it was interesting to note that it was the same as her mother's name, Therese. She found it endearing that he honored his mom with his boat.

"Is that one yours?" Anna asked, pointing to the *Christina Therese*.

"Good guess," Andrew answered. He looked out at the water, something pulling on his face, and perhaps would have been lost in thought if Marie hadn't chimed in as well.

"How's Lizzie doing?" she asked. "I've been meaning to catch up with your sister since we moved back from Buffalo last year. My husband, Mike, did his residency there, and I lost touch with everybody. Is she still as funny as ever?"

Andrew smiled and nodded. "As a matter of fact, she bartends here on the weekends. You should stop in and see her. She mentioned you have a baby, right? How old?" he asked as he took a sip of his beer.

"He's two and a half," Marie said. Her dimpled smile revealed maternal pride, her brown eyes shining. "That's so funny that she's been here the whole time—we'll have to come down and do dinner on the weekend. Henry would love it. We'll bring the fishing poles and fish off the dock. Actually"—she stopped, hesitating on her next sentence and catching Anna's eye as she spoke— "maybe Henry could head out on your boat sometime, during lobster season?" She looked at Anna with a guilty expression. Anna pictured her sweet nephew on the *Christina Therese*. There was something surreal about the way these events were unfolding. But she couldn't blame Marie. Henry would love the boat ride and the lobsters.

Andrew lifted his hands as an invitation. "You're all welcome, anytime." He seemed to look over at Anna cautiously after he said it, maybe gauging her response. Then he added, "It'd have to be after the second week in May, though; that's when the official season starts this year. I'm going to be busy before that anyway." Andrew reached into his pocket and grabbed his wallet. "Actually, I should be off now too." He glanced at his watch and finished his beer. "How about I give you my number?" he said to Marie. He grabbed a napkin and a pen from next to the register and scribbled his number down, his callused hands under his rolled up shirt sleeves triggering a wave of memories in Anna. "Give me a call anytime this summer; I'd be glad to have you and your squirt tag along. Maybe we could catch up with Liz too, do dinner here. And feel free to come along too," he said in the direction of Stephen, Anna, Sarah and Phillip. He handed the napkin to Marie, and then looked right at Anna and said, "Good seeing you." As they got up to leave, Andrew turned with a wave.

Anna watched him walk up the steep ramp that led out to the parking lot. She listened as the seagulls cried out, fighting over the fishermen dumping their scraps. The smell of the briny air and the sounds of the harbor washed over her like she was waking from a familiar dream, and Andrew walking away just added to the effect. She could almost feel a part of herself rising up like an anchor, like the tide coming into the harbor.

Later that night, after saying goodnight to Marie, she lay down in bed with a mystery novel, and tried to read. But her thoughts kept returning to Andrew. It had been such a surprise to see him. She gave up on the book, turned out the lights, and tried to sleep. Her mind involuntarily summoned up memories of him. Like putting the needle on the first groove of a shiny black record, she started playing the story of Andrew, from the beginning.

After that day on the dock when they saw the blue lobster, Anna tried to avoid him at school. Andrew was a senior, along with her brother, and she was a sophomore. Of course he would never notice her. Whenever she saw him, she froze. She couldn't believe the power one pair of eyes could have on her. Her school days started to become a running awareness of where he might be, and what he might be doing. If she bumped into him in the cafeteria, or in the hall, she almost detected a flicker of his attention turn her way, but then she talked to herself. "Forget it, Anna. He's a senior. He barely even knows you exist." She distracted herself with friends and soccer and a challenging schedule, and painting with her mom. And then, one day late in October, after soccer practice, she walked out into the parking lot to meet Stephen. His soccer practice ended at the same time, and he was her ride home. As she walked outside, a big fluffy snow flake fell onto her eyelashes, and then another. By the time she reached his car a light layer of white snow had settled on it. The cold air woke her senses up, and the snow was everywhere she looked, kissing her skin wherever the flakes landed and melted. Her cheeks were red when she saw Stephen coming toward her. "Can you believe it?" she laughed, holding out her hands. He replied by scooping up some snow, and making a tiny snowball, then hitting her with it. She looked down in mock horror at where it had hit her, and when she looked up, there was Andrew. He was smiling at her, the infectious fever of the snow lighting up his eyes. Freshly showered, his hair was damp, and his cheeks glowed red.

"We're giving Toomey a ride home," said Stephen. "Give him the front," he said, in typical brother fashion.

"*Whatever,*" Anna said back.

"*That's ok, you can have the front,*" Andrew offered.

"*No, really, it's fine,*" Anna said, flustered, her cheeks burning from his attention.

They drove the fifteen minutes back through Damariscotta to Pemaquid, the wipers beating back the clouds of snow, the boys bantering about someone on their team. Andrew looked back at Anna a few times, and their eyes caught. It felt so intense, she buried her nose in a book and stopped looking up.

When they got to Andrew's house, Stephen lunged out of the car and scooped up more snow, and chucked it at his friend as he tried to get out. Andrew shot back in rapid fire motion. "*Anna, help me!*" Stephen called to her. She laughed, and came out of the car, and with her bare hands, scooped up snow. But instead of throwing it at Andrew, she threw it at Stephen.

"*That's for hitting me in the parking lot at school,*" she yelled.

"*Let's take him down!*" Andrew shouted. Together they cornered him in front of Andrew's garage, a snow-covered row boat parked on the side of the driveway closing him in with no escape. When they had shown no mercy, and Stephen held up his hands in surrender, he shouted out, "*I give up. I need a towel.*"

"*Go look in the bathroom right across from the door. There should be some under the sink,*" Andrew said, laughing. He was breathing hard, and little puffs of steam floated out as he exhaled. Anna was in a similar state, and started to shake her hands which were red and wet, and almost numb. She put them together and breathed into them. "*Here,*" Andrew said as he came closer. He took of his flannel shirt, and wrapped it around her hands, holding it with his own hands to warm them up. Underneath it, he had on a white t-shirt, and she could see his biceps peeking out underneath them, and the solid mass of his forearms, the golden carpet of hair on them matching his eyebrows. He looked at her, and she smiled up at him. "*Better?*" he asked. She nodded, and then Stephen was back outside.

"*Ok, next time, I'm wearing gloves, and I am going to take no prisoners,*" he said laughing. "*But I gotta get out of these wet clothes before I get frostbite. C'mon, let's go,*" he said to Anna.

They broke apart, and Anna handed him back his shirt. "Thanks,"
she said. Andrew smiled from ear to ear. It was that grin. That smile
that undid her.

"Anytime," he answered, practically in a whisper.

The next day at school, in between math and chem, Anna closed
her locker, and he was suddenly standing there, his blond hair messy,
his blue eyes clear. "Hi there," he said.

"Hi," was all Anna could manage to say. She was positive he could
hear her heart racing, since the sound of it beating had suddenly flood-
ed her ears.

"I was wondering, do you have plans on Friday?"

"No, I don't...I don't think so." In truth, Anna had no idea, since
she couldn't think about anything other than the sound his voice.

"Oh, good, because I was wondering if you want to see a movie,"
he asked nervously, but with so much politeness it made Anna smile
as a reflex.

"Sure, you mean, with Stephen?"

"Actually, I thought it could just be you and me," he said softly,
tilting his head to one side.

"Oh, right. Sure, I'd love to," she said, nodding slightly.

"Ok, great. I'll pick you up at 6, ok?"

"Sure, 6 o'clock sounds good." She was still nodding. She actually
realized she hadn't stopped nodding since he had asked her out. She
willed her head to stop moving.

"Ok, great. I'll just...I have to run to history, but I'll see you then."

As Andrew walked away, Anna realized with a twinge that Fri-
day was still two days away, and she wondered how she was going to
handle her heart until then, which seemed to have turned into a bass
drum.

The movie was funny. He held her hand, and she tried hard to
make it stop trembling by holding her arm. When he dropped her off,
he kissed her gently, on the lips, once. Her first kiss. It felt simultane-
ously like ice and liquid fire floated through her.

"I had a really good time tonight, Anna. Can I see you again?" he
asked sweetly, his thumb gently brushing her cheek. His gaze felt like a
warm light glowing on her.

She smiled up at him. "I'd like that."

He kissed her again, briefly, and then she turned around and walked into her house, and headed straight to her room. Her mom might have said something to her but she couldn't hear anything, since she was floating in a bubble. She lay down on her bed, and replayed every second of the night in her head, over and over, until she fell asleep.

They were inseparable after that. Until Andrew left for college. And the years he was in college, they were inseparable on the weekend. Her mom joked that she had gained another child, since Andrew was always on their couch watching movies, or eating dinner over, or celebrating holidays with them. When they weren't at Anna's house, they were at Andrew's, watching TV with his parents or stacking traps, or they were out on the lobster boat, working his dad's territory.

And then she followed him to University of Maine at Orono. They studied together in library, ate dinner together every night. They grew even closer, if that was possible. Her dad was mad that she hadn't gone to a more prestigious school, but those years with Andrew were the happiest ones of her life. She just remembered laughing whenever they were together.

Anna opened her eyes, and looked at the glow the front door lights cast on the wall, the shadow of branches waving in the window dancing across the space. Remembering how much she had loved him felt odd, like remembering a dream. *A really wonderful dream,* she thought as she drifted off to sleep.

Chapter 4

"So there is going to be a reading of the will," her father said briskly into Anna's phone as she was filling her sister's car with gas. It was Wednesday, the day after Uncle Charlie's funeral, and they were headed back from the grocery store. She had been contemplating when to return to New York but wanted to hang around for a few days, to help their dad and aunt handle cleaning up Uncle Charlie's house, but she also just wanted to spend more time with her family, and soak up being together after losing Uncle Charlie. She felt comforted being in Maine, where she had loved him, where her family had spent so much time together when he was alive. This trip made her realize just how long she had been gone. She stood up and adjusted her Ray-Bans on top of her head before she balanced the phone and the pump at the same time.

"A will?" Anna asked. The thought hadn't occurred to her. Her main experience in the funeral-and-death department had been her mother's. There wasn't a reading of the will since everything just went to her dad, save a few smaller accounts for each of the kids. But Uncle Charlie had no wife or children—his brief marriage right after college ended sadly when his wife declared she couldn't live in Maine and went back to her parents' farm in Georgia. He just had his brother and sister.

"Don't you and Aunt Catherine just split everything?" Anna

asked, the logic from her last experience carrying over.

"I don't know what it says," her dad said. His voice sounded pained to have to explain this much to her. "I don't know what Charlie arranged, and I never thought to ask him." His father and his brother were close, playing rounds of golf throughout the summer and meeting up to watch big sports games. But by nature, John and Charles Goodrich were loners. While Anna's father had chosen academia, becoming a tenured professor of art history at Bowdoin College, his brother had been a banker, quietly running a regional bank and keeping it from takeovers until he retired, when it was subsequently taken over. Neither of them spoke about deeply personal matters very much, and Anna couldn't imagine them having a conversation about wills.

"Well, when do we need to be there?" she asked, climbing into the passenger seat. Her sister looked up, curious, having only heard a part of the call.

"The lawyer was asking if everyone could meet on Friday morning," he said. "I don't know if Stephen can arrange it, but I'll call him next and let you know."

"Hang on and I'll ask Marie." Anna put the phone across her chest. "Can you meet with Uncle Charlie's lawyer on Friday morning? Dad says there is a will."

"Sure, I can bring Henry with stuff to keep him busy, I guess. Mike doesn't need to be there, right? He's on this whole weekend."

"Hey, Dad, Marie and I can make it. Mike doesn't need to come, right?"

"No, just Marie," he said. "Let's make it ten o'clock, so Stephen can make it."

"We'll be there," Anna said. "Oh, and Marie said you have to come over for dinner tonight. We just got the makings for beef stew. Six o'clock."

Anna heard a silence and then, "Ok, I'll be there," and then the click of the phone, since he had hung up.

That afternoon, Anna left Henry napping and her sister contentedly making beef stew, her white apron tied neatly around her waist. Though Stephen was the professional, her sister shared his culinary prowess. Anna loved to eat good food but seemed to lack the good-cooking gene, which she ardently wished for every time she had a kitchen disaster. She started to feel hungry already as she drove Marie and Mike's red pickup truck into Damariscotta to get some art supplies. She wore her coziest pair of jeans, filled with holes and faded to a light blue, and a white long-sleeved T-shirt beneath her gray cardigan. Other than her uncle's wake and funeral, she hadn't put on any makeup or blow-dried her hair since she had arrived. Though she felt a sadness ready to pounce on her consciousness every time she thought of Uncle Charlie, she also felt clean and light, buoyed in the freedom or being in nature, away from the city, and being around family.

The day was gorgeous. Singing birds mingled with the sun-drenched sights of spring green buds and grass, the splashes of yellow from the daffodils and forsythia, and the red and white and pink tulips from eager gardeners. Anna noticed that even a concrete barrier in a parking lot had a creeping flower vine climbing over it, as if the ground itself was reaching up to cover banal with beauty. As she drove down the winding roads, her phone rang. It was Georgia.

"Hey Peaches," Anna answered. She pulled over into an empty lot on the side of the road, where farmers set up stands in the summertime.

"Hey Anna, God, how are you doing? I can't stop thinking about you guys losing your uncle. It's so sad, and so sudden. He was the one with the house on the water, right?" Georgia had joined Anna for a weekend home, and she was able to nod in wholehearted agreement that Anna's father was the difficult kind in all subsequent conversations they had. After a dinner on Uncle Charlie's deck of lobster rolls and cold beers one evening, they sat looking up at the stars, and heard Uncle Charlie tell the funniest stories, and played poker while smoking cigars until they were completely broke, her Aunt Catherine claiming he cheated and her brother Stephen demanding a rematch next time. Next time. She was glad her friend had been

..ere, that she had met her family.

"Yes, that was Uncle Charlie," Anna said. "It's been hard, but being around everyone is helping. Seeing my sister and my aunt have been great."

"How's your dad?" Georgia asked tentatively.

"I haven't talked to him much. It's been the same." Anna was hoping time at her sister's over dinner would help her discover the good vibes that she told Raphael she would try to find. "I also bumped into Andrew." Anna heard a pause on the phone.

"THE Andrew?" Georgia said in shock. Their friendship began right as they were breaking up, and just as Anna knew every detail of Georgia's relationship with her boyfriend Jake, from their first meeting to their repeat fights, to their bright future ahead, so Georgia knew all about Anna's history with Andrew and then Raphael. "What happened, how'd you meet up with him?"

"It was a coincidence; we bumped into each other when we went to a bar after the funeral. It's not that shocking, given how tiny my hometown is, but it still felt so weird."

"That's a lot to take in all at once. Well, I'm headed out now to meet a client who is buying some photos for his office, but we'll talk soon. You'll have to fill me in on all the details and you have to call me if you bump into Andrew again. Promise?"

"I promise," said Anna. She hung up the phone. As she stared out the window, a memory floated up.

Andrew, laying on the grass on campus, in the warm sunshine. They were supposed to be studying, but he was throwing grass at her instead.

"Stop, or I'll make you write this Plato paper for me," she said.

"What's it about? Maybe I will." Anna didn't doubt it – Andrew aced all of his classes with what appeared to her like no effort.

"Well, it's on one of his dialogues. The Symposium. They're all at a drinking party, and they start trying to figure out the nature of love. First all the men speak and say love is power, and romance. And then Socrates tells everyone that all of their ideas about what love is are wrong. He tells them that love was born of resource and need."

Andrew squinted his eye in the spring sunlight, his long muscular frame relaxed, his head resting in his palm. "I think that's a good explanation of love," he said.

"You do?"

"Yah. I need you."

Anna smiled. "Andrew, you're a portrait of resource. You tame the ocean and hunt for food. You cut down the egomaniacs who try to fish in your territory, and then go home and feed soup to your father, all with a 4.0 GPA. There is literally nothing you can't do." Anna stared at his soft almost blond eyebrows that were pushed together as he was thinking, and longed to reach out and touch them.

"Yea, but I still need you. I needed you since the first moment I laid eyes on you, when we were looking at the blue lobster." Andrew looked at her, his eyes serious. "Maybe that's why we love each other. We are each other's resource and need."

"Maybe," said Anna smiling, watching his eyes on her. Her heart felt like it a tectonic plate shifting. "I didn't think I could be any more in love with you, Mr. Toomey. But I was wrong. So now I have a need," she said. "I need a kiss."

"Thought you needed to write your paper," he teased, squinting one eye.

"I think I have to do some research first," she said, closing her book, and pulling him close.

She snapped out of her memory when a huge semi-truck drove past her, and pulled back out onto the road. A few minutes later, she pulled into the parking lot of Albright's Art Shop, the art store she and her mom had always shopped. It was still in business. Coastal Maine had always been a draw for artists. Streets were dotted with signs hanging out front that said Gallery or Art Studio. The northern light, the rocky coast, the drama of the seasons mixed with the power of the ocean, all made for constant inspiration. Add to that the charm of New England – lobster boats and tidy colonial homes with flower boxes and bakeries and restaurants with inviting facades. Plus, Mainers valued hard work, and they valued making things with their hands. Anywhere she went in Maine she found many hard-working crafters – in some parts they made bread or beer, in other parts they farmed. Here on the coast, they fished and painted.

And kept Albright's Art Shop in business.

She looked up at the familiar shop, and took a deep breath. It was the strangest experience, being home. Everything was stored somewhere in a memory that hadn't been used in so long, like she had lived another life in another dimension.

She heard a bell chime when she opened the door. The inside smelled faintly of turpentine and freshly cut wood. She saw an older woman with a thick middle, a colorful wool sweater, and a large white bun on top of her head. Though her hair was much grayer, Anna immediately recognized her. She had come into this shop almost every week during high school, especially in the summer. And every trip home during college required a stockpile shopping trip. Her school had supplies, of course, but she preferred her favorite brushes and colors from Albright's, plus they always sold their canvases unwrapped so they were used to the air. Anna loved being able to use them right away.

The woman was Frances Albright, and she had known her mother well. Anna suddenly remembered how she always had a poster of her mother's gallery behind the counter, with the name *McAllister Gallery* in large letters at the top. She had used her maiden name in the art world. Anna could still see the photo of her mother, smiling, head crooked, next to one of her paintings, with the text *Therese McAllister, Artist*, underneath. The space where it used to be was empty now, but she remembered how proud it used to make her feel.

The woman greeted her politely and then studied a pad of paper on the back counter. Anna hesitated to break her concentration. "Hi, Frances," she finally said. The woman looked at her for a long time. "Anna Goodrich?" She put her hand to her heart. "My word, Anna, it's so good to see you!" She dropped the glasses she had been holding up to her eyes, and they swayed gently on their chain. Her eyes lit up and crinkled, and she reached out to grab Anna's hand.

"Thanks, Frances, it's good to see you too," Anna said warmly. "Just here for some paints. I need burnt sienna, burnt umber, titanium white, indigo, cadmium red, cadmium yellow, and . . . mars black. Here's the list. Oh, and I need an angled and flared brush, and a few canvases as well."

Frances stared at her wall of paints and pulled out tubes efficiently as Anna spoke. Her arthritic fingers touched each tube tenderly. She looked at her nervously after she had found them all. "You remember that your mother loved Payne's gray, for doing the sky over the ocean, don't you? She used to always mix it with some blues and greens to get the ocean just right on a stormy day."

Anna smiled. Her heart ached so much at the memory, she had to remind herself to breathe. "That's right. I'm so glad you remembered that. I'll take Payne's gray as well."

"Have you been painting a lot yourself these days?" Frances asked while she handed her a receipt.

"A bit," Anna nodded. "I live in New York, so most of my paintings are scenes of the city now, but Maine comes out in them every now and then."

"Of course it does, dear," said Frances. "Maine will always be in you." She winked at Anna.

"Thanks for the supplies, Frances. It was so good to see you." Anna smiled.

"You too dear. Come back and see us anytime."

She walked out of the store with a large bag of canvases and a smaller bag of paints and brushes that made her enormously happy, and headed to St. Patrick's. As she drove down familiar roads, past their old high school, Lincoln Academy, and the parking lot where she had that October snowball fight with Stephen and Andrew, long forgotten memories started to crowd her head as she turned into the empty parking lot at St. Pat's. She set up a portable easel at the edge of the yard around the church. Her view was of the old nave and stained-glass window of St. Patrick, along with an old tree and garden that made the church look like it was from England. She sat with the church to her right, the late afternoon light streaming through the trees over the cemetery. She glanced at the far corner.

Third lot, first row, fifth headstone. Her mother's grave was a little more than a hundred feet away.

"I miss you Mom," she whispered, and closed her eyes.

She opened them again and started to sketch the church, her hands moving across the canvas, her mind free to wander. Back to her mother. Back to her life here. Back to when everything came apart.

The last time she saw her mother healthy, she was home from school for the weekend. It was the beginning of November, and she and Andrew had driven home together from school, the University of Maine at Orono. He needed to help his father winterize the boat. His MS was getting worse. They were happy on the drive home. They blasted Tom Petty and shared a bag of sour patch kids, and talked about classes they loved and roommates they didn't. Andrew kept making Anna laugh until she cried. Other than worries about Andrew's dad, they were carefree. That's how she remembered that drive.

Andrew dropped Anna at home, and she spent the afternoon painting with her mom in the barn – they were trying to capture the last sigh of autumn, and the way the colors of the trees reflected in the harbor. After they washed their hands and their brushes they cooked a big pasta dinner together and opened a bottle of wine. Drinking wine with her parents was still a novelty and Anna felt very grown up, on the cusp of living a life that seemed impossibly happy. She loved school, her boyfriend, her family, her work. Her mother seemed happy too – she was settling in to having an empty nest, and since she had more time to paint, she had weathered the transition well.

Perhaps the universe could not abide such happiness.

After that dinner, her mother said she didn't feel well. She couldn't eat very much the next day, and on Sunday she spent most of the day in bed before Anna had left to go back to school. She went to her doctor the next day, who sent her to the hospital. There she received a diagnosis: advanced ovarian cancer. The prognosis was 6-12 months.

They were in shock. Everyone except her mother. Her own mother had died of breast cancer when she was in her early twenties. She had been here before. She had always mourned the fact that they never got to know their grandmother, but now, she realized she had a model for how to handle her own death. She gave chemo a shot, but it was too late.

Once they realized how short their time was with her, Anna came home every chance she got. They spent weekends watching comedy shows and movies, playing cards, traveling to museums in Boston, her mother in a wheelchair, her favorite lavender cashmere knit hat on her bald head, her favorite oatmeal sweater over her clothes, since she was always cold. She had learned from her own mother that the way to die was to truly live. It freed them all up to enjoy each day as a gift, as it came.

When she had the strength, they would paint. Her last painting was a small canvas of the things that lay on her bedside table: a stem of purple lupine, the flower that bloomed everywhere in Maine in early summer. Her father had set in a glass vase, since he knew she loved them. Next to it lay a blush colored seashell, a photo of their family, and an ebony rosary resting on a Bible.

When she didn't have the strength, she rested, and held the same rosary from the painting, its beads moving through her fingers, her lips mumbling the ancient words.

She passed away in just nine short months. Anna was shocked at how fast it went, and though she and Andrew went home every weekend, she couldn't shake the voracious guilt that she should have been there more. Her mother told her she should stay in school. She remembered praying that they could have the summer together. Praying her mom would last till June. She died at the end of May. That was one of the last times she could remember praying. It was almost eight years ago.

When her mother died, Anna's faith and guidance in all things, but particularly in art, was suddenly gone. She could barely return to it. Something about the ritual of painting evoked memories of her mother and seemed to reintroduce her loss, each time from a fresh new angle she hadn't considered before. Her father couldn't understand this. There was hardly a worse crime in John Goodrich's world than letting talent go to waste. But in the wake of her mother's death, his ideas were distilled through his grief and anger at her mother's passing, until he was simply a tyrant.

Her mom had been gone a year and a half when they had a blow-out argument. She had come home from school, halfway through her senior year for Thanksgiving. After a bittersweet holiday at Uncle Charlie's, where her aunt and her uncle had tried to love them hard, she was home packing her bags to go back to school. She came into the dining room. Her dad was sitting at the table, looking through the piles of brochures and packets for art programs at grad schools, and for art shows across the country.

"What's this?" she asked her dad.

"I thought I'd help you get started on your applications. I know you've been distracted and maybe hadn't thought that they are due soon if you're going to grad school."

"I'm not going to grad school, Dad. I'm not going to submit to these shows, either. I'm going to take a break next year. I'll waitress or babysit. And I am going to help Andrew on the boat. That's my plan. But I'm taking a break from painting." Her blue eyes were fixed with a stubborn stare that was mirrored by her father's, only his eyes were brown. Andrew used to say that stubborn stare was the Italian and the Irish in them clashing.

Her father got up slowly.

"Goddamit, Anna, why are you doing this to yourself? Why are you throwing your life away? You could be a great artist. And instead you choose to be a waitress. You're just like your boyfriend. He could be a brilliant doctor or teacher, and instead he is going to be a fisherman. What is wrong with you? You could have gone to Brown, or RISD, worked with some of the best teachers in the world, but instead you went to Orono. It isn't exactly known for their art department—I should know. You just followed a boy. And now you're throwing your life away over a boy." He pushed the pamphlets and papers off the table in one sweep of his arm.

Anna shouted back, "I didn't need world-class art teachers! I had one of the world's best art teachers. I had Mom. But she's gone now. And I swear to you, I'm done painting. I'll never paint again."

That was about the worst thing Anna could have said. Her father's eyes were like those of a horse who had just broken a leg. Wild, in pain, wanting to fight, to keep going, but needing mercy. "For Chrissakes, don't you dare bring your mother into this!" But Anna didn't hear the rest. She stormed out of the room and slammed the door.

She grabbed her bike and rode over to Andrew's. *I wish mom were here*, she kept repeating through her tears. Her mother would have helped her talk sense into her dad. Instead he was going to squeeze her until he poured his sense into her. It was no use. She needed to leave. Get out of Maine. She thought of her teacher who had talked to her last week at school, saying she had a friend who was offering a paid internship at a gallery in New York City. She had recommended Anna, if she wanted it.

Suddenly that choice blossomed in her heart like a new beginning. She could stop painting. She could use all she had learned. She could earn a living and be free from her father. Andrew could go to grad school, maybe. Her father was right; he was smart. She just had to find him and figure out when he thought he could leave. Probably after lobster season was over, she thought.

But when she finally talked to him, out on the pier by the old fort, and told him about the gallery, he couldn't look at her. She could still remember the sound of the waves and the light on his face when he said, "I can't go to New York with you, Anna. I belong in Maine. We belong in Maine."

"But I need to leave," she told him. Her father's harsh words that she had followed Andrew to school made her stubborn side dig in. It was his turn to follow her.

She left after her graduation, and found her way to Genevieve's gallery. Still reeling from the hurt that he wouldn't follow her, and not having dealt with her mom's death and her dad's rejection, she told him they should take a break. Andrew seemed physically pained when she suggested it. She felt guilty then, but she was...frozen. She stayed that way for a long time—a year maybe?—before she finally realized she had made a mistake. As the shock and fog started to recede that her mother was gone, she realized how much she needed Andrew. *Love was born of resource and need.* Anna felt like a house that had been leveled by a storm. She couldn't even fathom her need until now. And she needed Andrew. She needed his sweetness and his humor, his strength and his smile. She needed to hold him. She left a message on his home phone that she was coming home, that she needed to see him, and hopped on a bus.

But when she went to the harbor to find him, to tell him how much she needed him, she saw him out on the boat, with another girl. The girl had reached up, and put her arms around him, and kissed him.

He didn't need her anymore.

She turned around, went back to the train station, and came back to New York the same day a wreck. Genevieve told her to take some time off. Marie came for a visit and gently told her it was time to move forward. To let him go. He chose his life in Maine. She needed to choose hers.

It was finally in a grief support group that she had found relief. They suggested doing for others was a way to heal, so she reached out the Boys and Girls Club. She started teaching art classes. In the slow brush strokes her mother had taught her, in the swirl of burnt sienna and Payne's gray, in the eyes of young children who still saw the world as hopeful, as new, she started to heal. And when she saw Miranda, so eager to learn and so talented, she found that the grief group was right. Giving to others did help her heal. Or at least, it had helped her find her way out of the dark.

When Raphael came into the gallery looking to decorate his Tribeca loft six months later, Andrew had been buried deep in her heart. Like her mother, like her father. Like Maine.

But here she was, unearthing them all.

All of a sudden, like seeing a photo in a clearer focus, she saw how much her choice to let Andrew go was influenced by her grief, and as much as she hated to admit it, her father's dislike of him. She was surprised by this. She couldn't picture Andrew in her life now in the least. Wasn't that proof that she had made the right choice? Raphael just worked in her life. Her New York life. He was smart and attractive and successful. Still, the memory of her years with Andrew gave her the gnawing feeling that she had known a happiness then that was more real than her life was now. Had she thrown that away because of her father?

She decided she wanted to ask her father, tonight at dinner, what he had so disliked in Andrew. She was home now; she might as well muddy the water, then go back to New York and let it settle after she was gone.

Chapter 5

When she arrived back at her sister's house, it was post-nap for Henry, and he was sprawled on the couch with a sippy cup, his blankie and a bag of Cheerios. She didn't dare disturb him, walking instead into the kitchen where her sister was just cleaning up.

"The beef stew is in the oven. There is nothing left to do but drink," she said as she poured herself a glass of red. "Why does thinking about Uncle Charlie make me want to reach for a glass of wine? And do you want some?"

Anna nodded. "Yes I do. I think it's either because we're Irish or because it is the universal prescription for grief." She joined her sister at the island.

"How was painting?" Marie asked.

"Good, it was great to be outside. I'm painting St. Patrick's." Anna took a sip of wine, which tasted so good after her afternoon of working.

"What a perfect thing to paint while you're here. Dad would love that. By the way, how's it going for you with him?" Marie asked. "I mean, when is the last time you guys came close to a real conversation?"

"I dunno. Eight years ago I guess?" Anna laughed. "I was just thinking about it all. Remember when we had that huge fight? The one that made me decide to move to New York?"

"You mean the one where he told you to go to grad school and you told him no? Then he screamed at you and you decided to move to New York?

"Yes, that's the one. Well, I just keep going back to that time, wondering why he disliked Andrew so much. I mean, everything about that fight was because Dad thought I was choosing Andrew over grad school. Just like I chose to go to University of Maine instead of RISD or RPI to be with Andrew. Which happened to be a great choice, by the way. We were so happy there. And after you and Stephen went off to big schools I saved dad a lot of money. But I just couldn't think about painting after mom died. I needed a break to figure out what I wanted to do. That's why I told him I was going to hang out with Andrew and waitress that summer. I knew I couldn't pick up a brush or go through those motions while I was grieving her. I guess Dad just couldn't hear that."

"Maybe he also couldn't let her die in you," Marie said. "If you stopped painting, everything she taught you, and what you guys had, would die too. I mean, he was having a pretty messed up time then."

Anna felt a twinge of guilt. "I know. And I beat myself up over it. I know that we were both hurting. But he was the parent, right? He was the one who should've heard me say enough, this hurts."

"But it was his wife. He couldn't hear you and your feelings when he was knee-deep in his own." Marie said.

"I did figure that out with my grief group a few years back." Anna nodded and took another sip. "It definitely helped me be less angry, having empathy for him. But I still don't get why he disliked Andrew so much. Sure he was going to be a lobsterman instead of a lawyer, but he was still a pretty solid guy. He didn't deserve the level of loathing Dad had for him. Maybe I'll ask him tonight."

"Don't you think we should avoid bringing it up? I mean everyone's so raw about Uncle Charlie," Marie said, her forehead wrinkled with concern.

"I won't make a big deal of it. I just need to know. I'm just starting to see how much his dislike of Andrew made me let him go so easily I guess."

"You're not having second thoughts about Andrew?" Marie said, her impatience hard to miss in her tone. "I thought we had that weekend where you let him go for good. Remember? Peter Gabriel on repeat? Several empty wine bottles on the floor?"

"It's not like that," Anna said. "I am not stewing about him. I think it is safe to say we've both moved on. I just need to understand what happened, I guess. Don't you ever think about how the events around mom dying impacted your life? As I recall, you decided to go to med school for oncology, right?"

"Yes, of course. And then I met Mike. But in my case, those were good things."

"In your case, Dad loved Mike because he was a doctor. He had done something with his life. He had achieved something, instead of sitting around in undeveloped potential like some people on Dad's list of people who suck. At the top of which were Andrew and yours truly."

"Stop, you are being ridiculous," Marie said, just as Henry ran in the room.

"More Thomas! More Cheerios!" he said.

"Am I?" Anna asked. She turned to scoop up her nephew and blew raspberries on his stomach. "Tell mommy Auntie is not being ridiculous! She is just asking some important questions!"

"'Portant quetchions!" Henry replied, laughing.

"See?" said Anna. "At least he understands me."

As her sister took care of her nephew, Anna poured another glass of wine and stirred the stew, and then wandered over to put another log in the fireplace. A picture on the mantle caught Anna's attention. It was a picture of her mom holding on to her children. It must have been summer, since her mom's hair was up high in a messy bun, her skin gleaming from a light glaze of sweat under her white eyelet sleeveless blouse. She stood in front of a fountain somewhere – Portland? Boston maybe? – with all three of them under her arms. No doubt her father was taking the picture. Her mother had the look of someone who was perfectly happy even while being mildly annoyed. Her father was a perfectionist at pictures, of course. But she remembered how her mother had always remained unflappable in those circumstances. Anna remembered her own stress at his loud voice, the stern reproachful look. But her mother always managed to sooth him - a hand on his arm, a warm laugh like Champagne that bubbled from her throat, and she could melt the moment, turn an iceberg into a stream. "Oh John," she would say. "That's enough dear." And he listened to her. That is all it took for him to turn his heart in a moment, to let his mood be softened. And he would look at her and smile. His love for her yielding to his best self so often that Anna didn't even think of him as overly harsh or stubborn, until she had died, and her ability to balance him was gone.

Anna saw herself in the photo. The long pig-tails flowing to one side, tied with white ric rac ribbons, the red and white checked shirt with white shorts. She squinted in the summer sun, her teeth revealing the wreckage of an adolescent mouth. Her shoulders showed the lines from her bathing suit, set off by a faint sunburn. Her father managed to capture her thick eyelashes, and knobby knees holding two thin reeds of long legs together. Anna remembered those awkward years anew. Marie looked beautiful then, in her jeans and billowy blouse and long, thick hair. And Steven looked exactly the same, tall, like her dad, with his hair messy and overgrown.

Anna remembered just how the world looked to those eyes, the little girl in the picture. This was how she remembered her family. Always doing something enriching, always in her father's gaze, always under her mother's arms. At least until her mother died. Then she saw her family as a group of people bonded together because they all missed the same person.

She put the picture back on the mantle.

That evening, the air was cool and moist, and the setting sun cast a glow on the room as Anna sat with her nephew, coloring and eating veggies while they waited for dinner. Henry banged on the table loudly with his sippy cup. "More ranch!" he yelled.

"Say please," said her sister as she swirled the creamy white goodness next to his cucumbers and peppers.

The house smelled heavenly, the aromas of the red wine it had been cooked in with the beef and onion and rosemary made Anna's mouth water. Mike was strolling around the house with Anna's father, discussing which plants to move, what things would make nice additions to the landscaping. Even though Mike had grown up in Minnesota, he had adopted the New Englander passion for keeping your yard looking pristine. They looked like they were deep in thought as they came into the house.

"Smells good, Marie," Mike said sweetly as they walked in, and he gave her a kiss.

"Goodness, it smells wonderful," her father agreed as he took off his shoes, poured himself a glass of Scotch, and sat down at the table next to Henry. Marie worked steadily behind them in the adjacent kitchen, and Mike tended to the fire. For a moment, Anna had to pinch herself. This night was just what her heart needed. If only her father's presence didn't put her on edge.

As if he could read her thoughts, he turned to her and asked, "So how's New York? How's your boyfriend?"

"He's good," Anna said. "He's as disciplined as ever, in early at work, and fitting in his crazy workouts. But we've had a fun winter trying out some of the new restaurants and art shows. And the gallery has had a lot of success lately," she said, realizing she meant her own shows, so she quickly changed the subject. She turned to Marie in the kitchen. "There is this new Brazilian restaurant we just tried, the meat melts in your mouth. I wish you could all come down and try it."

"Mmm. Meat." Mike said in his best caveman voice.

"Sounds amazing," Marie nodded.

Her father colored with Henry, and looked up at the mention of art shows. "I meant to tell you, there's a new artist who just opened a gallery out by the harbor. She's from away - came up from New York. She's quite good. You should go see her." He tilted his glass back. The ice cubes made a familiar clinking sound.

Anna felt her neck and shoulders tighten at the suggestion. She knew her father was just trying to share this information with her, but it felt heavy with the weight of past expectations. She tried to sound light in her reply. "Okay, I'll have to take a look. Where's the gallery?"

"Just down the road from Riley's market, before you turn to go to the harbor," he said. He looked tired, like he had aged a lot since the last time she had visited. No doubt the toll of Charlie's death added to the tightness around his eyes.

"I'll try to swing by," she said. "How's the magazine going?" In addition to running the Foundation, her father was a regular contributor for Art: Yesterday and Today, a magazine that kept art historians updated on contemporary art. He didn't really believe in retirement.

"Good, pretty good. Some crazy art teacher in L.A. hosted a crit where no one spoke for two hours, then just held hands. Like it was a damn séance. Drives me crazy when I think of the cost of that class." Anna was used to her father's criticism of the contemporary art world, mainly directed at conceptual art. His academic focus had been figurative art, and he was more comfortable with the masters of the Renaissance and Impressionism, though he respected a few recent artists, such as Lucian Freud and Luc Tuymans, a figurative painter from Belgium. And though she wouldn't admit it to him, Anna shared his dislike of the craziness of the art world, especially the overinflated ego of many contemporary artists and dealers. But she tried to turn the conversation to lighter stuff. She wanted to get into some of her questions and didn't want things to take a confrontational turn over the art world before she started.

"Want some help, Marie?" she said as she got up to help her sister serve in the kitchen. Anna came back in carrying plates of steaming beef and potatoes with parsley sprinkled on top.

"So, Dad, you'll never believe who we bumped into yesterday at Shaw's Wharf."

"Who?" he asked.

"Andrew Toomey."

Her father was silent he stroked his mustache thoughtfully. "How's he doing? And how's what's her name . . . that Marie was friends with . . . Liz?" he asked.

"They're doing well, I guess. Andrew is still fishing, on his own lobster boat. Liz is bartending at Shaw's Wharf. They said that Henry can go on a ride on his boat this summer."

At the mention of his name, Henry banged on his high chair.

"Boat ride!" he yelled, his blond curls filled with ranch, his eyes wide at the mention of a boat.

"Yes, boat ride!" Marie echoed him from the kitchen.

"So I see their family has really reached their potential in life," he said. He took another sip from his Scotch.

Anna looked up from the doorway. The comment hung in the air like a thick cloud. "What do you mean?" she finally asked.

"Well, they were both honor roll students, varsity athletes. Now they fish and pour beer? Seems like a waste of potential."

Anna was both glad and angry that the conversation had arrived here. This was the John Goodrich she ran from. Opinionated and ignorant, and obsessed with people's full potential as a righteous platform for judging them.

"Well, we can't all be academics. The world needs to eat," Marie said. She put the salad bowl in the center of the table and sat down, the corners of her mouth smiling in amusement at the hubris of her father.

"And drink," added Mike.

"I know, but that boy had talent. Gifts. And he threw it away," her father said.

"Just like I did?" Anna asked. Her hand was on her hip, her head cocked sideways. "He took me with him, right? What is it with you and what Andrew does with his life?"

"It isn't what he did with his life; it's what you didn't do with yours," he said.

Marie interrupted them. "Can we please sit down and eat? Don't do this in front of Henry." She motioned for Anna to take a seat next to her. Anna sat down and started to eat. Her pulse raced, and she started to think maybe Marie was right. It was a mistake to ruin this amazing dinner.

"Actually, this is a great conversation with Henry here," Anna's father said. He set down his fork and stared at them. "Imagine if Henry went to school, and they found he had the most amazing scientific gifts. They encouraged him to go to a special gifted school, and there he thrived. Won awards. Came up with amazing questions, and wrote amazing studies. Learned about medicine from both of you. But when it came time for college, he chose to follow his friends. Or maybe a girlfriend. And he went to the state school they went to. And when he was done, he announced he wanted to hang out with her for the summer. Maybe help his friend working on roof tops or new construction. Because it was comfortable. Easy. Somewhere along the way, he had lost his hunger to be great. His desire to excel. Because of who he was hanging out with. And you could say nothing at all, Marie. Even though you knew he wasn't truly happy. He spent his free time at the local bar, with his girlfriend. How would you feel?"

They sat silently at the table. "Dad, it was hardly the same thing," Anna started.

"How is it different?" he asked.

"His mom didn't die in the process."

"Marie? Mike? If one of you passed, would Henry's choice pain you less or more? Wouldn't it add to your grief? Wouldn't you be losing not one loved one, but two?"

Marie and Mike sat silently, and looked at Henry.

"I'm going to get some more wine," Marie said.

"Dad, I wasn't working construction and drinking at the bar. I was taking a summer to think about it. If Henry took some time off after college, maybe it will lead him to even better things.

"Not if he was influenced by those around him. He might never get back on track."

"Well, in your analogy, Henry would be about 21 or 22. Which means he gets to decide for himself what his choices are," Anna said.

"Yes. And people can still make bad choices. And the people who love them can try to keep them from continuing to do so." A vein started to pop out of John Goodrich's temple. "Maybe we even have a responsibility to help them when they make bad choices. Are you going to say it will be easy to watch him throw away his gifts?"

"Dad, calm down. Anna, let's get off this," Marie said.

"I didn't get us on this, Dad did. I'll make it easy for you. I'll leave." Anna stood up.

"Leaving is easy," said her father. "You should be good at it by now. But how would you feel if that was Henry's response? Leaving?"

"If Marie rode Henry the way you ride me, I would let him crash on my couch when he left," Anna said. She stormed up the stairs. A familiar wave of anger left her after a while, and she fell asleep as she heard her father's car start down the drive.

When she woke up the next morning, she headed down to get coffee and heard Henry and Marie up in the kitchen.

"Hey," she said. "I'm sorry about last night. You were right, we shouldn't have gotten into it."

Marie looked up from wiping the mess Henry had left under his plate and shook her head. "I just can't believe that red wine beef stew couldn't distract you guys from fighting. It was the best thing I have ever made!" Marie said. She put down the rag in the sink. "I can't believe you guys can get right back there so fast. I keep hoping one of you will let it go, but it appears that the stubborn streak isn't going anywhere."

Anna sighed. "I guess. I just don't get why that whole bit about 'freedom' escapes him. Why he feels like he has to decide what is right for others."

"I know," Marie said. "It is his version of loving, but it feels like the opposite of love. He just doesn't know it. But all you can do is not let it eat you up so bad, I guess," Marie said.

"I know," said Anna. "It still does. That is for sure. I'll try not to let it. I will be the big girl. Especially since we are going to a reading of the will together today. How weird is that?"

"Ugg, I'm dreading it," said Marie as she packed up snacks and toys in Henry's bag.

"Hey Marie?" Anna asked.

"Yea," she said, looking up from the sink.

"Can I try your beef stew for breakfast?" Anna asked.

Just as she had hoped, her sister rolled her eyes and laughed.

Chapter 6

The lawyer's office was a red brick house sitting on the main road just before heading into downtown Damariscotta. Its trees and bushes were almost electric with their spring green blossoms, setting off a black sign with gold lettering that read *Sloan, Ferris, and Wadsworth.*

James P. Sloan was Uncle Charlie's lawyer, a middle-aged, round-bellied gentleman with a full head of thick brown hair. He greeted them all warmly while remaining matter-of-fact about his duties. They gathered first in the front office. They were waiting for Stephen, who again had to drive up from Rhode Island, only to turn around promptly after lunch and head back for the dinner service. The attorney offered his condolences while Henry zoned in on the large water cooler. He walked over to it, grabbed a Dixie cup, and pressed the button. He giggled each time his chubby thumb managed to let out a few drops of water. The secretary eyed him as she pushed through some paperwork, smiling at Marie as both an acknowledgment that Henry was in fact cute but also was not free from her unspoken reign on the order in this space. Stephen walked in just as Henry filled the cup to the brim, and Marie beat the secretary to him, pulling the cup gently from his hands.

"Right into this conference room here, please," Mr. Sloan said. "This shouldn't take long. We'll do a reading of the will of Charles Goodrich and discuss a few matters regarding his estate." He placed a silver watch neatly next to the paperwork, and kept straightening the corners of his stack of papers. "Please take a copy to read along with me, and note that I will start reading at the middle of page three. The first few pages are just legal jargon and matters of health proxy, power of attorney, etc." *Things that would only matter if Uncle Charlie were alive*, Anna thought.

He spoke clearly, enunciating et cetera in an academic fashion. Anna felt as if she were listening to a professor. "As you can see on page three, we have an initial listing of assets and an approximation of their amounts as of last Monday. We must of course take into account market volatility. I will just begin to read them and announce the beneficiary designation of each." He cleared his throat as he began. "To Catherine Goodrich Kearns, we have the bequeathing of all family heirlooms, silver, china, furniture and such as designated by Charles Goodrich, in addition to fifty percent of assets held in a brokerage account in Damariscotta, Maine. To John Goodrich, we have the bequeathing of the personal effects of Charles, his automobile, library, and other itemized artifacts in his home, along with the remaining fifty percent of the brokerage account. Upon either of your passing, these amounts are intended to be dispersed equally among your children."

Though Mr. Sloan was not talking especially fast, Anna found herself a bit slow in absorbing the content of his speech. The amount listed on the page under "Brokerage Account" was $3.5 million. Half of that belonged to her father now. Before she could absorb this, she was sent reeling by the next item.

"To the children of John Goodrich, the paintings owned by Charles Goodrich will be equally divided by amount and preference. This should be decided among them, and if an arbitrator is necessary, Atty. James P. Sloan should serve in this capacity until a favorable outcome is decided upon." She recalled all the paintings that were at Uncle Charlie's from her mom's gallery. A strong desire to see the forgotten pieces came over Anna. She had most of her mother's work cataloged in her memory, as well as in an actual file at the gallery, but she couldn't recall all the pieces at Uncle Charlie's.

"To the children of Catherine Goodrich Kearns, the remaining shares of Bank of America stock from his firm's buyout are in a clearing account, and shall be divided between Sarah and Phillip as either an in-kind transfer or, if they prefer, a liquidation with the cash proceeds representing a taxable event for purposes of their income tax declaration." Anna looked down. The paper read $500,000 next to the stock value.

"Finally, this estate grants the ownership of Charles Goodrich's residence, Thirteen New Harbor Road, and those furnishings not previously listed in any other itemized gift to his niece Anna Goodrich. Mr. Goodrich wished to declare his intention for this perhaps inequitable distribution to his belief that she should return to the state of Maine. He has escrowed an amount to cover the cost of roughly five years' worth of taxes as well."

Mr. Sloane paused as he glanced over the remaining contents of the paper and, when satisfied, lifted his head, cleared his throat, and looked around the table at the stunned family members. Anna stared numbly at the shaft of light on the mahogany table in front of her, and felt the hair on her arms stand up. *Uncle Charlie was a millionaire? Uncle Charlie left her his house?*

"Are there any questions?" Mr. Sloane asked. The secretary entered just then, handing him a piece of paper, prompting a curt nod and dismissal before she backed away.

"When does all of this take effect?" asked Aunt Catherine, rubbing the area above her right eyebrow.

"The distribution of brokerage assets can be transferred as soon as you provide us with information about where you want it to go. If you have a broker already, feel free to provide us with their contact information. If you don't, we can certainly give you a recommendation, and then the transfer will be started as soon as you have an account opened with them. The contents of Mr. Goodrich's home can be handled anytime. The itemized section will be your guide, and if there are any discrepancies, a meeting at the house can be arranged where I oversee the distribution. I am not sure that will be necessary given your family's lack of previous discord or dissension, but at times these events can trigger some tension. I will let you contact me if you want to set something like that up. Any of you are free to contact me at any time."

They sat in stunned silence, as Mr. Sloan left and pressed on with his day.

After Mr. Sloan stunned them all with Uncle Charlie's will, they all went to lunch to process the news. She had been worried that her cousins would be upset about the house, but Sarah and Phillip were excited at the prospect of having her closer. Her father had returned to his neutral attitude toward her, and she did the same. He and Catherine discussed their amazement at their brother. By all accounts, Uncle Charlie was a frugal New Englander. He was very generous at Christmas and birthdays, but he hardly lived a glamorous life. Though his house was on the ocean, he had bought it from a foreclosure that had come through the bank for a great price almost forty years ago. His one vice had been his boat, and he had gifted that to his best friend last summer, saying he was getting too old to use it anymore. The fact that he had amassed that kind of wealth amazed them all. Having such a detailed will was surely because he was a banker, and consequently was aware what could happen without one.

She could barely start to process taking over her uncle's house, since she was still processing the fact that he was gone. She had to wait for the transfer to be official, but her father had a set of keys, and Anna, Marie and Aunt Catherine had gone over after lunch to try to sort through some of the belongings.

It had been very difficult. Seeing soap in the shower, milk in the fridge, his old sweater across the back of a chair in the kitchen made it feel like he had just stepped out for a bit. But he was never coming back. The hollowness of this fact, facing death in all the evidence of life, made Anna go into the bathroom and weep. She tried to hide it from her aunt, but Anna noticed she was crying as well on the back step, staring out at the ocean. Marie came in and hugged her.

Amid their grief, they barely finished cleaning out the perishable items at his house and hadn't made it to the items in the will, or the paintings. Marie and Anna had discussed coming back here in the evenings to itemize their mother's work, take pictures, and email with Stephen to decide what they each wanted. They went back to Marie's to eat, and while she put Henry down, Anna sat out on the deck and dialed Raphael's number.

"Hey Raph," Anna said when he picked up.

"Hey, sweetie, how are you? I'm just headed out to lunch now. How's it going? I miss you,"

"Thanks, I miss you too. It's going ok, I am just figuring out some things with my family. Think they might take a little while. Maybe a few weeks. Maybe a month," Anna said.

"Wow, I didn't realize you'd be gone that long," Raphael said, sounding surprised. Anna could hear the honk of cars and the squeak of buses breaking through the phone.

"I know," she said, heading out to her sister's back deck. The ocean chill wrestled with the spring sun, and it wasn't clear who was winning yet. "But there is a lot to do here. There are a lot of pieces to pick up from Uncle Charlie's will. Raphael, he left me his house."

"His house?" he asked. "The one on the harbor? Do you want to keep it?"

"I'm not really sure; it's happened so fast. I sort of want to give it some time before I decide. But the taxes are paid for five years so it won't hurt to wait. You should come up, stay there with me for a weekend or something," she said.

"That sounds really fun. It's so tough to leave work right now, but let me get through this week and see what I can do. How's Genevieve taking it?"

"She is fine with it . . . we sort of have an arrangement. She wants me to check out the local galleries, see if there is anything worth bringing back. I guess I want to make sure I have enough time to get everything with the house done so I don't have to worry about it down the road. I want to spruce it up, I guess. Get the gardens going. Uncle Charlie prided himself on his gardening, so just spring clean-up and getting rid of some stuff." Anna watched as a starling of birds flew over the pine trees in Marie's back yard. She remembered her mom used to call it a school of birds, since they moved like fish. "I think I want to see how it feels, too, staying in it. The house, I mean."

"Love, I just need to check - are you getting any ideas about moving back?"

"No, of course not. I just want to get an idea of what the house needs. I am just getting used to it all," she said. Marie called to her from the garage where she was waiting for Anna to leave for Uncle Charlie's. They were heading to the house to go over the paintings. "Look, I'll call you later. Marie is waiting for me, but I'll be back before you know it. You'll get a chance to focus on work. I'll set up our vacation spot before the summer." Anna tried to sound cheerful.

"Ok, sweetie. I'll talk to you soon. Love you," Raphael said.

" Love you too," she said.

"How's Raphael?" Marie asked as they drove over to the house. Mike was home with Henry again, and it was nice to have a moment alone with her sister. The spring evening was darkening quickly, and dusk settled in around them as they pulled up the road to the harbor.

"He's good. The house was just a surprise. I asked him to come up here soon and stay there with me," Anna said. She noticed the gallery her father had mentioned as they turned at Riley's market. It read *Perinault Gallery*, and there was a black sign with an oil painting of the rocky Maine coast under the name. The red barn had a sign that said *Open*. Anna promised herself she would stop by soon.

"I can't believe he left you his house," Marie said. "Think it was his way of trying to get you and Dad to make up? You know, make you come up here more?"

"I'm not sure," Anna said. She looked out the window at the neat New England homes, their flower beds tidy and their lanterns glowing. "How has it been for you to move back, to live near Dad? I mean, doesn't he give you grief for staying home with Henry instead of practicing medicine? We both know how our conversations would go if I lived nearby."

"Well, no, he doesn't ride me for giving up practicing medicine," Marie said. "I think he views what I am doing as valuable. And he views me as settled; stable. But we're totally different. You guys have years of hurt between you."

Years of hurt between you. Anna wondered silently if that hurt would be enough to keep her from returning home to Maine, to Uncle Charlie's house. It was enough to make her leave in the first place. It was just so exhausting. Even though a part of her felt very much at home here, felt as if it belonged in Maine, she was worried that having to face her father so often would be too hard. Her life in New York was easy. Safe. But being here was opening up her eyes to what a slower life looked like. The speed of life there was, deep down, not her speed. It was entertaining and glamorous, fast and sophisticated, but lately Anna had felt that something very essential about herself was shut off. At times she would try to listen for it, and other times – when she was busy, when she was distracted – she ignored it. But that part of her was alive here. She had to admit at least that much.

"Do you think you could be happy living in Uncle Charlie's house?" Marie asked.

"No, I couldn't imagine leaving my life in the city, leaving Genevieve and the gallery," she said as they pulled into the driveway. "I just like that I have this time right now. Like a sabbatical." She felt a wave of gratitude for the gift her uncle had given her. She wanted to stay in this moment, and because of the house, she could. She silently thanked him as they headed up his drive.

When they got inside, her sister started a fire in huge stone fireplace. As the warmth started to creep across the living room, they each turned to different rooms to take down the pictures. They designated the landing at the top of the stairs as a central place to pile them up. Anna's breath caught when she walked into her uncle's bedroom. There was a painting of white birches that her mother had done. It had exaggerated brushstrokes, so the whiteness and the dark lines popped, contrasting each other, and the background was a spring green color. It was beautiful, and Anna remembered her mother giving her a lesson in brushstrokes as she had painted that one. Then she had given it to Uncle Charlie for his birthday. Just as she was about to call Marie in to see it, she heard Marie shout.

"Anna, come here!" She walked across the hall into one of the other spare bedrooms and again caught her breath. It was a painting of the three of them when they were all in grade school. It was a masterpiece. The expression on their faces, the protective way Stephen's arm was around them, the serenity in the scene. Anna felt tears spring to her eyes as she took it in. The beauty of the painting was clearly the love their mother had for them. The lens you saw the figures through was pure maternal love.

"It feels like a piece of Mom, doesn't it?" Marie said quietly, looking at the painting.

"It does," Anna said, her voice heavy with sadness.

They looked through more of the canvases, and Anna could remember some of them hanging in the gallery in Damariscotta. Her mother's work sold sporadically when she had the gallery. In the years that had passed since her death, a secondary market had sprung up, and Anna knew collectors had inquired about the inventory on the market. They would be very happy to see these new pieces. She had never tried to look for them before, out of respect for her father and her uncle. Somehow they felt laid to rest with her mother. But here they were, staring at her. And they were beautiful. She looked at her mother's work with newly educated eyes. They were very good. Genevieve would love them. But Anna wasn't sure if she wanted to part with them. She would wait and work through with her siblings how to handle all these pieces.

She and Marie took a photo of each one, and they emailed them to Stephen to see what his top choices were.

As they searched through Uncle Charlie's bedroom for any other paintings he had lying around, Anna noticed a picture on his nightstand she had never seen before. It was her father, Uncle Charlie, and Aunt Catherine as young children. But there was a fourth child, a girl, who was clearly the youngest. "Hey, Marie, did you ever hear Dad or Uncle Charlie talk about a little sister, one younger than Aunt Catherine?" Anna asked.

Marie looked up quizzically. "No, why?"

"Because in this picture, it looks like they're with another child who looks an awful lot like Catherine but . . . younger."

Marie came over to glance at the photo. "Huh. That's weird." She stared at the picture. "I have no idea who that is. Probably another relative. We'll have to ask Dad." Her sister stood up straight and started rubbing her eyes. "Hey, I have to be up early with Henry. Do you mind if we leave in a few minutes?"

"Sure," Anna said as she put the picture back down. She took in the rooms upstairs and thought about Charlie living here a week ago. It was hard to believe. His shadow cast over everything.

As they drove home, Anna couldn't forget about the picture.

"Think we should ask Dad about the picture? With the young girl? Or maybe we should ask Aunt Catherine instead."

"Aunt Catherine might tell us more than Dad," Marie said. "Let's ask her when she is over for dinner."

Yes, Anna thought in her sleepy head, it was much easier to ask Aunt Catherine.

That night as she slept at her sister's house, Anna had a dream. Her mother was painting in the boathouse at Uncle Charlie's, down by the water, where she usually went when she was doing an ocean picture. She was sitting at the canvas, her brush busy working, when she turned around and beamed at Anna, her lips wide as she laughed. Her dark hair was piled up on her head, she wore a chambray oxford smeared with paint everywhere, and her blue eyes were laughing. Sunlight streamed into the boathouse. The canvas she was painting had the picture of the three of them that she had seen that day. But there was a little girl sitting in the corner, her mother's model, and Anna saw that her mother was painting her face in the spot where Anna had been. It was the little girl from the photo on Uncle Charlie's dresser.

Suddenly Andrew was there, urging them to get away from the boathouse, that the water was rising. Anna looked out the windows and the gray choppy water was covering three quarters of the window. Just as she was struggling to run away, she heard the water crash against the windows of the boathouse, and she woke up suddenly, the morning light streaming through the window.

Chapter 7

The next day, Anna went over to the house early. Marie had let her borrow the pickup truck that Mike used for dump runs, and she was grateful to have it.

"Just, um, make sure you drive carefully," Marie had said as she handed her the keys. Anna knew this reminder was because her brother and sister had always teased her about being a bad driver. Which was unfair. She just didn't have a lot of practice; living with them as the youngest and now in the city, she didn't have a ton of opportunity. And she had a few accidents when she first started driving. They were just mean older siblings, Anna though defensively as she grabbed the keys from Marie and slide into the truck, glaring at her like the slighted little sister she was. But by the time she pulled out of Marie's driveway, she sat back, relaxed. Her body felt amazingly rested as she sipped coffee driving to the house. It was the fresh Maine air, she thought.

She went down to Riley's market to grab a few things to bring over to the house. The store's wide pine boards stained almost black brought back memories of being a kid and picking out candy here. Mr. Riley's son had taken over and very little had changed. If anything he just polished the store up.

There were men in the shop with bright orange fishing overalls on. Her thoughts instantly went to Andrew. Everything near the harbor would remind her of him if she let it. As she stood in front of the produce, her mind went back to taking Andrew's skiff around to Back Harbor, hanging out under the old bridge that was completely covered by water when the tide came in, lying in the sun and laughing. It seemed to Anna whenever she replayed a memory with Andrew that she was laughing. And in every memory, they were always surrounded by beauty. She could only appreciate that now, having been in the city for so long. But there was no denying how beautiful mid-coast Maine was, especially Pemaquid. No wonder the artists and tourists flocked here.

Pemaquid was actually a peninsula that stuck out into the Atlantic Ocean. New Harbor lay to the south and Round Pond to the north. They were all technically villages of Bristol, though most people from out of town referred to the area as Pemaquid. The name was given to it by the Indians, and it meant "a point of land running into the sea." The Indians were there long before the settlers were, though both were drawn to it for its abundant fishing and hunting. The road leading all around the rocky coast was lined with bed-and-breakfasts, giant boulders, white picket fences, and sea roses. Everywhere your eye fell, there was beauty. Maybe that's what drew her mother here. Maybe that's why Andrew wouldn't leave. She thought briefly of her strange dream with both of them. It had been so long since either of them had visited her dreams.

She put her bags on the seat next to her—more ground coffee, clementines, and their famous cheese bread, which she remembered well—and started up the noisy pickup truck. The town was quiet this early on the way to her uncle's house. She was glad. She needed to spend some time alone out here, in the quiet, and let the reality of his death sink in. She also tried to ignore that she made a six-point turn to get out of the parking lot. She was a fine driver. Just out of practice.

Once she was on the road, her thoughts were buoyant. Grief had purified her heart somehow. Everything that had been bothering her in New York—Raphael's workaholic tendencies, Genevieve's constant competition with other galleries, the frequent ache of wishing she could call her mom—were quiet now. In their place was a kind of emotional spring, and it felt real and honest, unlike the persona everyone, including Anna, wore in the city. She felt light as air.

The sunlight nearly blinded her as it bounced off the water. She dug her Ray-Bans out of her purse and put them on as she drove carefully along the curvy rocky shore road. Finally she pulled up to her uncle's house, a few hundred feet after Shaw's Wharf. She had been out here with the other family members, but this was her first trip alone.

Though it was bright out, the morning air was crisp. Anna was glad she brought her winter jacket, the ocean breeze making it even cooler. She got out of the truck and looked up at the white colonial with the purple lilacs just starting to blossom on both sides of the yard. Anna walked up the brick path to the front door, and noticed that her uncle had planted bulbs—tulips and daffodils. They were popping up now, and he wasn't here to see them. I wonder if he knew his time was running out, she thought.

She was eager to get inside and start working. As she walked up the path, she saw sunlight bounce off the upstairs window. She realized that the window was in her uncle's bedroom. He would've looked out of it every day for most of his life.

Inside, the house was musty and smelled of a mix of the cigars her uncle smoked and the fire her sister lit last night. Though it was tidy—her uncle was a New Englander, after all—there was a thin film of dust covering most of the tables and bookshelves. Anna stepped from the front hall into a cozy living room and rolled up the sleeves of her plaid flannel oxford. The large picture windows faced the water, and the sunlight warmed the room. Putting down her art supplies next to a knotty wool sofa the color of strained peas, she walked straight toward the kitchen to set down her groceries from Riley's.

Anna stood there staring at the outdated cabinets and walls, the rug underneath the sink that was a faded map of Maine, imagining her aunt and mom bustling around, getting a meal ready for a holiday. She walked into the back pantry, which was down the hall from the kitchen, the linoleum floor uniting it with the kitchen as well as a bathroom off to the other side. She hated the linoleum. She put her snacks in the fridge, she set up the coffeemaker and brewed half a pot, the aroma filling the air. This was a perfect morning for lots of coffee.

She grabbed a notepad from her bags in the living room and stood up, taking in the view. The ocean waves were crashing into the rocks, and the sky was so huge, she was sure the clouds she was looking at must be hanging over London. Seagulls sailed effortlessly before they dove down to skim the water. Buoys were scattered throughout the waves like toy tops left behind by children. To think that this view was now hers was hard to process. She stared at the boathouse at the end of the long wooden pier. Grabbing her art supplies and a cup of coffee, she went down the steps and walked inside the boathouse, the old wood creaking underneath her feet, and the swell of the water making splashing noises against the dock. She opened a travel easel, laid out some pastels, and started to draw the rocky shore in front of her.

What she had kept from Raphael, and from her family was that she wanted to stay to paint. Something had jolted her system since she had returned home, and everywhere she turned she wanted to capture the image. Maine had breathed into her nostrils, her lungs, awakening something in her so that she saw with fresh eyes, and what she saw was beauty everywhere.

As she looked out on the ocean, she remembered lines from a Keats poem Andrew used to quote sometimes when he was driving his boat out on a particularly beautiful day.

"O ye! who have your eyeballs vexed and tired,
Feast them upon the wideness of the Sea…"

Those words echoed how she felt – like her eyes were vexed and tired by the city, by becoming distant from nature. She thought back to when she first arrived in the city. Genevieve had been college roommates with one of Anna's favorite art teachers, who told Anna her friend in New York City needed a new person to help run the gallery. She was exhausted with the girls she kept interviewing for the position who asked about being invited to parties in the Hamptons and if they could have Fridays off in the summer, all with lackluster experience about art. She asked her friend to send down her brightest, hardest working student, in the hopes that they would know something about art and help her build her gallery.

"Oh Anna, you are exactly what I was hoping for," Genevieve gushed, getting up from her desk, her gray suit impeccably tailored, her neat blond blonde bob razor sharp, when Anna interviewed with her. She hired her on the spot and she started that day. And every day after that, she showed up at 9:00 am with a vanilla chia latte for Genevieve, and a dark roast with milk and sugar for herself. The structure of her new days carved out space for Anna to breathe, let her think about something other then cancer and grad school. The gallery gave her exactly what she needed, even if her father and Andrew couldn't understand.

At first, Genevieve came off as a total New Yorker, tough and strident. In time, Anna learned that she was fiercely loyal, maternal, and very competitive. Once you were in her grasp, she took care of you. "You're amazing, and I can't live without you, you know that right?" she said whenever she left for a meeting or when they closed for the day. They fell into an easy rhythm, finishing each other's thoughts, looking up from catalogs with possible new acquisitions with the exact same pieces circled. Anna knew a lot, thanks to her parents, though she never breathed a word about them to Genevieve. What she didn't know she was hungry to learn.

Anna was relieved to dive into the fast-paced art world. It was the best distraction. She didn't paint at all that first year, just worked until six or seven at the gallery, then went home to Georgia and take out and whatever cable show they were binging on, swatting away thoughts of her mom, Andrew, her dad. She still talked to Marie and Stephen, but they were busy with med school and restaurant work. All the Goodrich children seemed to be using hard work as therapy, and she let herself be swept up into her new world.

But then one November, they got a painting in. It was a picture of the sea, with a café in the foreground, a rope fence separating the solid ground from the rocky coast. Out on the water, there was a boat with a fisherman on it. It looked foreign, like a view of the French Riviera or the coast of Italy. It knocked on her heart until she bought a whole set of art supplies on her way home a few weeks later, and packed them in the travel easel her mother had given her.

Since they were open on weekends, Genevieve kept the gallery closed on Mondays. Anna took the train to the Connecticut coast, to Rowayton, a commuter town just outside the city, where Georgia had taken her one weekend to visit her sister. The downtown was nestled on a harbor, with gorgeous boats and piers and a jagged coastline. The houses reminded her of Maine, with their weathered gray shingles and lobster buoys hanging from the sides.

She started to take the train there every Monday, the commuters to the city headed to the train like worker bees to the hive. She smiled to know she was going in the opposite direction. She would head to the Rowayton Market, which reminded her of Riley's, and get a hot coffee and a flaky chocolate croissant. Then she would set up on a pier, at a beach, or even in her car when it was raining, and sketch until her hand hurt.

She gravitated toward the lobster boats, and the fishermen working. The wideness of the sea.

A few years later, the gallery was having a slow summer, and Anna could see how stressed and anxious Genevieve was getting. She got burned when several new artists she had her eye on chose to sell through her biggest competitor, the Turner Gallery. When Anna read the email out loud to her announcing their show, the vein on the side of her neck pulsed as she pulled out her phone and left the owner a message.

"Thanks a lot, Richard. The artists I've been wooing for the last six months just happen to have an opening with you next week. Right after I mentioned them to you. Don't think I won't remember, darling." She slammed her phone down and paced the floor. Anna could still recall the moment when she let out in frustration "I need new blood!"

Anna looked up and said, "I know some new pieces."

Anna took her to her apartment, where she had a dozen large oils and at least twice as many smaller oils and pastels leaning against the wall in her bedroom. She liked to wake up early and work before heading to the gallery, or sometimes she would take walks through the city to take mental snapshots of images she wanted to paint, then return home and get them down as fast as she could. Her collection—though she hardly thought of it as one—was made up of scenes from Rowayton, a few from Central Park, portraits of faces at restaurants and shops in the city. She loved to capture intimacy—a mother and child, friends, lovers, even someone alone with their passion. But her favorite pieces were of the sea.

"Unbelievable!" said Genevieve when she saw them. She put her tortoiseshell eyeglasses on top of her head and leaned in more closely, her hazel eyes sparkling with delight. "It's astounding how mature your work is! I had no idea you could paint like this."

Of course, Genevieve had no idea that Anna's mother was Therese McAllister. Anna wanted it that way. They had had some of her paintings come through the gallery, and Anna found she couldn't muster the energy to tell her. It felt like a truth that rested deep in her heart, and digging it out would be too painful and messy. Except for the times her eyes fell on her mother's name on a list she was reading, or the scroll of her 'T' and 'M' stared at her from the corner of one of her paintings in the gallery, Anna felt like her mother's death was in another universe, or had perhaps just been the worst kind of dream.

"Can we have an opening with these? Next weekend?" she begged Anna.

Before she even answered, Genevieve had out her phone, and was taking pictures of Anna's paintings. "Of course," Anna said, happy to see relief and excitement on Genevieve's face instead of worry.

"Wonderful! I just sent these pictures over to the printer – can you tell them I'd like 1000 copies of a glossy card. And 100 posters. Actually, let's make it 200 and put them up around the Met. The usual format. Let me know when you get the proofs," she said.

And just like that, Anna was a commercial artist. Every painting sold that night, to Anna's great surprise. The first large pieces sold for between $10,000 and $15,000. The smaller pastels sold for $3,000 to $7,500. She was in such shock, she was glad she hadn't invited Georgia to the opening. It was just a fluke, just a favor for a friend, she kept telling herself.

The next day, there was a buzz. Several articles ran in different newspapers, and a few well-known websites ran features on the new young artist in Mid-town. When she showed up at 9:00 am with a vanilla chia latte for Genevieve, dark brew for herself, Genevieve spun around in her chair, her long thin legs crossed under her navy pencil skirt, and put down one of the reviews she had just finished reading.

"What's wrong with you, darling? Why aren't you bringing me your resignation or opening a bottle of Champagne?"

"But I don't want to stop coming here," Anna had said. She stared at Genevieve with her stubborn gaze and refused to blink. "I need this. The routine of coming here helps me paint."

"Ok, fine, but I am hiring someone else to answer the phones. You're working less hours and making more of those gorgeous paintings."

Sarah started in the Gallery the next week, a petite girl with strait black hair and perpetual red lips who had been trying to break into the art world since she graduated from Brown, and was eager to help them both. Anna was relieved. She split her hours with Sarah, keeping connected to the art world – the buyers, the egos, the markets – through the gallery. Then retreating into her own world to create new works.

After Raphael had come into the gallery, enlisting her help to pick out art for his loft, he had sent flowers every day and called twice a day until she had dinner with him. When they became a couple, she spent a lot of her time with him, but kept up her routine of painting in the morning and on her days off from the gallery. She managed to work while he did, and soon had enough pieces for a second opening. But she couldn't bring herself to invite him, or Georgia. She wanted it low key.

As they got ready for the opening, she gasped when she saw the prices Genevieve had listed for her works. This time with the larger canvases going for between $40,000 to $125,000.

"Genevieve, are you sure those are priced right?" Anna had shouted into her office when she saw the prices.

"Oh, don't worry, dear. That's a bargain compared to the garbage they're getting down at The Turner Gallery."

They had all sold. She was shocked and surprised at the check Genevieve handed to her. She was happy for Genevieve, and for the gallery. And for the Boys and Girls club, who got new supplies for their art program from an anonymous donor. The next day, Anna showed up with a chai latte for Genevieve, a skinny mocha for Sarah, and a dark roast for herself. As she walked to work, she noticed a woman on a bench in the park who wore a scarf in the shades of a sunrise, and mentally noted what she would be working on tomorrow.

Without her closest friends and Raphael knowing about her openings, she stayed grounded. The routine of going into work at the gallery kept her days ordinary enough to notice the smallest things, and she wanted to keep it that way. A few times, Anna worried that her dad would find out. Either through the magazine he worked for or a stray article he stumbled on. It was immature, she knew, but she wanted him to think she had still given up art. She was still hurt by his criticism of her choice to go to Orono. To follow Andrew. He had been wrong. Her years in Orono had been so happy. She had been surrounded by real life – real friendships, the woods and rivers of Maine, and the simple, pure love from Andrew. Sometimes, she wondered if she had ever been as happy as she had those years. Then she remembered the girl on the boat, and reminded herself again that Andrew didn't need her anymore.

She had been immersed in her painting for over an hour, her fingers and cheeks red with cold, when she heard the car door slam. She finished the last few strokes around one of the rocks before she put down her pastel and brushed her hands together, standing up. She figured it might be her dad or Aunt Catherine. She turned around and was shocked to see Andrew walking toward her. She awkwardly put her hands in her coat pockets. That feeling of shock flooded her just as it had at Shaw's Wharf, and she felt her hands shake for some odd reason.

"Hi there," she called out. Her voice seemed hoarse.

"Hi, Anna," Andrew said quietly as he walked closer to her. He looked good, his hair messy as usual, wearing jeans and a white T-shirt with a dark green plaid wool flannel over it.

"I hope you don't mind that I stopped by. I just heard from Liz that you got the house. I guess she talked to some neighbors at the bar. I saw the truck out front and wanted to see if you needed a hand with anything." He seemed like he struggled to get the last part out, as if he wasn't sure if his excuse was good enough. Anna tried not to let her reaction show. She felt pulled toward him, but she tried to tell herself it was just the familiar habit of him coming back to her mind, firing old, long-unused synapses.

"Thanks, that's really nice of you," she said. She racked her brain to think of anything he could help with, just to make him feel better about stopping by. "How about helping me move a couple of paintings to the back of the truck? I have to bring them back to Marie's, and I don't want to risk damaging them. We could carry them out together."

"Can do," he said. Andrew put his hand in his pockets, and Anna was reminded of how broad his shoulders were when he turned to go up the front walk with her. She fought the urge to grab his arm.

They walked silently into the house. The upstairs creaked as they headed toward her uncle's room. Anna grabbed a stack of towels and blankets that she found in the closet to put around the pieces. She was conscious of the small space at the top of the hall, and having him so close.

"You were painting outside, right? How's it going? Your art, I mean," Andrew said, draping a framed picture with a blanket.

"Good, I guess. It's strange being back here. Ideas have been coming to me, because, well, I just see a lot of stuff I want to paint," she said. "I forgot that Maine was so beautiful. If I try to focus, I think I could get a lot done while I'm here. Before I head back," she added.

"To New York," he said, carefully wrapping a blanket around a painting. "Do you like living there? I mean, besides all the people and traffic, of course." She was surprised he was opening the door so easily. The standoffish Andrew of the other day was gone, and the funny Andrew she remembered was standing in her uncle's hallway.

"Yes, I guess," she laughed. "Besides all the people and traffic. I like the gallery where I work. Everyone is really great, especially the owner." She shook out a quilt and pointed to a few pieces down the hall. Andrew took them down and carefully wrapped them. She and Marie had cataloged all of them and were taking most of them to her house until they decided where they were going to go. If no one was living in the house, the cold and the heat could damage them.

"Wow, did your mom do this one?" he asked, holding the one of Anna, Marie, and Stephen. "This is amazing."

Anna nodded, thinking of her dream and how surreal this moment was. He was so close to her she could breathe him in, and his smell was so familiar, yet it threw her off guard.

Andrew put the painting down. "Sorry I had to shove off so quickly the other day at Shaw's Wharf. I had to be somewhere. But I had a chance to think through some things that I wanted to say to you. Since then, I mean."

Anna saw how he was struggling. "It was a surprise to run into you too," she said, smiling, trying to make him feel at ease.

"I have thought about you a lot, you know." He looked up and met her gaze. "I wish I had stayed in touch. It feels strange. I barely know anything about your life now."

Her life now. Why would he want to know about it? She thought about how to answer him. Besides painting, and working at the gallery, she could only conjure up a string of glittering New York moments. Art shows and parties and expensive stuffy dinners where the only beer they served came from a foreign bottle. Things she knew he wouldn't care about at all. She worried her insides were too thin, too shiny for Andrew to be interested in now. And then she remembered Miranda.

"I have a student that I help mentor. She's becoming a great artist. She'll be in high school next year, and I am trying to help her get into a really good art school."

Andrew wrapped a painting, smiling. "That sounds like something you would do. You're like your mom. Good at teaching art." Anna was struck by how nice it was to be around someone with memories of her mother.

"How's your dad?" she asked.

"He's not great. He has some months where he's in bed. Other months he can walk with a cane, and even come out on the boat with me. They have some new meds that are helping to slow down the MS, but it's still pretty much downhill. My mom's good though. Still teaching at the elementary school in town. Doubt she'll ever retire."

Anna smiled thinking of his parents. They were like family to her once, and she had made good memories with them. But almost as a protection, her mind started replaying the hard memories for her as she stood wrapping up a painting. She remembered their last conversation here at home. The one at the pier by the old fort. The one when she had tried to convince him to come with her to New York. When he finally said no, that he couldn't leave Maine, something broke inside her. She felt that he should have picked her, picked their relationship, over his homebody tendencies. And she remembered the long bus ride she took, trying to tell him that she had made a mistake, that she knew they needed each other. But she was wrong. She remembered the exhaust and the chemical smell of her seat mingled with her grief, making her nauseaus. She walked around after that in a daze, her heart broken, her mind numb. It was only through Marie and Georgia, and her grief group, that she found a way to return to herself. After that she had been very disciplined in not thinking about him. She tucked the pain she felt about losing him in with losing her mom, being angry at her father. She wrapped up her life in Maine carefully and left it buried in her heart. The stubborn streak she inherited from her dad came in handy when it came to shutting out the pain.

But now here he was, suddenly right in front of her, and her heart had a completely different story than her mind did. There was no rational closed door, only a strong gravitational pull towards this person.

"I was wondering, do you, would you like to come out with me on the boat sometime? We could catch up on life, or something," he asked, scratching his head on the side like he always did when he was thinking deeply.

Anna stopped working. "I – I've got a boyfriend. His name is Raphael. He lives in the city." She shifted her weight from one foot to the other.

"Oh. Right. I guessed maybe you didn't, since you were alone the night of the funeral. I guessed wrong, huh?" he said, smiling wistfully, his cheeks turning a light shade of rose.

"Do you?" Anna asked, her voice a few octaves from normal. "Have a girlfriend?"

Andrew stood at the top of the stairs with a large painting in his hands and stared at it. He shook his head slowly. "No, there is no one serious," he answered. Then he looked up at Anna. "No one who lives in Maine, that is." Then he headed downstairs.

Anna wrapped up another painting. She thought of what Andrew just said, trying to understand what he meant by it. She could see him out the window from her uncle's room, setting the frame carefully in the truck. He seemed deep in thought, his eyebrows furrowed. It was surreal to Anna that she was standing here in her uncle's house, having a conversation with him. Catching up. She heard his feet coming up the stairs.

"So how's your dad doing?" Andrew asked. "This has to be hard on him, his brother passing, right?"

"Yes, of course." Anna nodded. "You know my dad. The controversy has to be somewhere. For him it is with the board of directors of the bank that my uncle was on. He thinks they gave him the heart attack, with all their stressful mandates they kept putting on him. It had nothing to do with the fact that he had a penchant for steak and Scotch, or ate a fish fry every Friday," Anna said. She tried to make things light, because with Andrew around, everything felt intense.

"Your dad loved the heat of battle," he said. Anna suddenly felt protective, like she had said too much. Her confused feelings about her dad's dislike of Andrew flooded her, and she found herself feeling just as she did when he said he couldn't come to New York. The look on his face, the sound of the waves came back to her as if it just happened yesterday.

"Well, at least he stands by the things he loves," she said quietly. She hadn't meant to go back there. It had only been a few minutes ago that she was happily painting, and now she was confronting Andrew about his choice seven years ago.

Andrew set down the painting he was about to carry to the car. He turned around slowly and looked at her, his face showing her that he understood what she meant.

"Anna, it wasn't about me not standing by you," he said. "It was about me helping my dad, about building the life I saw for me, for us. I don't belong in New York City. Could you imagine me there for one day? I didn't think you did either, but obviously I was very wrong."

He went downstairs, and while he walked out to the truck again, Anna flared up at his response. What does he know about her? What did he know back then? Nothing. He was trying to blame her for wanting to leave when all she had ever done was follow him—to college, back to New Harbor. Her life was in New York, her friends, her work, Raphael. Then why did what he just said sting so sharply? She put her hands on her hips and stared out at the ocean. She felt like she would rather it swallow her up than continue this conversation. She walked out to the car with a painting and set it in the back of the truck, then turned to face him.

"If you felt like that, why didn't you pick up the phone and call me? Tell me how you felt instead of waiting this long, when there is absolutely nothing I can do about it. Hell, why didn't you bother to call me after I left you a message?"

The wind from the ocean was whipping at her hair, her chambray shirt. Andrew stood next to his truck holding the door open. He closed it and turned around to face her. "I never got any message from you," he said.

Anna felt again the black wave of hurt and fear on her ride home. She couldn't tell him what she had said, and what she had seen. She couldn't let him know how hurt she had been. "It's fine. Really not a big deal. I just called to catch up but obviously it wasn't worth it."

His eyes were so full of emotion, a part of her wanted to comfort him. Then he frowned and walked to toward his car.

"Well, I'm glad I didn't get it. I'd probably just have to feel all over again how wonderful it is when the person you love chooses a city over you when we talked. Why would I put myself through that again? There was no changing your mind, Anna. You were going to leave. And I could never have kept up with you. It was easier to imagine you had changed, that you were a different person than the one I was in love with. But you're here now and . . . you're still you. I just can't believe you've really picked something else over what we had," he turned to her, his eyes looked right at her, desperate, pleading, and then a cloud came over them. "But you have. So I have to deal with that." Andrew turned towards the water, and looked out at the ocean before he turned back to her. "I've got to go."

"Wait, Andrew," she shouted as he pulled away, but the roar of his engine drowned her out. She stood there staring as his truck disappeared from view.

Later that afternoon, Anna looked up from her painting in the boathouse and looked out at the harbor. She watched the boats rise and fall with the swells of the ocean. She closed her eyes, and thought back to a summer afternoon, when she and Andrew were on his boat. She lay with her head in his lap, the rhythm of the waves as the tide came in gently lulling her, bringing on sleep.

She opened her eyes and saw him looking at her. Patient, ardent, quiet Andrew. "Why do you love me, Andrew?" she asked, reaching up and running her hands through his hair.

He stroked her cheek, then looked up out onto the water. "Because your good, Anna. Your everything that's good and beautiful," he said, kissing her knuckles gently. He laughed and then asked, "Why do you love me?"

Anna wasn't sure she could answer him very well. Discovering that Andrew loved her, looking up and seeing his straw-colored hair and piercing blue eyes, his eyebrows so light they almost disappeared in the sun. He was strong and smart, beautiful and simple, and he was hers. It felt like she was inside of a dream.

"You know how a mussel is just two shells stuck together? It feels like we're each one of the shells," she said, and smiled up at him. "Like we're only whole when we're together."

After that, Andrew started leaving mussel shells for her – in her coat pocket, on her back steps.

Anna sighed and opened her eyes, and looked down at her painting. She had intended to paint the sea, but instead she had painted mussel shells lying open on the sandy ocean floor in shallow waters, the ripples obscuring them slightly, the light bouncing off the ripples. The shades of iridescent pearl white and cobalt blue were copied from the mussel shells that sat on the table next to her. She noticed, for the first time, that each shell was the shape of half a heart.

Chapter 8

Anna stared at her computer open in front of her on her uncle's kitchen table, a large coffee from Riley's in her hand.

Miranda Rivera exemplifies the type of student that we need to nourish, tend, and till in order for the next generation to flourish. With her enthusiasm, dedication, and talent, she has the brightest of futures, if given this opportunity.

She was trying to get her mind off everything and writing Miranda's letter of recommendation was the perfect excuse. She re-read the letter and changed *flourish* to *blossom*, decided it was done, and emailed the letter to both Miranda and the admissions director at the school.

She sat back with a big sigh. If it wasn't for being able to channel her energy into something to help Miranda, she would probably still be under her covers. She didn't know how, but everything about Andrew felt reopened and up for discussion. *I tried so hard to let you go,* she thought. *Please stay gone*, she pleaded into her coffee.

When Anna returned to her sister's house, the late afternoon air was clear and bright, and smelled of wet dirt from the rhododendron bushes Mike had transplanted that afternoon. When she walked into the kitchen, her sister was pounding a mound of dough.

"Hope you're in the mood for pizza," Marie said. Henry was sitting at the island with her, tearing apart his own little ball of dough.

"Auntie! We got cheese," her nephew said, holding up a bowl of mozzarella.

"I'm starving, that sounds great," said Anna as she took a bite of the freshly grated cheese. "You'll never believe who came to visit me today at Uncle Charlie's."

"Who?" Marie asked, wiping a bit of flour from her cheek with her shoulder. Anna noticed she had flour in her bangs but decided not to mention it.

"Andrew."

"What? For what possible reason did he come over?

"He said he thought I could use some help. And then he sort of asked me to go out with him on his boat. But I told him about Raphael. And I think I might have blamed him for all of our problems too. Either way he did not leave happy."

"Well, sounds like you were your normal self. I think getting Raphael up here would help you out right now. Think you could get him to come up for the fundraiser for the Foundation in a few weeks?"

"What fundraiser?"

"Well, we have a big gala every April, to raise money for the coming summer tuitions for kids from the city. I never invite you because I know how you feel about it."

Anna shook of her coat and sat down. "Well, I don't know how I feel about it. I didn't know it was happening."

"Well, Aunt Catherine always organizes it, I'm more of her wing man. Along with Sarah. It's at the high school but it's supposed to be black tie. This year's theme is the Great Gatsby."

"And you've never invited me?" Anna said, her mouth hanging open.

"Well, you did say you wanted nothing to do with the Foundation after dad asked you to help out with it."

Anna chewed on more cheese. She started sprinkling some in front of Henry, teasing him with one of his favorite foods, welcoming the distraction.

"Is Stephen going?"

Marie skillfully spread out the pizza dough and started spreading the sauce. "He came for a few years but he's been too busy with the restaurant since last year. So he won't be there." She layered toppings – artichokes and zucchini and onions – as she spoke. "It'll be fun, you and Raphael coming would mean so much to everyone. Especially with the funeral and everything."

"Well, I'll have to talk to Raphael. I'm not sure if we're up for it, but since I'm here, I'd feel bad not going. Although are you sure dad even wants me to go? He is still icing me out. No surprise there." Anna joked, but the truth was she suddenly felt very confused and raw about everything, including her Dad.

"Never mind Dad, he'll come around sooner or later. I think it's good that you stayed. He'll have to get used to you when you are always around. And I think coming to the fundraiser would be a nice step towards you two getting along." Her sister smiled at her reassuringly. "But Andrew is another story. And I kind of already asked Liz to see if he could come to the gala."

Anna pushed the bowl of cheese toward her sister. "I don't know, I can't even think about it right now. Is Mike home tonight?"

Marie nodded. "He had early morning rounds, but he's off tonight."

"Think he'll let you sneak out to Shaw's Wharf for a drink?" Anna said.

Mike walked in, muddy from the yard. "I'm sensing there's a trade in there for me. Like free babysitting sometime while we go out?" He rubbed Henry's head and grabbed a pile of pepperoni from the counter and popped it in his mouth.

"You should have been a lawyer not a doctor with those swift negotiation skills," Anna answered, laughing. "That sounds like a fair trade though," she said, hugging Henry.

While Marie put Henry down, Anna curled up on the bed she'd been sleeping on and called Raphael about the gala. As she listend to the phone ring, she flashed for a moment to Andrew climbing into his pickup truck, and then just as quickly she pushed it out when she heard his voice answer.

"Hey sweetie, how's it going?"

"Hi hon, it's going pretty good. I cleaned out my uncle's house and got some painting done. How are you?"

"I am working my tail off while you are gone, and I've been going to the gym almost every night. Except for tonight – the guys are coming over to watch the Yankees play Boston."

"Sounds like a dream night for you. I just wanted to ask you a quick question. My sister was wondering if you would come up for a gala the weekend after next. It's to raise money for my mom's foundation."

"I'll have to double check, but I'll try to come up, if it's important to you."

Anna thought for a moment, and tried to think through how she was feeling about it. Then she thought of Miranda, and all the students who would benefit from the fundraiser, and said, "Yes. I would like to go and it would be great if you could be there."

"Ok, love, just let me check my schedule. The guys just got here. Call you tomorrow?"

"Sure, talk to you tomorrow. Love you," she said. She held the invitation her sister had given to her and ran her finger over the raised letters. *The 5th Annual Therese McCallister Goodrich Foundation Fundraiser.* She couldn't believe there had been a party in her mother's name for so long without her knowing about it. Though if she had, she was confident her dad would want her to run it every year. Still, she couldn't help but feel the smallest degree of peace in this idea, peace in the knowledge that the foundation existed. That her mom's name lived on in it. Too bad it had a tyrant for a director.

They drove into the gravel parking lot of Shaw's Wharf, the evening air making everything feel cool and damp. The smell of wet earth mixed with the salt water, and Anna breathed in deeply. The somber sound of the harbor bell rang out mellow and low. They could hear the laughter of a small group coming up from the bar. It was Saturday night, so the bar was busy with locals—the tourists would come once the weather turned warmer. Anna was looking forward to a cold beer and time with her sister to help her smooth the rough edges of the last few days.

As they walked into the bar, Marie laughed out loud. "What's so funny?" Anna asked.

"Well, if you wanted some space from your issues, you might have come to the wrong place." She pointed toward the bar. Behind the long, wooden counter stood Liz, Andrew's outspoken sister. Her blue eyes were the same, and her dirty blond hair was pulled up in a ponytail. Underneath her sweatshirt and jeans you could see her muscular, petite frame was still just as lean and strong as it had ever been. Liz had always been a runner. She was a life force. Her loud voice boomed out at the customers while she counted money for a customer's change. And her face still held a compelling sweetness— maybe it was the roundness or the dimple on the right, but you had to love Liz, even if she was yelling at you.

"Can I help you?" she said, not glancing up until the end of her question. "Oh my gosh, what are you guys doing here?" Her shock was genuine, just as Andrew's had been last week. She came out from behind the bar and gave them each a hug.

"Sit down and have a beer, on me," she said, her face lit up. She poured two Pemaquid Ales and set them down. Anna took a long sip and smiled at their friend. Liz's reception had been warm, and she hoped it would continue this way. Liz and Marie had been friends, but she knew that Liz disapproved of Anna's choice to move to New York, to become a big-city snob. To leave Maine and her brother only added to the injury. But tonight it appeared to be long forgotten.

"Sorry to hear about your uncle, you guys. He used to come here all the time. Can't believe we won't see him around anymore." Her sadness was so genuine, it once again hit Anna that her uncle was really gone. Anna looked down the row of bar stools and could just picture her uncle sitting on one of them.

"Thanks, Liz," Marie said. Her eyes filled up a bit even as she smiled. "It's very kind of you to say so."

"So my brother mentioned he saw you." Liz turned to Anna. Anna squeezed her glass a bit tighter. She smiled lightly.

"It was really great to see him. It's great to see you too," Anna said. "Makes me miss home." She pushed up the sleeves of her sweater nervously and took another sip of beer. Out in the harbor, the *Christina Therese* sat a few yards from the dock.

"Since he's been back he's been really preoccupied or something. Like something happened on his last trip maybe," Liz said. She stood with one hand on her hip and one on the bar, a motion so familiar to Anna that she had to blink to remind herself that any time had passed at all since she last saw Liz.

Anna found her curiosity stoked. "Trip where?" she asked.

"He's been traveling around testing ocean levels. South America. Alaska. His last trip was to Brazil last winter break, for a couple of months. I don't know, it seems like something happened down there, but he's been so busy finishing his semester and setting up the boat for the lobster season, I haven't had a chance to talk to him."

It sounded to Anna like Liz was describing a totally different person than the Andrew she knew. Andrew who didn't want to leave Maine? Andrew, who was a lobsterman through and through, in Brazil? It made no sense. She shot Marie a glance, and Marie just shrugged. More surprises, it would seem.

"Um, what do you mean, *semester*? Is Andrew back in school?" Anna asked.

"No, he got his PhD two years ago. But now he teaches and does research at the DMC in Walpole."

Anna stared at her with a blank look on her face. "The DMC?"

"DMC stands for Darling Marine Center. It's University of Maine's school of marine sciences. Like their marine laboratory. It's on Clarks Cove Road, about twenty minutes away."

"So he's like a professor?" Anna struggled to put the thoughts together.

"Pretty much. But he's more interested in the research. He really went to school to figure out how to make sure Maine lobstering could stay healthy and sustained. He wanted all the families who rely on lobstering to not have it be threatened by pollution, warmer ocean temps, or radical environmentalists. So he does research on it now. That's why he had to travel, to get a bigger perspective on what was happening to the oceans all over. But he always came back for lobster season. Never missed a season. He made sure of that. Andrew says that with the seasonal fishing laws in place, we should have the Maine lobster industry for another hundred years. Says there's lots of bugs down below. They like these waters because of the rocky ledges on the ocean floor here, from the glaciers passing through. From here all the way up through Canada. Best spot on earth. They have a whole city for themselves under Maine's waters. Hang on one second." A few new customers sat down at the other end of the bar, and she went over to take their drink order.

Anna picked up her beer and swallowed a large gulp. "Are you kidding me?" she said to Marie. "Andrew is the ocean's new protector? He didn't just drive a boat for the past seven, eight years? He went and got his *doctorate*?" She finished the rest of her beer in one sip. "I'm going to need yours too till Liz comes back," she said, and grabbed her sister's beer.

That night, Anna dreamed of the ocean floor. It had cavernous spaces and rocky ledges, and piles and piles of lobsters. On a far-off ledge, there was one lobster that was blue. Around it, the ocean waters seemed to glow, or maybe the glow was coming from the lobster itself.

Chapter 9

It had been a relaxing Sunday with church at St. Patrick's, then brunch out with Mike, Marie, Henry, Aunt Catherine, and Uncle Joe. Anna realized she was feeling good about going to Church again, and she added it to the list of changes she felt since she had come home. Her anger at God had melted considerably, she noticed, and thought it might be time to get in His good graces again.

She spent the afternoon in the boathouse painting. Afterward, she headed back to her sister's house. She had made an amazing lamb curry for them while Mike was at work. He hated Indian food, but Marie loved it and made it often when he had to work at night. Anna filled herself with the delicious stew, flavored with ginger and garlic, and dipped her fingers into the warm pile of naan bread Marie served. She let the comfort food distract her and tried not to think about Andrew. She had called Raphael both yesterday and today, but said nothing about Andrew or the Fundraiser.

On Monday morning, Anna woke up with a pressing thought—Andrew was a professor. She went to the computer, looked up the Darling Marine Center, and in less than five minutes learned that there were in fact two weeks left of classes, and that a Professor Andrew

Toomey was teaching Invertebrate Biology at ten a.m. After borrowing Marie's truck and promising to drive carefully (with an eye roll) she drove the twenty minutes to the campus, which was easy to find. Class didn't start for twenty more minutes, so she grabbed a coffee at the cafeteria and then made her way across campus wearing a baseball hat and nondescript clothes - Mike's navy blue hoodie and jeans. Anna reached the classroom and sighed with relief since it turned out to be lecture room. She could hide in the back.

What are you doing? Are you crazy? Stalking this place where Andrew teaches? What's next, are you going to hide on the boat before he sets off? Wandering into the ladies' room to kill the last few minutes, she splashed some cold water on her face, suddenly very nervous. She overheard two girls talking next to her. They were grad students, probably, in jeans and sweaters. They were reasonably attractive, clearly very academic and confident.

"So only two classes left with Toomey. How are you taking it?" the shorter, dark-haired girl said to her taller friend with blond curls.

"My hearts gonna break a little bit at the final. Maybe I'll have to rearrange my fall schedule to fit in one of his classes," she said as she lathered Chap Stick on her lips.

"I know. I almost want to volunteer to be his skipper this summer just to have some more face time with him. Could you imagine being in a boat alone with him out on the ocean?" Anna was very glad her face was resting in a paper towel as they spoke, because her reaction was completely involuntary. She started to laugh out loud, but managed to make it sound like a cough. She found herself feeling oddly . . . protective? Angry? *Jealous?* Of *Andrew?* Dear Lord, what was happening?

Anna quickly rushed into the back of the classroom and pulled her cap down low over her eyes. She spotted a tall, rotund guy and sat right behind him. Not long after she sat down, Andrew walked into the room. He was wearing old jeans and Top-Siders, and a blue oxford with a white T-shirt underneath it. After a minute of staring at his stack of papers, he looked up and started to speak.

"Okay, everyone, we are two weeks out from the final right now. If anyone hasn't completed their last lab they should have it in to me by the end of the week. I'm not accepting any more as of Friday at five p.m. Just slide it under my door before that time." Anna felt an electric shock go through her body at the sound of his voice. He spoke with his hands in his pockets and the effect was casual, but Anna had to admit that he was extremely attractive as a professor. Who could blame those girls? It was hard to concentrate on tidal charts or exoskeletons with Andrew teaching.

"Let's go over the items that will be covered on the exam. Consider this class and next week a review. We'll follow the syllabus as we review since the exam will follow it pretty closely. First we have anatomy, habitat, and reproduction. Who wants to tell me about the lobster's brain?"

Anna looked down hard at the floor as Andrew walked around the front of the class. Although the lecture hall was big, she noticed with a slight sense of panic that it was not that full. He could spot her if he looked around the giant in front of her. She pulled out her sketch notebook in her purse so that it looked like she was following along, and put her hand on the side of her face, covering her profile.

She listened for a few more minutes in her silent panic. *Okay, seriously, what were you thinking? Do you think you are going to get out of this moment without him recognizing you? Are you prepared for the humiliation you are about to experience?* She couldn't believe her internal alarm did not go off when she had first considered this idea. It was such a strong reaction, when she saw his name next to this class time she decided to check it out. She almost didn't believe Liz when she first told her. But here she was, sitting in her old boyfriend's classroom, hiding like a criminal in the back.

And then it happened. Andrew walked over to pull down a roll-up chart hanging at the side of the classroom. "Let's review habitat. Tell me about the relationship between migration and water temperature." His eyes cast over the room when the large guy in front of her bent down to pick up a pen, and he spotted Anna. Andrew's face grew confused, then stunned; then finally a faint smile crossed his lips. Though the students might not have noticed, Anna did. She tried to sit lower in her chair, but it was too late. I'm an idiot, she thought. Andrew regained his focus and continued on as if he hadn't noticed her at all.

—

"So are you planning on taking the final exam too?" she heard Andrew say after the last student had left the classroom. Anna could hardly move from her seat. The humiliation weighed down on her. She had picked the edges of the sweatshirt hoodie through the whole class, and now there was a good-sized hole along the seam. She took a deep breath and stood up to face him.

"Why didn't you tell me you were a professor?" she said. "I mean, why were you trying to hide this?" She put one hand on the desk next to her, and the other rested on her hip.

"Anna, we haven't exactly sat down over a cup of coffee, have we? It didn't occur to me to mention it to you," he said, picking up handouts and books. "Besides, what difference does it make to you? So what if I am a professor or researcher? I'm doing this to help other lobstermen. Lobstering comes first for me, and you already know that's what I do." He put his things into his bag.

"Well, you could have mentioned it," Anna mumbled. She felt even more humiliated by the fact that he was right. What business was it of hers? "I'm sorry that I interrupted your class. I didn't mean to bother you. I guess I was just shocked when your sister told me you taught here. And there have been so many surprises lately that I can't seem to think clearly anymore." She couldn't look at him as she spoke. "I should probably go." She walked toward the door, pulling her baseball hat down tighter around her head.

"Wait," he said. "At least let me buy you lunch. I have to eat now anyway. We will officially catch up over a sandwich. No more surprises."

At first Anna thought the invitation was a bad idea. Somehow it seemed like it would confuse her even more to spend more time with him. But then she realized she was curious. She wanted to hear how he had become a professor while remaining a lobsterman.

"Okay," she said, heading into the hall. "But let me buy lunch. I crashed your class. It's the least I can do."

The large windows of the cafeteria filled the room with sunlight, and the tree boughs around the window swayed lazily in the wind. Anna stared at them while she waited for Andrew to sit down with his tray. She had grabbed some soup and crackers. Her stomach felt a little too nervous to eat a sandwich or salad. She saw him crossing the cafeteria, walking toward her with his confident, slow stride. Her thoughts drifted back to their days in college, when they ate together in the food court every night for dinner. They were broke then so they had to stretch every dollar they had on their meal cards. They would sit there for hours eating frozen yogurt and doing homework, or talking with friends, laughing until their sides hurt.

She didn't think he wanted to become anything other than a lobsterman after college, although he always excelled at his studies. A biology major, he graduated magna cum laude, something her father often pointed out when they talked about how he was 'just' a lobsterman. Anna could hear her father now: *How can he throw his education and talent away like that? For what? Some romantic occupation?* She snapped out of her daydream just as he sat down. His tray was filled with a large sub and chips. She remembered he didn't like tomatoes, and she saw some sticking out of the sub. "You know there are tomatoes on there, right?" she said.

Andrew promptly picked them off. "Thanks."

Anna took a bite of her soup, a delicious clam chowder. She noticed the two grad students from the bathroom staring at them and she had to smile. She cleared her throat. "So when I left for New York, you were determined to keep up your family's lobstering rights, or your territory at least. Keep the tradition alive. How did you end up getting your PhD while doing that?"

Andrew took a bite and rolled up his sleeves, thinking. "Not long after you moved, there was a bunch of fighting between the fishermen and the lawmakers. They wanted to increase the minimum size for lobsters that you could keep while they were shortening the fishing season. The local newspapers were carrying articles about the debate almost every day. The lawmakers were listening to shoddy facts from environmentalists. It just really made me mad. I knew these waters. I knew there were plenty of lobsters down there. They thought they were trying to keep lobstering sustainable, but they would have easily pushed out the fishermen we had at the time by making those changes. So the one thing I kept thinking was they needed someone who understood both sides of the debate. Someone who understood the ocean and the lobstermen. I took some classes thinking I was just going to get my master's degree, and by then I had become close with a few professors who shared my view. They encouraged me to keep going. So I did. And I was lucky. They understood the constraints I had during lobster season and they never required me to do anything during that time. If I had to take a trip for some research, they scheduled it in the winter or spring." Andrew waved hello to a group of students that walked by.

"What about the fights between lawmakers and lobstermen? Have you been able to make a difference so far?" Anna asked.

Andrew shrugged. "Well, the oceans are definitely getting warmer. We've had record catches because Long Island and Connecticut lobsters are moving north. But I think with bigger boats, and lobsterman going out farther, we can keep this industry in Maine. I just published a few papers on it, so we'll see."

Anna nodded. They ate in silence for a few minutes. "How's your brother doing? I heard he opened a restaurant in Rhode Island?"

"Yes, he seems pretty stressed at the moment and we don't get to see him that much. But I think he's good, from the little I have gathered. He's upset about Uncle Charlie too." Anna felt another twinge of guilt that she hadn't visited and check in on her brother since he opened the restaurant. Anna looked up at Andrew's face, and she suddenly found herself wondering what experiences he had had, and if he had loved anyone else besides her. "So what about your grad school years. Any girlfriends?" she asked.

He sat back and crossed his arms, silently thinking for a few moments. "A few. I just came from a trip in Brazil where I grew pretty close to a colleague. But it didn't work out," he said soberly. "She wanted to go back to the West Coast. Seems like I have a bad streak of luck with girls who don't want to live in Maine." He gave a shy, crooked grin, and the effect was so disarming Anna was grateful she was sitting down. Surely her knees would have buckled at this moment.

"What about you and your guy in New York? Where's that headed?" he asked. His voice was very direct and took on a serious tone. He wasn't grinning anymore, but instead sat holding his drink in his hand, his eyebrows furrowed. His shirtsleeves were rolled up and Anna could see the scar on the bottom of his right forearm. A lobster trap had come up too quickly and dug into his arm, scraping his flesh almost to the bone. She had taken him to get stitches at the hospital in Bristol.

"He works in finance, on Wall Street. He's from Argentina originally, but his family has lived in Connecticut since his school days." She nibbled on a salty cracker as if to say she was finished talking about it, but Andrew pressed on. "Well, how come you're still here in Maine? I mean, how much time can you take off for a funeral? Did you take a leave of absence or something?" he asked. He leaned toward her with great interest, his arms crossed and his shoulders forward.

"I have a great job at the gallery," Anna said. "My boss is like a mentor. I've learned so much from her. She let me stay here in Maine and I promised her I would look into the galleries here, see if there was anything worth bringing back." Anna hoped her answer sounded convincing. She again promised herself to visit the gallery her father had mentioned so that her story about scouting out talent looked good to Raphael and her family. She still wanted to be under the radar about working on several pieces while she was here.

As if he could read her mind, Andrew asked, "What about your painting?" His face seemed to soften a bit, and in his eyes she saw a friend, and something else. Longing. That was what was getting to her. She could see Andrew's longing. Since they first saw each other at Shaw's Wharf. It seemed to stir up her own.

Anna tried to hide her thoughts. "I still paint. I can't help it. It's just . . . always going to be something I do, I guess." She wasn't sure why she wanted to keep her commercial life hidden. She liked the creative freedom that came from no one thinking she was trying to sell her art, that it was just for her. And for some reason she didn't want Andrew to know about her agreement with Genevieve, although it would be easier to tell him then her father. For now, she wanted to keep things the way they were.

"Tell that to your dad," Andrew said, laughing into his plate of chips. "He must be really sad that you keep your lantern hidden under a basket. He wanted you to be a direct link to the Old Masters, right? No offense, I just remember the pressure you had to deal with. I don't know if he just relaxed as he got older, or . . ."

"I wouldn't say that," Anna said. Talking about her dad put her on edge again. "He's still the same as always. We just don't really talk much now." She grew sad at the thought, and the whole situation made her depressed. "I sort of swore to him I'd never paint again when I left. To cut off that pressure once and for all. I would rather he think that I stopped painting than for him to know that my apartment hardly has room to hold any more art. It's easier that way. Raphael is always teasing me that he has nowhere to sit—we don't . . . we don't live together. I have a roommate." She wasn't sure why she was telling Andrew this.

Andrew wiped his face with a napkin and was quiet for a moment. "Do you love him?" he asked. Anna suddenly felt very uncomfortable, and the room became so hot that she felt a drop of sweat roll down her forehead. Maybe it was the soup overheating her, or sitting in the sunlit window. Or maybe it was having Andrew shine a light so intensely on her life. She wasn't ready for this kind of scrutiny.

"I would say that falls under the category of none of your business, kind of like your getting a PhD is none of mine," she answered. She crossed her arms. Her pale skin grew flush under her cheeks.

"But you're here, aren't you? And I told you that story." Andrew answered, smiling slightly. The effect was disarming.

Still, Anna couldn't answer him. He quickly added, "I'm sorry, I didn't mean to make you uncomfortable. And, I'm sorry for driving away so angry the other day." His eyebrows furrowed as he spoke, and he played with the salt and pepper shakers nervously.

"No, I'm the one who owes you an apology, I shouldn't have blamed you for everything, and I did," said Anna. "We just, we needed different things. And it was a hard time for me, with my mom gone."

His face was tight with emotion. "It's not your fault. It was my fault. When I . . . when I saw you again, I just . . ." He sighed and pushed his hands through his hair, the perpetual mess of Andrew's light brown locks. "Look, I have office hours that start in a few minutes." Andrew glanced at his watch and avoided her gaze. "I'm done with my semester in a few weeks. If you're still around, why don't you bring your sister and nephew out on the boat?" He stood up suddenly and grabbed his tray. "I should run. I'll see you later, Anna," he said. He made eye contact quickly, his gaze intense, but guarded. He nodded as he walked away.

Anna sat watching the leaves blow in the wind outside, though the sun had disappeared behind a cloud. She couldn't seem to forget the feel of being under that gaze.

Chapter 10

She drove back to her uncle's house (she had resigned herself to the fact that it would feel like her uncle's house for a while, so why fight it?). The sky had turned dark gray, and the ocean acted as a mirror to the sky, making it hard to pick out the horizon.

Why did she go to Andrew's classroom? Why did she feel unsettled about everything? Andrew and Raphael, her dad? She could feel the weight of her emotions pulling her down as she pulled into Riley's market. She grabbed some tea, wine, and chocolate—she wasn't sure which one she needed. On her way back to the car she spotted the new gallery again. She put her things in the front seat and walked over. She listened to the sound of the small rocks crunching under her feet. The sea roses lined the edge of the road, and she tried to steer clear of the thorns.

As she walked up to the gallery, she saw the *Open* sign was hanging in the window. She climbed the front steps and pushed open the door, which creaked loudly. The inside had a narrow white staircase to the left.

She followed the stairs and found herself in a large loft with pictures hanging on three walls, the fourth wall being a large window looking out at the road behind her. She didn't see anyone inside. She walked up to the first section of paintings and took them in. After working in a gallery for so long, she trained herself to go from left to right around a room, paying attention to the images that grabbed her attention. She already felt a painting of a large brown and white cow hanging in the center of the second wall pulling at her, but she tried to stay focused. She was immediately taken in by the artist's bold, round brushstrokes and use of color. The pastoral and landscape images were touched by an exaggeration of color that made them feel electric—the green was too green to be real, the eyes of an elderly man were too blue. She could see that the beauty of the coast called to this artist, as images of Monhegan Island, the lighthouse, and the rocky shores were mixed with images of a city.

Her dad had told her that the artist lived in New York, and she began to notice images that looked like Brooklyn and Chinatown, perhaps Central Park. As she went around the room, along with the brown cow, an image of a woman sitting on a porch with the sun setting on the ocean behind her grabbed her attention. Just then, she heard footsteps. A tall, dark-haired woman came up the stairs. She wore a loose white oxford, jeans, and moccasin slippers, and she had a stylish layered bob. She somehow exuded elegance and comfort at the same time.

"Hi there," she said, her voice deep and gravelly. Anna detected years of smoking had added the patina to her voice.

"Hi there. Hope I didn't intrude," Anna said. "The sign said you were open, so I let myself in."

"Of course, the gallery is open. Let me know if you have any questions," the woman said.

"Are you the artist?" asked Anna. She still had on jeans and her navy hoodie and realized she must look very young—too young to buy artwork, or at least too poor.

"Yes, I am. My name is Abigail Perinault. And you?" Anna was struck by her formality. She had a complexity that was part sophistication, part intelligence.

"My name is Anna. Anna Goodrich."

"Oh my word. I know you!" Abigail looked shocked. "Or I should say, I knew your mother well, and I knew you when you were a little girl. And I know your father too."

"Really? You were a friend of my mother's?" Anna was surprised. She used to know many of her mother's artist friends, but she couldn't remember ever meeting Abigail.

"In fact, this one . . . yes, this painting right here was one I painted of your mother years ago." She pointed to the picture of the woman on the porch. "She was pregnant with one of her children, not sure which. I think she had a toddler at the time."

"Then it was Stephen. She would have been pregnant with Stephen." Anna looked at the painting, and her eyes took in the line of the woman's face. It was so nondescript, just the outline of a woman's form, that it would be impossible to be certain it was her mother, but somehow the scene and the ambiguous figure seemed familiar. "I wonder why my mother never mentioned you."

"I moved to New York shortly after that. I came back to visit here and there, once when you were little. I remember your long dark pigtails." Abigail laughed. "But we lost touch. She was an extremely talented woman."

"Thank you. She was." Anna smiled. "Your art is beautiful. I love how you capture the color in the rocks. And your sky here"—Anna pointed to the picture of Monhegan Island—"it's really breathtaking. You know, I could bring some of these back with me. I work in a gallery in Manhattan, the Genevieve Keller Gallery."

Her face revealed some resistance, then softened. "Thank you for the flattering offer. I'll think it over. I sort of came up here to escape all that. I don't paint well when I think of the art as a commodity. But here, take a card, give me a call when you get back," she said, handing her a card from the nearby table.

Anna found herself wanting to tell this woman yes, she knew what she meant. She wanted to show her the painting she was working on and discuss her technique on the rocks and sky, and tell her that she agreed with her that art for sale was spirit-crushing at times. But all she said was, "Sure. I'll be in touch, though I don't know exactly when I will be back in the city." Anna smiled and took the card. She waved goodbye as she headed down the stairs.

When she reached the outside air, she was met with her thoughts of her earlier funk—Andrew, her father, Raphael. These were now mixed with a strange optimism after meeting Abigail. She was a fine artist and would be a great discovery. But more than that, Anna was reminded of her mother. They would be roughly the same age. Being around another strong female artist—one who rejected the "noise" of the city and art scene—reminded Anna of something she had gotten from her mother. That same strength. That sense of painting for oneself.

She thought about what it would be like if her mother was still here. How she would feel about Anna's life in New York? Would she be as disappointed as her father was? Anna thought that maybe the answer was yes, though for different reasons.

As she walked to her car, she remembered how her mother had stood next to her after Anna showed her a painting she had done.

It's beautiful, darling. But keep going, keep going. Push yourself to match up what you see and feel as closely as possible. How do you see? That is what the picture should tell us.

The answer always made Anna a better artist. It also made her thick-skinned. She expected a critique, first from herself, then from some trusted source, for each painting. She wished she could have the same perspective on her life, the ability to ask someone, *Have I made the right choice, living in New York? What is the next brush-stroke?* There was no answer, she knew. She was a big girl now.

She drove back to her uncle's house, and settled her bags. She decided to have tea first and grabbed a mug off the shelf, looking at it and realizing it was her uncle's favorite mug, with the faded logo of Hardy Boat Cruises on it. They ran the boat that took everyone from Shaw's Wharf to Monhegan Island. Almost every time she was over he was sipping coffee with extra cream out of it. Even if it was hours old, with the cream hardened in swirls on the surface, rings left at different levels, he would still sip it. She put it back on the shelf and grabbed another. While the tea steeped, she called Marie to say that she was going to try to sleep there, and would it be okay if she kept the truck. Her sister didn't mind, she said, as long as she was careful – Anna rolled her eyes once again - and reminded her that their dad was coming over for dinner tomorrow. Anna said she would be there.

She headed out to the Adirondack chairs at the top of the dock with her tea and sketch pad, wearing a fleece over the navy hoodie.

It was impressive how being in Maine for a short time had taken her desire to be fashionable out with the tide. The Earl Grey tasted wonderful but it didn't help her stop feeling annoyed for some reason about her lunch with Andrew. She was mad at herself for going to his class. It was humiliating, to say the least. And he was different than the other day. He was more guarded, closed off. Maybe it was the fact that she was on his turf. Or that he was very busy. But she had a feeling it had to do with Raphael.

She had to admit that there was a part of her that came alive around Andrew. It was just that she had worked so hard to bury that part of herself when he didn't choose her. Her head hurt thinking about it.

She looked out at the churning ocean waves, soothing in their rhythmic dance, and took a deep breath. She thought of Raphael. He hadn't called her in a few days. *I think he is mad at me for being here*, Anna thought. She worried about it for a minute and then remembered that the last time they spoke, he said he was going to use the time she was away productively. Catch up at the gym, with his friends and family. She looked at her phone for a minute, then dialed his number and got his voice mail. It was still 4:30; maybe he was still at work. She left a message. She dashed off a quick email to Genevieve about Abigail, and then headed into the house.

Anna wanted to sketch some ocean pictures for her next painting, but her head was too unsettled. She stared out at the trees around her uncle's house. An idea occurred to her – she had not yet visited the forest near Pemaquid State Park. The quiet in the woods might be the closest to knowing quiet in her heart. She grabbed her running shoes from her bag and jumped in the truck.

It was a few miles from her uncle's house. As she turned into the familiar parking lot at the edge of the park, she took a deep breath. God, she loved it here. She had come to these woods often after her mom died. It was a space that was both insulated in the trees, but vast too, for when the woods ended, it turned into dunes and then the enormity of the ocean. It felt both big enough and intimate enough to handle her sadness then. Surely it would be able to handle her confusion now.

As she walked along the dirt trail, going deeper into the woods with each step, she thought of her life back then, and her life now in New York. The city seemed so far away. Raphael, Genevieve, parties and amusing friends. It was so different being here. She had built a life in New York over time. But it wasn't like she had dreamed of a life there. She wasn't sure she was cut out for the competition. Everyone had a constant need to impress with more money, better positions, more influence, more contacts. It was convenient to hide among workaholics who partied hard. Like them, she was purposefully ignoring parts of her life.

But from this distance, she could see how anxiety-producing that life was. It was one of the main reasons she struggled to let herself become known as an artist. It would get even faster, and she wanted to avoid that at all costs. Being a lowly gallery girl meant people around her could feel important at her expense. She would rather hide in her apartment than live a public artist's life. Why? Partly because of her father. But mainly because she had learned from her mother. Art had a simple and pure path. As long as she had been able to follow that in the mornings, while she worked, she had held on to all that her mother had taught her. She had held on to the girl from Maine. But she could see how much she had wandered from it.

From this distance, deep in the woods in Maine, she could see clearly that she let things that didn't matter fill her mind and her heart by living in New York. The pace of the city, once so helpful when she was trying to forget, seemed hectic and noisy now. Something about this trip, this time here, had opened her eyes. It had to be her uncle dying. Her grief opened up feelings she hadn't considered in a long time. She stepped on the wet, dead leaves and looked out at the spring green woods, noticing the green ferns peeking up between the leaves, still curled. She remembered a painting her mother had done: *Spring Ferns*.

She looked through the pine trees and stared out at the ocean. The endless steel gray reminded her of her grief. The grief she had left right here, in this space. She preferred to ignore it, close the door, run away from it. The problem was that in doing so, she kept shutting off those parts of herself. They were knocking, clamoring, calling at her. They had started the second the plane landed in Maine.

Some of her grief rose up as anger when she thought of Andrew. She sat down on a rock and closed her eyes. *Okay, just feel it. Feel all of it.* And then a thought rose up.

I still have so much love for him.

She opened her eyes in shock when she realized what she had just admitted to herself. *When I'm around him, I feel this happiness just because he exists, that someone so beautiful exists. And yet my head says he'll hurt you, disappoint you, because he didn't choose you. But then there is the look on his face when we're together. Part of me thinks he feels the same way. That he still cares.*

Her heart swelled at the thought. Then she remembered how guarded he was after his class. *Don't be silly,* her head told her heart. *You are loving someone from the past.* She knew nothing about his life right now. Nothing about his feelings. And he knew nothing about hers. *You'd better move on from these feelings. It was a long time ago.*

Right. It was a long time ago. So what mattered in her life right now? At 28, what did she really want?

Walking back to the truck, listening to the crunching of dead growth under her feet, she felt the first few drops of rain on her cheek. Once she was safely inside the truck, her cheeks flush from the cold, she turned up the heat and checked her phone. She had three messages—one from her father, one from Raphael, and one from Genevieve. All three wanted to know the answer to that exact question.

Chapter 11

Anna picked up the phone and heard her dad's voice first. "Anna, it's your father. I could have talked to you tomorrow at your sister's at dinner, but I didn't want to sit on this that long. One of your uncle's neighbors called me. They're interested in the house. Said if you wanted to sell it, they could offer you more than the market price for it. Make it worth your while. So think it over and let me know tomorrow, okay? Bye."

Anna put the phone down and stared out the window. The rain was coming down harder now. Sell the house? She was just wrapping her head around owning it. She wasn't sure if she wanted to think about selling it right now. On the other hand, if she had any doubts, she should contemplate this offer. It would be comforting knowing it was going to a local who really wanted it. She wanted to talk to her sister and brother before she could really decide what to do.

As she started to drive toward the house, thinking it was time to open the wine she had bought now that she had that issue to think through, she listened to Raphael's message.

"Anna, it's me. Call me when you get this, but most likely I'll be free after five so call me then. I miss you. I was thinking of coming up that weekend if you want me to. Think it over and let me know." His voice sounded sweet, full of the charm that he used on her that was so persuasive. She was touched by his message and found herself missing the comfort of him too. She dared herself to hope that seeing him here in Maine might help put her doubts to rest, that he would see her for who she truly was here.

Before she called him back, she listened to Genevieve's message.

"Hi, honey, it's me, Genevieve. Listen, when you get a free minute, call me. Something big has just come up and I need to talk to you about it ASAP. Don't wait even two minutes to call me, call me right now. Okay? Did I mention call me right away? Okay, love you, sweetie."

She waited until she pulled into her uncle's driveway to call her back, a place she knew she'd get decent reception. There were a million dead spots along the coast. Probably why she was just getting the message now, at a little after five. That or she had been too consumed about her morning with Andrew. It was Monday; whatever it was it must be important for her to open the gallery on a Monday. She heard the phone ringing; then Sarah, the other gallery worker, answered it. "Hey, Sarah, it's me, Anna. How're you doing? Listen, Genevieve just left an urgent message on my phone, said I had to call her back right away? Okay, sure, I'll hold."

Anna listened to the hold music. She was a full minute into Mozart's "Dies Irae" when Genevieve picked up.

"Genevieve Keller," she said quickly, with a slight New York accent.

"Hey, Genevieve, it's me, Anna. You called me about something urgent?"

"Okay, God, Anna, what took you so long to call me back? I've been on the edge of my seat all day. Are you sitting down?"

Anna looked at her denim lap. "Yes, what's up?"

"Three words for you, honey. Art. Basel. Miami."

"The American version of the European art show. Lovely, what about it?" Anna's eyebrows smushed together, confused.

"We are invited. You and me. The gallery and you. I need you there, to represent us, this December. What do you think?" Genevieve said, her voice staccato in its excitement. "My guess is the success of the new artist at my gallery threw our hat in the ring. There is a buzz about you."

"God, Genevieve, are you kidding? Seriously? The Art Basel show, us showing in it?" Anna felt the blood rush to her head. She felt almost like she was under water. With the tide coming in. She put her forehead in her palm, trying to absorb the information.

"First of all, you cannot say no. I won't allow you to say no. This call is not to see if you are interested, it is purely to discuss logistics, how many pieces, what do you want to show, what are you working on up there?"

"Yes, but, God, Genevieve, I really do need to think it over a bit. This would change everything. It would change the way I do art. I need to think it over."

"Um, sorry, I don't think you heard me correctly. Art Basel Miami." She said these three words very slowly, like she was talking to a child.

"I know. But I am working on . . . a lot right now . . . and I need some time to think it over. Just give me a chance to sleep on it. I like showing in New York – it's far enough away from my father to fly under the radar, right? I need to think about what it would be like to change that." Anna ran her fingers through her hair. She tried to breathe slowly but she could feel her anxiety creeping around her heart like vines. "I'll call you back tomorrow morning, ok? And don't worry, I know how much this means to you. I know you are offering me a big opportunity."

"At least that is clear," said Genevieve. "Okay, call me tomorrow. Bye hon,"

"'Bye Genevieve. Thank you."

She sat in her car, the windshield wipers still going, the heat on full blast, making her start to sweat. Or maybe it was the news from Genevieve. If she said no, she could possibly be taking away the biggest opportunity of Genevieve's life. But she would also be irreconcilably changing her life. She wished she could talk it over with someone. Raphael didn't get it; his head was too far up in the stock-market clouds. He would blindly say yes to making money. That was the reason she hadn't told him about her other openings. The specialness of each piece would be lost and he would just equate each title with the price it fetched. He would start to brag to all of his friends about it. Art Basel Miami would be the same thing, more bragging rights. Why would there even be a question?

She also wondered if showing at Art Basel might reveal the fact that she was Therese McAllister's daughter. She had so enjoyed everyone being unaware that her mother was a well-known artist. And of course, her dad would find out she didn't just work at the gallery. She would call Stephen but her brother was super busy with the restaurant. Her eyes drifted down to the business card on the seat next to her. The Perinault Gallery. Abigail was from New York, and she knew her mother. Anna didn't think she would tell anyone, least of all her father. Yes, she could talk to her. She would stop by tomorrow when the gallery opened. The offer on the house would have to wait until tomorrow.

She went inside and built a fire, and opened the wine. She was glad she had picked it up, but she wasn't sure even it could touch her stress now. She stared at the fire, wine in hand, for a long time. The truth she had realized about Andrew had put her into a fog. *I tried so hard not to feel this. I had buried this. And there is no chance he feels this way. He does what he wants. If he wanted me he would have done something.* Suddenly a jolt of guilt snapped her out of her thoughts, and she remembered she hadn't called Raphael back. She reached for her phone and dialed his number.

"Hello," he answered. His voice sounded raspy.

"Hi, Raphael, it's me," she said. "How are you?" She walked over and poured another glass of wine.

"Hey, Anna, how are you, sweetie? I was just going over some numbers and practically falling asleep. One second. I am walking out now." Anna heard him talk to someone in his office, and then he was back. "So how are you doing? It feels like ages since we talked."

"I know, I have been tied up at night with family stuff and you're so busy during the day, I didn't want to disturb you. But I've been good. How about you?" She sat down at her uncle's kitchen table and stared out at the ocean, dusk settling over the waves, hypnotizing her. She pushed down her guilt about Andrew – *he didn't matter*, she told herself. *Raphael matters.*

"Good, good. The markets are crazy but we've had a few good days. I've been rocking the gym. Looking strong for you when I see you next," he said with a laugh. "Speaking of that, what do you think if I take a flight up next Friday night? I could leave at four on the dot, grab the 6 o'clock flight, and be there by 7:30ish."

"That sounds great," Anna answered. She felt hope rise up in her chest. Maybe this period of confusion would clear up once she saw Raphael. "I can pick you up anytime. Just tell me your flight info and I'll make sure I'm there."

"Okay, I am meeting up for drinks with Dave and Mac, so I'll look into flights when I get home and I'll text you. It will be so nice to see you, Anna." There was that charm. Anna wasn't immune.

"It'll be great to see you too," she said. "Love you."

"Love you too."

She put the phone down on the table and looked out at the sea. She watched one of the lobster buoys rise and fall with the ocean swells.

That night she had another dream about her mother. She was in the barn at home, where she had grown up and where her dad still lived. Her mom was painting with her when suddenly the barn caught fire. She and her mother ran around trying to pick up their canvases; then her mother grabbed her by the shoulders and looked at her intensely. "They don't matter. They are inside you anyway." She repeated this over and over until they headed for the door. Anna looked back to see a self-portrait curl up in flames.

Chapter 12

The next morning, Anna woke to the sound of ocean waves. She'd slept in the guest room, where she usually slept when she used to visit. She wasn't ready to take over Uncle Charlie's room just yet.

The sound was so deliciously soothing, she was in a complete state of relaxation until she remembered her dream, and her task for the morning. To go to Abigail's gallery, to discuss if she wanted to change her life as she knew it.

She headed downstairs to brew some coffee and stared at the painting she had finally started the night before. The clouds needed a bit more definition, she decided. She grabbed her pallet knife and added a few dark lines while she listened to the coffee pot gurgle and choke. Painting in the morning was such a habit for her. It was nice to be able to leave out her supplies at Uncle Charlie's and get into her routine here.

Marie called her after she had been working for a while, procrastinating her trip to talk to Abigail. "Hey, can you bring wine and some bread tonight? And also, dad told me about the offer on the house. What are your thoughts on that?"

Anna wiped her hands with a towel and mulled over the choice. "I am thinking Dad and Aunt Catherine want me to keep it in the family. Don't you think? But also, how much could I realistically come up? Three times a year? Five?"

"I would talk to them tonight and see how they feel. I personally like the idea of seeing you three or five times a year better than what we were averaging, which was basically never," Marie said. Anna felt a pang when she realized her sister was right. Her distance from her dad had put distance in their relationship too, and this time together was therapeutic.

"I'll ask them tonight. And we have to ask them about the picture -the one with the little girl in it," Anna remembered suddenly.

"Right. Lots to chat about. I better get cooking."

"See you tonight at 7?"

"Yes, 7 sounds good, see you then."

She showered and dressed, putting on jeans and a long sleeved white T-shirt, her winter coat, and boots, and headed to Riley's for an egg and cheese sandwich. When she got to the counter, there was Millie, the wife of the former owner and mother of the current owner. She had to be well into her eighties, but she still stood there as happy as could be, greeting customers and making their breakfast. Anna smiled when she saw her, remembering her from when she was little. The old woman smiled warmly at Anna and gave her the sandwich with a wink.

"Hello there," she said to Anna. She didn't remember her at all, Anna thought, but why would she? It had been almost ten years since she last saw her.

"Hi Millie, remember me?"

She squinted at Anna. "Oh, my, you do look familiar. Aren't you the Goodrich girl? At first, I thought you were from away."

"Yes, that's me. It's good to be back," Anna said smiling. She didn't know how she fit into the group that the locals gave to everyone not from Maine – they considered anyone not born here was 'from away'. Did it apply to her now that she had been gone so long? Or was her childhood here enough?

"Well, enjoy your breakfast, honey." Millie seemed unfazed by her answer.

She decided to walk down to the harbor and watch the boats while she ate. The day had started out warm, and the heat made the air foggy, covering the entire harbor under a gray blanket. Pea soup, the locals called it. The seagulls screeched as if trying to navigate by sound waves. There were a few lobster boats in the harbor, their skiffs tied to them like little children. One of them was the *Christina Therese*. Just the sight of it made her pulse quicken, her lungs tight. Andrew was surely at the campus today. She was surprised at how much she would have liked to see him here, waving to her from the boat, a familiar scene from so many summers in the past. She tried to push him out of her mind, and a twinge of sadness followed.

All of a sudden, a thought occurred to her. The boat's name was after Andrew's mother, Christina. Could he have named it after her mother too? She couldn't remember his mother's middle name, but the likelihood that it was Therese was pretty small. The thought erupted like a geyser in her heart. He had cared about her then, when he named the boat. That was a huge honor to bestow on anyone. Had he really given that honor to her mother? She already knew the answer.

Anna looked out at the harbor. Most of the other fishermen had been out since daybreak. There was no doubt about it, the fishermen worked hard. They were busy hauling and dropping traps before most people had even pulled back their covers. They were devoted to their labor. It was a lifestyle for them. Andrew was right—cutting back their ability to make money would mean some of them would have no choice but to find a different job. But finding a different job was finding a different life for most of them. They certainly weren't doing it for the large salaries. It was the honesty and integrity of hard work, and the love of the ocean, that kept them fishing. It was more than their own identities—it was the identity of their families and community, too. Anna thought about the Connecticut lobster boats she painted last summer. She wanted to capture the spirit of that quality of life. She knew it was possible to love a life such as fishing, and a place such as the harbor. She had loved them both through loving Andrew.

She took off her coat, finished her sandwich, and drank the last sip of coffee before heading to Abigail's gallery. She found herself feeling very free on the heels of thinking about the fishermen. She felt that way about her art—that it was a simple life she was after. Anna walked slowly along the rocks toward the gallery, her hands in her pockets, the wind whipping at her hair and chilling her despite the warm sunshine. *Wouldn't Art Basel take that away?* The thought roared in, and Anna sighed. She could practically feel Genevieve waiting at her desk for Anna's phone call.

She looked toward Abigail's gallery. She was relieved to see the Open sign posted. When she opened the door, she heard bells chime that she hadn't noticed last time. She walked up the stairs and took in all of the artwork again. The brown and white cow still peered down at her majestically. The pastoral painting fit perfectly with her mood, and she had a desire to meet that cow more than anyone in New York. She stood staring and smiling when she heard Abigail's footsteps on the stairs.

"Can I help you? Oh, it's you, Anna. Good to see you again," Abigail greeted her warmly.

"Hi Abigail," Anna said. She noticed her black button-down shirt and jeans were covered in splotches of paint. Her studio must be right downstairs, and she had just come fresh from work. "I'm so sorry to bother you while you're working. I've actually come with a question I wondered if you could help me with."

"A question? Sure, I'll try to help if I can," she said. She wiped her hands on a cloth as she spoke.

"Well, you're familiar with Art Basel Miami, right?" Anna asked.

"Of course. I don't know if there is an artist in America who doesn't know about Art Basel. The shows in Miami are very exciting."

"Well, I have a dilemma, and I didn't know who I could go to with it. I thought since you used to live in the city, you might be able to help." Anna sat down next to the window "Like my mom, I paint quite a bit, and the last few years, I've shown my paintings at the Genevieve Keller Gallery, where I work. Have you heard of it?"

"I think so, it's in Midtown, right?" Abigail said, cupping her face with her fingers. Anna noticed how long and feminine they were, even without any polish. She wore a small gold ring with her initials on her pinky.

Anna nodded, and felt confident she would understand her situation. But she was nervous too. What if Abigail told someone in the art world she was Therese McAllister's daughter? What if she told someone here she was a professional artist in New York? She crossed her arms and took a deep breath. "Well, I've had two very successful shows, and the Keller Gallery has been invited to Art Basel Miami. And the owner, Genevieve, who is my boss and close friend, wants me to show. But I'm really not sure if I want to."

She had Abigail's full attention. She silently walked over, sat down on a bench under the brown cow, and looked at Anna. "Well, dear. That's a very big honor. You must have inherited your mother's talent," she finally said.

Anna joined her on the bench. "Thanks. I appreciate you saying that. More than you know. That's why I wanted to talk to you, I guess. Because I haven't told anyone in New York that I am Therese McAllister's daughter. My mother kept me all to herself when she was alive, and we just painted. I went to the University of Maine at Orono for many reasons, but also because I could stay close to her, and to Andrew – my boyfriend at the time who went there. After school, all summer, I got to study with her. She taught me so much. But after she died, my dad went crazy. He wanted me to be a success, to go to the best grad schools in the country. But I told him I was done painting."

"I see," Abigail said, listening very intently.

"I went to New York to be a gallery worker, not an artist. That world is night and day from this one here in Maine. The one I started painting in." Anna gestured toward the window.

"I understand. It's why I moved back too," Abigail said. She rubbed at the paint still on her hand distractedly.

"Right. You know both sides of the coin. I don't know if I can ever go from Art Basel to . . . this." Anna held her hands up around Abigail's gallery. "I'm afraid I will get stuck where there is a lot of noise. At the very least, the freedom I enjoy when I work would be gone. If I show, and if anyone finds out who my mom is, I'm not sure I'll be able to go back to how it is right now. I'm afraid that the outside world will impact me more than I want it to. But how do I tell my friend Genevieve, who owns the gallery, that my answer is no? She has wanted to show at something major like this her whole life. It is her magnum opus. I just don't think it's mine. On the other hand, I know it is a great honor. Am I going to wish I took that opportunity?"

"Well, I guess that is a dilemma. But I am confused. You say you don't want the outside world to impact you. But as an artist, we are always talking. We are communicating with our images. We can't help but have a conversation. Do you think you might be shutting off the outside world because of your mom?"

"More like my dad," Anna blurted out before she could keep it inside. "I mean, yes, it is complicated, and it is partly because of how hard her death was on me, on all of us. It was very painful to have that piece of her in me. I guess I don't quite know if I want to bury it or share it."

"Well, what do you think that part of you has tried to tell you?" Abigail asked, taking Anna's hands in her own. "Has it stayed buried?"

Anna shook her head, and tears welled up in her eyes. "No," she said. "That part is alive and well every morning, itching to pick up a brush."

Abigail smoothed out the wrinkles in her pants. "Well, that is something worth listening to. But there is one more thing you should know."

"What's that?" Anna asked.

"I have shown in some fantastic shows. But nothing is quite the same as having your own space. Your own gallery. Especially here in Pemaquid. Even if you are the toast of the town in Miami, you can always return here. The world will have other people to favor or despise. When you want to leave the limelight, you can. Anytime."

Anna stood up and rubbed her eyes with the palm of her hands. She sighed and looked up at the cow painting. "How much for that painting?" she asked, smiling.

"Depends on how much you sell in Miami."

"See, that is exactly the kind of attitude that makes me not want to do it," Anna answered, laughing.

Chapter 13

"Go pick some tomatoes from the garden, would you honey?" her mother said, laying down brushes and opening paints on the table in the barn. Her white linen shirt looked cool in the heat of the sun, and the humidity had made the dark hairs around her face curl up.

"Yes, mom," Anna replied, her eleven-year-old eyes shining brightly in anticipation of what was to come.

She went behind the barn where the garden grew, and before she could even reach the lush, verdant postage stamp of earth, she could smell the tomatoes. The fragrance was like an invisible liquid in the air, heavy like golden honey, yet still ethereal, like a cobweb, like lace. When Anna picked the round red fruit, the scent intensified, and she loved that where her fingers had brushed the plant, the smell would linger for hours, allowing her the pleasure of drinking it in again and again.

She brought the tomatoes around to the barn, and her mother set them in a bowl. "Ok, sweetheart. We already prepped our canvases yesterday with the burnt sienna background and the white table cloth in the foreground. Now we're just going to paint the tomatoes. First we're going to mix our colors. Find the combination of red and yellow and white that matches what you see. And let's do a little green for the stem, too." Her mother held her palette and made tiny pools of mixed shades, circles of red and orange and dark green.

Anna went into her head, focusing on the colors before her, and on

the white spot on the fruit where the light hit it first. Her mother gave her
pointers every so often, tips for capturing a feature of the tomatoes on the
table. An hour passed in what felt like a minute to Anna. As she worked,
she noticed the metallic smell of the paint mixed with the fragrance of
the tomatoes, and the smell from the grass outside as the summer sun
scorched it. This must be what happiness smells like, she thought.

Anna drove past her old house on the way to her sister's. She pulled
over, and looked for a long time at the old barn, at the part of the
backyard she could see where the garden had been. Her dad had
kept up everything nicely. He was already at her sister's house, she
knew. Anna sat staring and thinking about the house and how many
memories it held. It was amazing that eight years had passed since
she left. It had all started in that little barn. And that little girl might
one day show at Art Basel.

She pulled away from the house and headed toward Marie's. As
she drove, she thought about what Abigail had said, and could feel
herself slowly coming around to the idea of showing in Miami. She
had avoided calling Genevieve back, although she did send her an
email saying she was still thinking it over but that she needed more
time. She was able to drop all thoughts of it when she walked in,
however. Her sister's house smelled delicious, like roasted meat and
vegetables and balsamic vinegar. A small part of her wished she
could talk it over with her father. He knew so much about the art
world and would no doubt have a strong idea about what she should
do. But that was exactly why she didn't want to talk it over with him.

She took off her boots and scarf and jacket. She heard little feet
running toward her before she even caught a glimpse of Henry.
"Auntie Anna!" he shouted. She had only been away two days but he
looked bigger than before she left. "Hi there, Henry! How's my sweet
boy? Hi, Marie," she said in the direction of her sister, who was stirring something on the stove, her hair in a knot on top of her head,
her tunic and leggings making her look like she would fit right into
a dinner party in New York.

Anna picked Henry up under the arms and swung him around the kitchen. He giggled happily. "Did you bring me a 'prise?" he asked, his eyes shining brightly.

Anna thought quickly and remembered she had a piece of chocolate left from the bag she had bought in her pocket. "I do! Do you have a kiss for me?" She pointed to her cheek, and the little boy patiently gave her a peck. She knew it was extortion, but it was worth it. She gave him the candy, showing him how to unwrap it, and tousled his hair. He had managed to put her in a great mood, despite her angst over her big decisions.

It was just then that her father brought up her other one.

"Hi there, Anna, how goes it?" he said as he walked in from the family room. He was in tan cords and a red-and-brown plaid cotton oxford. Like usual, he was impeccably groomed. Aunt Catherine followed him in the room, her bright blue scarf matching the color of her eyes. She was glad she could ask her about the house and the photo in person.

"Did you get my message yesterday about the house?" her dad asked. "The O'Rourkes called me two days ago begging me to talk you into selling it to them. I had no idea what to say other than I'd pass the message along to you."

"I did. Thanks for letting me know, Dad," Anna said. "Sorry I didn't call you back. I—I just had a lot come up all at once. I am surprised they called you." She walked to the counter and poured a glass of wine. "Seems a little soon after Uncle Charlie died, don't you think? I'm not sure right now exactly what I should do." Anna was quiet for a moment. She took a sip of wine. "Just for the record, do you all have any strong opinions about it? Would you like the house to stay in the family? What about you, Aunt Catherine? Marie? Do you have any sentimental attachment to it?"

Marie answered with her characteristic diplomacy. "I think you should do what you want, Anna. Yes, it holds family memories, but if it's not something you want to take on in your life, you should have the right to back out."

Catherine nodded. "The house is not going to bring Charlie back. You should do what you want, dear. Though we would love to have you close, that is for sure."

"Well, if you need a place to live, you should keep it. If you don't, sell it," her dad said with his usual directness. "But where will you ever find a view like that, hmm?"

"Right, good point, Dad, though do I detect the fact that you don't want to worry about me, and if I have a roof over my head?" Anna joked, trying to make the moment light, surprised that she was able to find the humor in it. Marie chuckled while she ground pepper into a pot of mashed potatoes.

"Well, that is amazing. You understood me perfectly. My, that feels novel, to get through to you for once," her dad replied, joining in the jovial tone. Something had changed in him, Anna sensed. He wasn't as heavy as he usually was.

"By the way, I think Raphael is going to come up for the gala. Looks like we can make it," Anna said, sipping her wine, waiting to see how the news would hit her dad.

"That's great!" Marie said. "You can find a flapper outfit if you want. I can help you find a '20s style suit for him too."

"It will be great for you to be there," her dad said, seeming stoic but pleased.

"Oh, by the way Anna, Mike's schedule for May was just put up and there are some Saturdays that he has free. Would you mind if I called Andrew and took him up on his offer to have Henry go out on the boat?" Her sister looked up at her, her eyes a mixture of guilt and hope. Anna could hardly blame her for asking a favor like that of Andrew. She knew Henry would love it.

"No, of course not," Anna said. Her face grew flush, though, thinking about him playing with her nephew for the day.

"Do you want to go too?" Marie asked.

Anna picked up a cucumber from Marie's salad and munched on it nervously. "I'm not sure where I'll be on the weekends, but I'll think about it," she said.

Anna sighed as she realized she was no clearer on any of her dilemmas than she had been that morning. At least there was yummy food and delicious wine to enjoy tonight, and she and her dad had their first semi-pleasant exchange in years. The rest she would try to figure out in the morning.

Anna remembered the other thing she wanted to ask her dad and Catherine about. "So, I was wondering about something and wanted to see if you could fill me in a little. When Marie and I were cleaning out Uncle Charlie's house, we found a picture of you all with a younger girl in it. I never heard you talk about another sibling, so was it a cousin or something?"

Aunt Catherine and her dad exchanged glances. "Yes, it was a younger sibling," her aunt said quietly. "She died young." Her tone indicated that she wasn't willing to talk about it anymore.

Her dad said nothing, but picked up his Scotch and finished it in one sip. "I think I'll go check on Henry," he said, walking toward the stairs.

"Well, he didn't say much," Anna said to her sister and aunt when he had left.

"It is a very difficult subject for him," said Aunt Catherine.

"Enough to keep it quiet for thirty years?" Marie asked.

"Yes, I would imagine he would stay quiet for many more. It was Charlie who still talked about her. He was more open to sharing about her."

They all stood quietly, absorbing the news that seemed impossible.

"So Uncle Charlie wasn't the first sibling you lost," Anna said, feeling a sympathy for her aunt.

"No, he's not," she said, dabbing the corner of her eye with a napkin. She walked into the dining room and sat down at the table. They didn't ask her any more.

"Why don't we all sit down at the table," Marie called out.

"Yes, great idea," Anna seconded, and grabbed the wine she had brought and set it down.

They tried to change the topic, and talked about the gala, and Sarah and Phillip, and how Uncle Joe would be retiring from his post at the Lobster Co-op. They might throw him a surprise party next month. Anna wondered where she would be next month. She didn't have the faintest idea if she would be ready to leave Maine yet. They also filled Anna in on how large the Foundation had gotten. There were over 50 students who came up every summer, and had two weeks with some of the same art teachers who had taught Anna.

She was heartwarmed to think of the opportunity for those kids. She thought of Miranda. She should get in touch with her, see how the high school decision was sitting with her mom.

It was so good to be around her sister's table, with her dad and her aunt and uncle. It was healing after the intense few weeks they all had to have nothing more urgent then a bread basket to share.

As Anna left her sister's house that night, she turned to Marie and asked, "So that was illuminating, right? They clearly didn't want to talk about the girl in the picture."

"I know, they shut down pretty fast, huh? I wonder if Dad would share more sometime, if I got him alone. But on a lighter note, have you noticed that Dad seemed semi-pleasant tonight?"

Anna nodded, holding her keys. "I know. I was going to ask you about that. He must be mellowing with age. Or lightening up since Charlie's death, maybe? Something's changed in him."

"Or maybe it is because you're here for longer than a weekend," Marie said.

"Maybe," said Anna, smiling at the idea that her dad was happy that she was around. "All I know is I like the feeling of being in the same room with him and not having to be ready to defend myself. It felt like the old days, when mom was alive." She hugged her sister goodbye, and walked out the door, thinking that maybe Maine wouldn't be so hard to visit after all.

Chapter 14

Raphael was on his way to Maine.

He had sent Anna a text late Tuesday night. He bought the ticket and would be waiting in Portland at six p.m. Anna was excited and strangely nervous. She planned to eat with him at one of the great restaurants in the Old Port. He wouldn't feel too far from the city with the amazing chefs and lively residents of Portland. The whole city had a cool, funky vibe. It was a good strategy to ease him into Maine. Plus she could catch up with him without all the confusion she had here.

In the last week, Anna worked hard to finish the painting she was working on before Raphael got there. She'd had a few days of solitude to focus, and she took advantage of them. She loved the piece—it was one of her best, she felt. It was a landscape out her uncle's window, and even though it had simple elements, she gave the sky and the pine trees an injection of her feelings about being back here. It felt vibrant and powerful.

She managed to put Genevieve off, saying she needed more time to decide. Genevieve decided to spin this to the organizers of the show, saying her gallery would be there, and the new artist was trying to decide if she had enough for a show. If not, she would have other works to show from her gallery. "*C'est vrai, ma chérie,*" she said to Anna. "Though you know I want it to be you."

Anna changed into jeans and a black sweater. She realized she was out of clothes, and hoped that Raphael didn't mind. She made a mental note to go shopping soon. In New York, she picked up pieces at the amazing boutiques or at Barneys on her way home, but here, she had been too busy, and her only choices were Maine tourist sweatshirts at Reny's, the chain of discount stores beloved by all who traveled through Maine, or the overpriced knit sweaters at the boutiques in town.

She borrowed the truck again, and drove the hour and twenty minutes to Portland, and stopped by their hip and trendy shops to grab a few outfits. She changed into one, watching her jeans and sweater fall to the floor, staring at herself in a gray A-line dress and bright tights she had pulled off the racks. Her ballet flats would do with this. She threw a big cozy scarf over the whole thing to ward off the chilly wind from the ocean, and drove to the airport.

Not long after she pulled into arrivals, her phone rang.

"Hey, sweetie, I am walking out now," Raphael said.

"Great, I'm right outside," she said. "I'm in the large beat-up pick-up truck."

"You're in what?" He laughed. "A truck?"

"You're in Maine now, honey. The truck works." She laughed back.

She saw him walking toward her. His perfectly groomed soft brown hair, his olive skin, and his dark eyes. She knew girls turned their heads when he walked into a room. He wasn't overly tall; at five feet eleven he was just a few inches taller than Anna. But he was very fit, and his muscular physique gave him the illusion of being bigger. He smiled when he saw her, and Anna smiled back, glad to see him, like laying eyes on a long-lost friend.

They drove downtown, the skyline scattered with cranes, barges, and bridges under construction. They wove through the city streets to the Old Port, and could hear the seagulls crying out as Anna parked the truck on a cobblestone street. Anna self-consciously noted that the pedestrians all looked interesting, artistic. It was a good call to bring Raphael here first.

In a red brick bistro in the Old Port, they settled into their table next to a warm fire and ordered their meals. They sipped an Argentinean red that Raphael had selected, which was, of course, delicious. The chef here had won a James Beard award, and they eagerly awaited their curried crab bisque and lamb meatball appetizer. After a lull in the small talk, Raphael asked, "So how was the funeral?" He held his glass at the bottom of the stem and looked at Anna.

The question brought Anna back to a reality she had pushed away the last few weeks. "Depressing. Sad and cold. At least it was good to see my brother and my cousins," Anna said. She felt like it had happened months ago. "How's work?" she asked, trying to divert the subject away from the awful feeling in her chest that was by now familiar.

"It is crazy as always. The European banks are a mess. They are scrambling to come up with money to pay for the debt facing Greece, but it's like blood from a turnip. The Euro is looking like it was not the best proposition for many Europeans. Could've told you that years ago, but no one was listening to me." Raphael's eyes twinkled with enthusiasm, which made his accent more pronounced. "Anyway, everyone's sitting on the sidelines until the uncertainty goes away. Once Europe decides on a plan, things will probably settle down. But until then, we are trading on commodities and currencies and getting by. Avoiding the bloodbath. But enough of that, how have you been here? Do they have electricity and running water yet?"

Anna laughed at his joke, and noticed how interesting it was to be around the New York pace once again, the idea that the whole world revolves around where you stand. Anna hadn't been around that intensity for a few weeks, so she noticed it more. She was reminded of his drive, focus, and intelligence, all things that drew her to Raphael. She just wondered if he would be able to melt into the Maine pace, to relax with her just a bit this weekend.

She took a sip of wine and enjoyed sitting by the fire with him. She had missed him. Her face was warm and she smiled.

"So how are the guys from work?" she asked.

"They're the usual. They swear you're going to leave me and move here for good." His eyes were suddenly serious, and pierced into hers. The waiter appeared, and set down their appetizers and refilled their wine. The glimmer of the fire danced on Anna's glass, making the red liquid look like a jewel.

"Should I be worried, Anna?" He was smiling, but his eyes were serious. "Is there something here that you want?"

Even though his question was so open, Anna felt her heart pounding. Her mind flashed to Andrew's eyes. She worked at keeping her expression even and met his gaze. "What do you mean, Raphael? You know why I'm here. What are you afraid of?"

"Not afraid," Raphael said. "Just confused. But I am here now. We'll visit, you can show me the house, and we'll spend some time with your family. It'll be fun."

Anna smiled and put her hand in his. "I don't know if I would call my dad fun, but my sister and her family, sure. Of course it will," she said. "You'll love it here."

After their ride up to New Harbor, she begged Raphael to go to Shaw's Wharf with her for one beer, even though he said he was exhausted. Anna wanted to see him in her element, show him her Maine. "It's my favorite bar. You have to go to someone's favorite bar when you visit their hometown. Besides, tomorrow night we're going to the gala, so this is your only chance."

She couldn't wait to show him the harbor, and she had calculated that Liz bartended Saturdays, so if she wanted to fly under the radar with Raphael, they should go tonight. She thought about the possibility of Andrew being there, but he was tied up with exams. They pulled into the parking lot and Anna made him stand behind the painting of the giant clam with its face cut out, a photo op for tourists that would have a line next to it in a few more weeks. She laughed out loud while he stood sheepishly, his face resting in the circle cutout, the rest of him a painted blue and gray mollusk.

"You can show this to the guys at work when you get back!" Anna said, laughing as she pulled him up to the bar. She double-checked the bartender and didn't recognize the older man with gray hair pulling the tap.

"Oh, right, like they will ever let me live that down," Raphael replied. He grabbed her hand as they stood waiting for their beer.

Anna found two stools and made herself comfortable at the bar. He ran his fingers through her hair. "So this is where I grew up," she said.

"Your parents raised you in a *bar*? Wow, must have been some childhood," Raphael said, grinning, his voice dripping with sarcasm. Anna slapped his arm. It was working; Raphael was relaxing with her.

They ordered two Pemaquid Ales, again in plastic cups. Anna was glad to share the local brew with Raphael. "Cheers," she said as she tapped his glass, beer spilling gratuitously down the sides. She took a sip, and then lifted up her eyes. There, sitting at a table at the edge of the dock, was Andrew. Their eyes met for an instant, and she knew that he had assessed the situation already. His expression was taut, not sad or angry but full of emotion. *Oh Lord*, she thought. *Why did I come here? I am an idiot!*

Raphael didn't seem to notice the expression on her face. "This beer is good," he said. "It definitely tastes better next to the ocean." He looked out at the harbor, the lights from the houses and docks glistening onto the water. The waves made the lights move constantly; it was easy to get hypnotized staring at them. The harbor bell called out, its low iron drum soothing.

Anna sat frozen, wondering what she should do in this moment. She didn't have to wait long. Raphael said he had to run to the bathroom, and while he was gone, Andrew got up to leave. He came over to Anna, who was sitting alone with empty seats on either side of her. His cheekbones were pulled tight, and Anna could see the restraint he was using. "Hi, Anna. Just wanted to say you two look great together." He waved, then put his hands in his pockets and walked up the ramp to the parking lot.

Anna fought the urge to run after him, to hug him and tell him it wasn't what he thought. Only it was. It was exactly what it looked like. But why should she feel guilty? He was the one who chose to let her go. Why did she feel like sitting here with Raphael was a direct assault on him? And why did she have the urge to console him? She sighed as she took a sip of beer. Why did he get so under her skin? And as she watched Raphael walk back to her. She was here with Raphael, but she couldn't get her blood pressure under control from just seeing Andrew. She focused on Raphael's face as he sat down, the familiar warmth of his eyes.

"So I was thinking that you should come back with me on the flight

Sunday night. I already checked and there is plenty of room." Raphael took a sip of his beer with a mischievous expression on his face.

Anna thought about what it would be like to get on that flight. She would leave two paintings unfinished, as well as the tidying she wanted to get done at her uncle's. And she would say goodbye to Henry and Marie for who knew how long. She also felt something else, some unraveling inside her. She needed to be here to let it keep unraveling. She felt like she needed more rest, more reflection. "I can't, sweetie. I'm not done fixing up my uncle's house."

"We can come back in a few weeks, on the weekend, and do it together. There is an opening at John's gallery this week that I know you would love. And I have been dying to take you to the new restaurant that just opened around the corner from there. And I want to hold you. Isn't that an offer you can't refuse?" he said, his eyes glowing. He pulled her close and kissed her cheek, moving slowly toward her ear. Anna felt the silkiness of his offer. Something in her resisted it, though.

"I know if I go back now, I will get sucked up in the busy schedule and life there, and I will leave all these things undone. I should just stay for a few more weeks and then go back," she finally managed. It was not easy to disappoint Raphael.

He sat back. His face looked equally handsome and quizzical. He said nothing, but looked around the bar at the other patrons. One looked back in his direction, a female. Anna could guess why.

"I don't get it," he said, turning back to her. "What is here for you? What is the big draw?" He put his glass down, and she could see on his face frustration that hadn't quite turned to anger. Anna was suddenly very relieved he hadn't seen Andrew talking to her. She stared out at the harbor. She noticed the big red house with a large yard facing them on the other side of the harbor. The property was outlined in trees. Maine pine trees. They looked so majestic next to the big house and the barn next to it. She had always loved that house. It had belonged to one of Charlie's coworkers.

"I don't expect you to get it," she said. "I grew up here. The draw is just to be home, in the place where you came from. There is something about Maine that calls you back, I guess. When you go back to

Connecticut or Argentina, don't you plan a long stay?" she managed. Anna had visited his parents' house in Connecticut for weekends and holidays, but remembered as she said it that he tried to keep it to a few days when they did. His brother and sister lived there too, but usually came into the city to see him. She hoped the Argentina angle would be more helpful.

"No. We stay for a week, I line up everyone I need to see, then take the first flight back to New York. I wouldn't want to stay there this long. I can't leave my real life alone that long. The worry that I have is where you feel like your real life is." He held her hands in his and looked at her for what felt like an eternity. "I can only hope it is with me."

When they arrived at Uncle Charlie's—Anna's—house, Raphael was asleep on one of the twin beds in the guest room before Anna could even show him where the bathroom was. He had always been a morning person, and the adrenaline rush of his days made him exhausted by ten. Anna covered him with blankets and crept downstairs. She poured a glass of wine and sat outside, watching her breath form bulbous clouds in the night air.

She tried to stop seeing Andrew's face.

She looked up at the sky, stars hung like lights at a party. And in the glow of the moon on the harbor, the stars like a wreath around it, the night sky seemed an alter to all that is good and holy. The black sky and the water in the harbor melted into one and wrapped around her like a blanket. She sat in silence, and after a few moments, she noticed that even though the stars were so bright, they were not the most powerful thing that assaulted her senses. What hit her the most was the far-off sound of waves crashing, on the other side of the harbor, behind the houses across the harbor. The waves she could not see were crashing, and the sound was at once violent and peaceful, turbulent and serene. A reminder that somethings turn without you, even when they are out of sight.

Chapter 15

The next morning, Anna rose early, made a pot of coffee, put on a sweatshirt and walked down to Riley's to get the paper, a loaf of their delicious cheese bread, and eggs. When she returned, Raphael was still asleep. She went out to the boathouse and looked at the piece she was working on. It was a lone boat on the water, like the one that had sold the day Uncle Charlie had died, but there was a different color pallet – softer, pastel colors - that echoed how peaceful she felt here in Maine.

She thought of Raphael's fear that she would stay here. In her head, Anna kept feeling like her time in Maine would run its course and she would feel compelled to go back to New York. It had been almost three weeks. But each morning she woke up excited to do what faced her that day.

She thought of waking up in New York in a few weeks. She was happy painting in the city. She enjoyed going out at night. But often she felt like a boat tied to an anchor. Just floating. Her anchors were Raphael, the gallery, and her painting. But here in Maine, she didn't feel like she was drifting. She felt more like a part of the rocks, the dirt and the trees. Her senses and her heart floated on the fresh air. This translated into some of the best work she had ever done. All of her felt alive here. Maybe that would change in the next few weeks, but she wanted to ride out the wave while it was happening.

When she got to the house, she opened the back door that had white paint peeling off of it. Uncle Charlie would no doubt have already stripped and repainted it with the first few weekends of nice weather. Anna added it to the to-do list. When she got inside, she found Raphael in the kitchen, in shorts only, his bare chest café-au-lait-colored. She walked up and hugged him and put her face into the nape of his neck. "Good morning," she said.

He put his arms around her. "Good morning, beautiful. Wow, it is amazing how good you can sleep in the fresh air here. I can't remember the last time I slept that well," he said, rubbing his eyes with the palm of his hand. "Where were you this morning? I wanted to reach over and hug you but you were gone," he said. "And I was in a twin bed," he laughed, kissing her gently.

"I went to the store to get us some breakfast. You need to try Riley's cheese bread. There is nothing like it in the city," she said, smiling. Raphael raised his eyebrows at the challenge.

"So do you want to go check out the galleries near the harbor or head down to Damariscotta? There are lots of shops and restaurants down there."

Raphael put his arms even tighter around her. "Or we could stay here." He smiled.

"I want you to see downtown. Please." She smiled back at him and quickly kissed him. She pulled out of his embrace and turned to toast the bread.

"Okay, but it will be difficult. The air up here is making you more beautiful, if that is even possible." Raphael had learned the art of chivalry very well in Argentina. It was definitely one of the things that attracted Anna to him. They ate in front of the picture window, the sunlight bathing the kitchen. She pointed out some of the projects around the house that she wanted to do. "What do you think of having this become a summer place for us?" she asked, brushing the crumbs off her hands.

"Well, it's pretty far," Raphael said, "but very beautiful. Realistically we could only get here a few times a year. But it's your house; you have to decide."

"The neighbors want to buy it from me," she said, putting their plates in the sink. She saw Raphael's eyebrows go up, interested in the prospect.

"You mean you could get the money out of the house and then come up here and rent something else?" he said, his voice sounding like it was an easy proposition.

"So I take it that is what you think I should do?" Anna said, putting her hands in her pockets, her hip resting on the sink.

"I think it is an opportunity. It's your choice, but there are such things as missed opportunities." Raphael's confident sales voice was full of persuasion. "Besides, they're a very hungry buyer, to have contacted you all so soon after your uncle's passing. So you have that on your side when you negotiate."

Anna suddenly felt sick to her stomach. Talking about sweet Uncle Charlie's passing so indiscreetly, as a bargaining chip, made her queasy.

"I can't handle that decision right now," she said, running her hands through her messy dark locks, sighing. Her pale skin seemed a shade paler. "I'm gonna go take a shower."

She should have never thrown that debate onto the table with him, she thought as she showered. She knew how he would feel even before she said it. Something in Anna fiercely defended her choices here. It was her life, her family. Raphael was happy just having their life in New York City. But she didn't feel like being that Anna anymore. She wished he could open up his world to include this – Maine, the house, time away from the city – but she was doubtful.

She dressed in jeans and a sweater, and came downstairs. "Do you want to shower too?" she asked, her voice neutral. Raphael was at the table, *The New York Times* spread out all around him.

"Sure, I'll be right back. Listen, whatever you decide, its ok with me." He gave her a quick kiss and headed upstairs.

Anna sipped her coffee while she perused the headlines. She opened the arts section and saw a small piece in the corner about the Art Basel Miami. She tucked the section in a drawer in the kitchen just as Raphael came down the stairs.

Half an hour later, they walked down the main street in Damariscotta. They hit a bookstore, then a discount store. When they found a wine and cheese store, Raphael found some Argentinean wine that he bought to take back to the city.

It was almost one o'clock when they came upon a small English-style pub that overlooked the estuaries. They ducked in and sat down, each ordering a pint of Guinness. While they waited, Anna could feel the slight awkwardness that had settled in around them. She tried to keep things light. "They have a great burger here, and oh, you have to try the crab cakes with the frisée salad. Amazing."

Raphael managed a smile. "They have crab cakes in New York, too, you know."

"Then order something else," Anna said. The sourness of his comment was echoed in hers. She looked down at the menu and only glanced up when the waitress put down her drink.

"So you said your mom had a gallery down here?" Raphael asked, his tone light, ignoring Anna's crankiness.

"Mmm-hmm," Anna answered, nodding. "She had one in the barn at home, and one downtown."

"How is your dad doing, with his brother passing away?" He seemed to sense that he had been unnecessarily confrontational. He was trying to ebb back into calmer waters with some compassion.

"He is doing okay, I guess. I am not sure since we aren't on deep talking terms, but he seems like he has been handling it well." She hadn't told Raphael about her dad's inheritance. She didn't feel like talking about money anymore. The pub quickly became crowded, and there seemed to be people surrounding them. Their food was set down in front of them, and as she started to eat her delicious crab cakes, she noted that Raphael had ordered the burger and the crab cakes. He was trying. Anna suddenly thought of an idea. Something they could do that would be sure to be fun and maybe break the tension between them.

"After this I am going to take you somewhere special." Anna looked up and smiled.

Raphael knew not to challenge this one. "Waitress," he motioned. "I'll take another beer."

Anna drove them down Route 130 through Bristol, back to Pemaquid. They parked near a boat launch next to a cozy restaurant. They walked slowly up the rocky path to the docks, in the new rubber flip-flops they had just bought at Renys. Their lunch and the beers gave them an invigorated energy, and the wind whipped at Anna's hair. They came to a small wooden stand with canoes and kayaks propped up against it and lying all around it. Anna looked for someone, and in a few minutes a man came out of the restaurant and stood behind the stand. Anna chatted with him, handed him some cash, and turned to Raphael. "Ready to go sea kayaking?" She buckled on a life vest, grabbed a paddle, and pulled a large yellow kayak down to the boat launch. Raphael grabbed a kayak and followed her, running to catch up.

They headed out onto the Pemaquid River, which was really brackish water fed by a series of ponds and rivers, mixing freshwater with salt as it headed out to Pemaquid Harbor. Anna was reminded again why she loved being out on the water here. The motion of their paddles mixed with the ocean swells, relaxing her. They paddled for several minutes, eyes looking out at water that enveloped them, a cold wet tapestry that was all they could see. There were a few landmarks on the shore that got smaller and smaller, and the green and brown coast followed them along the left side.

Soon they came to a bend in the land, and Raphael noticed the large brown structure that was up ahead, a landmark that was long familiar to Anna. It was the fort at Pemaquid Harbor. Beyond that it was the wide ocean, dotted with colorful buoys.

It's beautiful, Anna thought. *If this doesn't win over Raphael, nothing will.* She hoped he would fall in love with this stretch of water, one of the most pristine places she had ever experienced. It didn't help that her memory kept conjuring up times when she and Andrew would paddle out here for hours at a time, after he had come in from fishing. You could see herons, frogs, ducks, and turtles here, especially in the summer. It was about as far from the city as you could get. Anna waited for Raphael's reaction.

But as he paddled his boat up to hers, he asked, "So what are you going to do about Art Basel Miami?" Anna's mind reeled in from the serenity of this place to the stress of her decision, and more importantly, how Raphael had learned of it.

She grabbed the side of his boat. "How did you hear about *that*?" she asked. Her pulse quickened, and she couldn't tell if it was nerves or anger that Genevieve told him. She was playing hardball—apparently she wanted this bad.

He looked out at the water. "Genevieve called me this week. Asked me to talk you into doing it," he said, smiling. "I think it is a big honor, so at the very least, congratulations are in order." He spoke respectfully, but then added. "I have to say, I am a little hurt you never told me. About your openings at the gallery."

She took a deep breath and stared at the shore. She watched a fish jump, leaving concentric circles growing wider in its wake. "I'm sorry I didn't tell you. But I didn't say anything for the same reason I don't want to do Art Basel. It would change everything to operate as a successful artist. I would have to schmooze and talk and be exposed, I guess. When I made all the pieces, it was really private. I only know how to work like that, when I think it will be just me who will see the painting. The more people I let in, especially those close to me, the more it will change. I didn't tell Georgia either."

"I understand, I guess. But you get instant credibility, plus a really wide audience for less than a week's worth of being in the public. What artist doesn't want that?"

"Apparently I'm the only one." They paddled in silence, and Anna tried to let the rhythmic motion of rowing relax her. "So I guess you saw the short article in the New York Times, huh?" Raphael nodded, looking sheepish.

"Look, let's just enjoy the rest of this paddle. I am thinking about it and I'll let you know when I come up with an answer." Anna's stomach twisted in knots. Then they rounded the corner.

Suddenly she saw the dock where Andrew had told her he wasn't going to New York. The memory flooded her, and she could picture sitting there that day in an instant. Like no time had passed. How many hard emotions could she handle? She looked out at the amphitheater of sky and water, which offered no answers, just a vastness, an impartial kind of wisdom that surpassed her present state. She watched two seagulls fly together overhead, their movements effortless. She envied them in their ease.

"Hey, Raphael, let's turn around at the next bend and duck in for a beer at that restaurant near the car." It was called the Contented Sole. Anna had anything but.

They paddled back in silence and returned the supplies to the man behind the wooden stand. Inside, the restaurant was quiet. Tourist season hadn't picked up yet, but there were a few locals. Anna would have loved to sit here by the water all afternoon, having fun with Raphael, the way they used to spend Saturday afternoons in New York. She knew they needed to get ready for the gala, but there was also something confusing and hard about having Raphael here. She had been hoping it would be easy. She thought she'd give it one last chance to be fun.

She watched him sit down across from her at a table in the corner, his rugged good looks fitting in here as much as they did in the city. The windows were large picture windows, making the ocean look touchable with just an outstretched hand. A skinny girl with dyed black hair and black nails came to get their drink order. Anna did a double take—it almost looked like the girl could have been a New Yorker. Then she read the back of her T-shirt: Lincoln Academy. That was where Anna had gone. The girl could have been her, if she had stayed here.

Raphael sipped his beer. After he put it down, he said, "Anna, what's wrong? Something is different about you, and I don't understand it." His accent was more pronounced, and Anna couldn't tell if it was from being angry or tired. "You seem really on edge, and it's not like you. I am wondering if it was a mistake that I came up."

Anna took a sip of her beer. She looked up at Raphael, and tried to word her thoughts carefully.

"Look, I'm very confused right now. I'm not sure what I want, but I know I was hoping that you could share in what I am feeling here. I am feeling very alive and amazed by life here. I was hoping if you had a taste of it, you would feel some of that about this place too. Instead I wonder if you came up here to win some pissing contest, to convince me that New York is better than Maine. You act like there is nothing here that is worth anything. I just need to be here right now. Please at least respect that instead of trying to fight it." She felt relieved to get that off her chest. Even though she didn't include how confused she was about Andrew, she was still glad to speak up and ask for Raphael to understand that she was going through a lot of things. In a way, it was conveniently true. She took a large sip of her beer and exhaled slowly.

Raphael was quiet for a few moments, thinking. "You are right. I'm sorry. I was acting like a jerk. I was completely afraid that you wanted to leave our life, to come here. And in my being afraid I . . . I was just defensive." He put his hand on the table and looked into her eyes. She noticed again the caramel-brown color of his eyes, just a deeper shade of his skin. His perfect hair was blown a bit by the wind, and his cheeks were red. Anna felt her anger melt, and a familiar pull toward Raphael settled over her. "I promise I will try to be supportive to you about this place. Can you forgive me? Can we start over now?" he asked, smiling, his charm oozing.

"Yes. Let's try to start the weekend over." She kissed him and smiled gratefully. "On that note, ready to go see my family?"

Chapter 16

When they entered the gym at Lincoln Academy, Anna was stunned at the transformation. A large white mansion was painted onto canvas that stretched across the whole back wall of the gym in a deceptive tromp l'oeil style that made you feel like you were walking onto the property of a Newport mansion. Lights were strung up that added to the effect, and a band was set up in the corner, playing big band '20s music. Ladies were dressed in their flapper best, and Anna suddenly wondered if her dropped-waist, pleated dress she had ordered online was enough without a headdress or shoes to match. Raphael looked dashing in a white tux he had rented in the city, though, so he would have to make up for it. Marie and Mike looked like they could have passed for F. Scott and Zelda, with his bow tie tux and her crimped hair and bangs and headband with a plume. Her white satin flapper dress and long necklaces looked like a movie costume.

"Marie, you look amazing!" Anna said over the saxophone.

"Thanks, I bought it all soon after we planned the theme. I don't think I would have had the mindset to find it after the funeral."

Their dad strolled up to them, in a black tuxedo, looking gala-esque.

Marie reached up and hugged her father. "Hey dad, how are you feeling?" she asked.

"Good, good. Those students did an impressive job painting the canvas for this. And you and Catherine did an amazing job, my hat's off to you," he said with obvious pride.

Anna couldn't help but feel a tinge of exclusion. Her sister had helped, she had turned her back. She couldn't blame anyone, and she tried to shake it off. Now that she was here and saw what they had pulled off, and why, she realized the Foundation was a vibrant, healthy entity, despite what she had thought about her father. She was also stunned to hear that the students had painted the backdrop, which was masterful work and transformed the space.

Marie turned to her and explained, "The culmination of the Foundation is the last two days, the students paint a backdrop for the fundraiser the following spring. So it means we have to pick out next year's theme soon!" she patted her dad's arm with a gentle prod.

"Let's enjoy this year first," he said with his typical stoicism.

Anna looked over and realized she had forgotten to break the ice for Raphael with her family. "Dad, you remember Raphael," Anna said as he leaned in to shake hands with her dad.

Her dad reached out a hand for Raphael to shake. He sipped his Scotch, then cleared his throat. "How's the world of finance holding up?" he asked amicably enough. His firm gaze seemed to look through Raphael.

"It's certainly a rocky time. But people are still making money, here and there." Raphael kept it to small talk, but you could see he immediately got animated talking about his work. "And how is the world of academics? I understand, aside from the Foundation, you are still in an advisory role?" Raphael's eloquence and charm were not lost on her father.

"Yes, just a bit. I view myself as a final harbinger of a belief in quality. This period of art can become more than a little crazy. They have forgotten that the great artists don't care about the consequences of their art—people's reactions, evoking an emotional response, trying to shock and change society. All pure crap. Narcissistic at best. It is the quality of the individual work itself that matters."

Anna blushed at her father's outspokenness and looked to see how Raphael was taking it. She was surprised to see him nodding in agreement. "I think you are absolutely right. After all, living in New York, you are bombarded by this. But every once in a while, a

contemporary artist can make you excited about art all over again."
He smiled at Anna. "Your daughter sold me some wonderful pieces
when we first met, and I am happy to say that even years later, my
heart is warmed by the sight of them on my walls each day."

"Well, that's good to hear," Anna's father said, waving hello to
people that walked by.

Raphael smiled mischievously at her, then said, "As a matter of
fact, your daughter is quite the artist herself." Anna pleaded with her
eyes for him to stop. She shook her head covertly and felt a familiar
tense grip reach around her heart.

"Oh?" Her father's interest was suddenly focused, and he turned
his head to stare at them.

Anna shook her head a bit. Did she just hear him correctly? "So
Marie, what's on the menu for tonight?" she interrupted, hoping to
change the subject.

"The pub in Damariscotta is catering. Little cups of clam chowder, fried calamari, beef tenderloin on top of garlic toast," Marie said
quickly, picking up on the conversation.

"Yes, she –"

"Raphael, do you want to come with me to get a drink?" Anna
interjected, pulling his arm so he had no choice.

Marie leaned over and whispered to Anna, "Does Raphael know
what he is doing? That he is opening up a whole can of worms between you two? And also, are you really painting again?"

Anna felt a slow ember of anger burn next to her heart. Yes, he
knew. He was bringing it up so that he could convince her to do
Art Basel. If her father knew she had been invited, no doubt Raphael thought that he would encourage her to go. But the fact that he
hadn't warned Anna that he was about to expose her made the anger
she felt previously in the day return in full force. She was happy to
have him with her but so torn about how he was acting.

"I'm sorry I didn't mention it, it seemed like no big deal. And I don't
know what he is thinking, but if he doesn't cool it, he is sleeping at the
airport." Anna whispered back as she kept pulling his arm. Her sister's
face looked like it was processing something, but she gave Anna's arm
a quick squeeze and tried to help her distract the conversation.

"Isn't this band great, Mike?" she said loudly, as Mike put his arm around her, nodding.

Her father ignored her question, and leaned into Raphael. "So tell me, how is it you've come to know about Anna's art?" He spoke slowly and deliberately. Anna could feel her arms and chest tremble slightly. She and her father waited eagerly for Raphael's answer.

Raphael took a sip of water and slowly set his glass down. "Oh, I've seen a few pieces here and there," he said smiling, and winked at Anna.

"So you've started again?" Her father looked at her from underneath his imposing eyebrows.

"Just for fun, Dad. For myself. Not for anyone else," Anna said, her words staccato.

Her father sat quietly and stroked his chin.

"C'mon, Raphael, I really need some wine," she said again, pulling even harder.

"Thank God," she heard her father say as they walked away.

"What the hell were you doing?" Anna asked Raphael as they pulled away from her dad. "How dare you tell my father that I've been painting? That is not your news to tell, it's mine, and I wasn't ready." Her face was hot.

"Anna, calm down. I didn't tell him anything major. Don't you think he guessed that you dabbled in it now and then?" Raphael's calm made Anna even more upset.

"No, I don't, not if you knew the last conversation he and I had about my painting. He is an overbearing, pushy, unrelenting hound when it comes to 'my gift,' as he calls it. He loses sight of the fact that I am his daughter and goes into some psycho realm about following your calling, using your gifts and potential. His opinion of what I should and should not be doing about my art is not something I want to invite into my adult life." She tried hard to remain calm, but she could feel her volume escalating. It was a good thing the music was so loud.

"Look, Anna, you can downplay it to him if you want. I don't think any harm has been done. But speaking of crazy, it doesn't make a lot of sense to completely hide what you are doing in your spare time from me, from your family, from everyone, for God's sake! Why, because you have a grudge with your father? Your dad is not the only one who is acting a little crazy here. You didn't even tell me you had two showings at Genevieve's! And I am your boyfriend! How do you think I should feel?" Raphael's free hand was waving in the air.

Anna sat quietly. He was right. How was that fair to him? It wasn't. But she still wouldn't have done it any other way. So what did that mean? "It is my choice, isn't it?" she finally answered.

"Yes, it's your choice," Raphael said, his voice exasperated. He turned toward the bar, and ordered a scotch and a glass of red wine for Anna.

Anna turned around to face Raphael as he handed her a glass of wine. "Thanks," she said, setting the glass down at a table next to them. She didn't even want it after the beers they had earlier and her frustration at the moment. "I'm sorry if you feel like I kept you in the dark. I didn't mean to. Now, will you wait here for me while I go to the bathroom. Please don't say anything more to my dad, Ok?" her eyes pleaded at him, and he stroked her cheek.

"Ok, I won't," he said, and quickly kissed her.

In the bathroom Anna looked into the mirror. Her confusion was all over her face. She suddenly longed to lay down, on her bed, and curl up and go to sleep.

Suddenly, out of the stall behind her, she saw Abigail emerge, looking lovely in a black gown with gossamer beading.

"Oh, hello, Anna. So nice to see you again," she said, her formal and elegant way striking Anna once again. She welcomed the sight of her more then she knew.

"Hi, Abigail, it's wonderful to see you here," Anna said, giving her a quick kiss hello on the side of her cheek. She suddenly realized she hadn't employed that New York greeting in several weeks.

"Your family has just done such an amazing job on this gala. It feels like we have transported ourselves. And I bet everyone is blown away – this doesn't happen often in Maine."

Anna smiled and nodded. She was right – fancy dresses and tuxs were very un-Maine. But it attracted all of the people from the south, from Portland and Portsmouth and Boston who had lots of money to donate to the Foundation, so it was a very smart move for her aunt and sister to go black tie. "I know, they've done an amazing job," she agreed.

"Are you all right sweet heart? You look upset."

Anna took a deep breath. "I am – I'm alright. Just thinking about that situation I'm in," she flashed Abigail a genuine smile, truly grateful that she had her to talk to.

"Any further along on your decision?"

"Not really, I think I put it out of my mind for now. My boyfriend is up from the city, though he is doing his best to lobby that I show in Miami. And I'm not a fan of some of his tactics. I'm still not quite sure what I want," she said. Now that her dad knew she was painting, half of her anxieties were realized anyway, though she kept that part from Abigail.

"Either way, darling, just try and stay true to you, to your voice. Whether you show or don't show, it doesn't really matter if you know what's important."

Anna smiled at her wise new friend. "Thanks, Abigail. That sounds like something my mom would say. And I think I really needed to hear it tonight." She took a deep breath, and realized she felt much better. Just the memory of her mother was enough to center her.

"Anytime," Abigail said, giving her a wink as she walked out the door, the music streaming in through the opening.

Anna looked at herself in the mirror and took another breath. She was her mother's daughter. This night was about what truly mattered. Kids doing art. Giving back. She touched up her makeup and walked back outside. As she strolled across the gym-turned-mansion, she suddenly thought about Miranda, and realized she owed her a text or an email saying she was still in Maine. As the band started to play 'In the Mood' an idea occurred to her. She should see if Miranda could get into the Foundation's summer program. She could spend time with her up here, and give her access to painting the beauty of Maine. Perhaps even teach a little herself at the Foundation this summer.

She went over to Marie, who was chatting with the caterers. When she was done, Anna asked, "How hard is it for a student to get into the summer program?"

"Well, not that hard. They have an online application. And they are evaluated based on three art samples. Deadline is soon, though. Of course, you know some people, so we might be able to help." She smiled and winked. Anna smiled at her sister, and couldn't wait to help Miranda get her application in. She would have to talk to her mother though, and hope that she said yes to this idea.

"Hey hon, there's some people from the hospital I'd love for you to meet," Mike said, holding out his hand for her.

"Thanks, Marie," Anna said. She headed over to Raphael at the table where she left him, scrolling on his phone. *The poor guy knows no one and was left alone*, she thought. She tried to put herself in a forgiving place, tried to overlook the conversation with her father. She was focusing on what was important – *Raphael. The Foundation. Helping Miranda.*

"Talking to a friend?" she said, smiling.

"No, just checking the Yankee game score. They're up by 10," he smiled.

Anna put her hand on his cheek and smiled back. "I'm sorry I got so mad. I am sure you didn't realize how crazy my relationship with my dad really is. Besides, now that I can see the work he's doing with the Foundation, I am trying to find a way to bridge things with him. A little." She held up her thumb and first finger an inch apart, showing him the distance she was yielding to her father. Or at least the Foundation. "Let's just dance and have a good time," Anna said.

"Ok, my dear," he stood up and took her hand, sipped his drink, and set it down. "It looks like you were able to find your *bueno onda* in the bathroom," he said with a grin, and handed her a glass of wine.

Anna laughed. "Yea, I guess I did," she said smiling, taking a sip, then pulling him to the dance floor and putting her arms around him. She stayed there, in her good vibes, with Raphael for exactly one song. Then, as the last notes faded she looked up, and saw Andrew in the corner of the gym, in a white tux with polished shoes, his golden hair still wild, but in a more contained way than usual. A gorgeous blond woman next to him in a red dress, with spaghetti straps and a dropped waist, a gorgeous diamond necklace strand around her neck. Her hair was down in lose, big golden waves, and her lips were a shade of red that matched her dress. They were talking easily, Andrew waiving his hand animatedly about something, and she was relaxed as she smiled at him, the corners of her eyes were crinkled as they laughed. Was she the same blond she had seen years ago? The weekend she came up to talk to Andrew? She couldn't be sure, but she felt a familiar pang of hurt.

Marie came up to Anna just then, with Liz by her side.

"Hey Anna, look who I found," she said.

"Hey hon," Liz said, giving her a quick hug. "So good to see you! Your sister was right when she told me we should come. This place looks amazing. I convinced Andrew to come too. I hope you don't mind! Who's this?" she said, pointing to Raphael.

"Liz, meet Raphael, my boyfriend. Raphael, this is Liz, an old friend of my sister's."

"Andrew is Liz's brother," Marie awkwardly interjected over the music.

"Nice to meet you," Raphael said, taking her hand, his eyebrow raised slightly. "Um, I'm gonna go get another drink," he said pointing at the bar. "Looks like you could use another too, yes?" he asked Anna. "I'll be right back."

After he was gone, Marie looked sideways at Anna, then asked Liz carefully, "So, who did Andrew come with? I don't recognize her."

"Oh, that's Stephanie. She was his partner on his last research trip. I'm not sure exactly what their status is, but she came to visit. I'll have to get the scoop from him."

Anna felt something twist again inside. So it wasn't the blond from the boat. But it was nevertheless a lovely girl. *Let it go*, she whispered to herself. *Remember what's important.*

She might have had success with that if Andrew hadn't walked up to them all right at that moment. The minute he was standing across from her, Anna could feel her heart pound, and looked around to see if anyone else seemed to hear it.

"Hello, ladies," he said. "Marie, you've done an amazing job tonight. The Lobsterman's Association may have to tap you when we need a fundraiser."

"Thanks, Andrew," she said, laughing. "I don't know if I have more than one of these a year in me. But I could pass my Excel spreadsheet over to someone and help them pull it off."

The blond woman came up to Andrew, and Anna's face suddenly felt warm, and her head became so light, she was afraid she was going to pass out. Memories from her train ride home after seeing him with the blonde from the boat flooded her. Rational thought seemed to recede, like a wave, and the pure pain of rejection wrapped around her heart, like barbed wire. She needed to leave. "Excuse me, I'm going to go see what Dad and Aunt Catherine are up to," she said quickly. As she pulled away, she caught Andrew's gaze. The look he gave her hit her hard. It was that same gaze that seemed to jump right inside her lungs, making her breath sharp. She stepped away, unsteady, and went out to the hall. Breathe, she told herself. Breathe.

She stood there in the empty school hallway, in front of a glass case filled with trophies. She could see her reflection in the glass, her black hair contrasting with her pale face and red lips. She stared at the gold figures of girls swinging a bat, the names on the rectangular plates under the title "MVP". Angela Hopkins. Jennifer Walters. *Is this what having a breakdown looks like? Reading the names of girls who were good softball players while you quietly lost your mind?* Molly Malone. Ashley Reichl.

The door from the gym opened, spilling light into the dark hall. Andrew stepped out, and slowly walked towards her.

"Anna, can we please talk."

"I – I don't think that's a great idea," she said. "Raphael's going to look for me, and your, well, your gorgeous lady friend will probably look for you."

"Look, I asked her to come when I heard, when I heard you were coming with your boyfriend. I had already agreed to come and it was going to be too hard for me to watch you – to see you together if I came alone. She's just – she's a colleague."

"Well she looks an awful lot like your type. Like the blond you were with in your boat after we broke up."

"What?" Andrew looked confused.

Anna turned around to face him. She crossed her arms, holding on to them as if they would give her some kind of support right now. "We had only been broken up for a year. I came up to Maine to tell you I had made a mistake. I took the bus to surprise you. And when I got to the harbor, you were out on your boat with some blonde girl. You guys were kissing." Anna realized she was crying now. "I got back on the bus and went back to New York. I couldn't believe you had moved on so fast, and it really hurt. So, I think it's better if we just leave it alone, Andrew. Just leave it in the past," she said. She was suddenly shivering.

Andrew looked confused, and stared at the wall. Then his eyes opened wide. "You're talking about Sam. Samantha. She's Chris's little sister. He couldn't help me one day, so she came out to help. She kept flirting with me, told me what a huge crush she had on me," he stopped, remembering, his hand cupping his chin as if it would help him remember. "We kissed for like a second, but I pushed her away and told her I didn't feel that way about her. She kept trying. It was a nightmare. You – you were there that day?" he asked, bewildered.

"Yea. I was there. I came back." She wiped her tears, positive her eyes were probably resembling a raccoon at this point. "But none of it matters now." She took a step towards Andrew. "You should've come to New York if you weren't over me. You should've come to New York period." She walked passed him, and headed back towards the bathroom. She didn't think she could find her good vibes this time.

After she put cold toilet paper wads on her eyes, to bring down the swelling from crying, and wiped as much mascara away as she could before touching up her make up, she started to worry Raphael would wonder where she was. She came back into the gym, and breathed a sigh of relief to see him standing with Marie and Mike, her dad and a few other people she didn't recognize, along with Aunt Catherine and Uncle Joe, and Sarah and Phillip. Her family had taken him under their wing. She headed in their direction, and overheard their conversation as she reached for Raphael's arm.

"Interest rates aren't going anywhere. You're going to want to look at High Yield at the moment," she heard Raphael say.

"That's a great opportunity if you can buy in at a low," said a gentlemen who Anna guessed was a colleague of Mike's. They all seemed to nod their heads.

"I see you've met Aunt Catherine," she said to Raphael, feigning a bright spirit. He nodded and put his arm around her.

"Yes, your aunt is a lovely lady," he said, winking at her.

Aunt Catherine smiled at them, and leaned over to Anna. "You didn't tell me your boyfriend was so handsome and so smart," she said.

These words made Anna feel better suddenly. "I didn't? Well, he's very modest. I didn't want to embarrass him too much." She fought every thought of Andrew as she joined in on the conversation about investing the Foundations assets and the hospital's 401(k) plan. She was so grateful Raphael's attention was on something other than her.

Later, as they headed home, Anna driving the truck down the winding road back to Pemaquid, they sat in silence for a few minutes. The headlights lit up a long rock walls as they drove. "Aren't the stone walls charming around here?" she asked, trying to make conversation.

"They are," he said half-heartedly, nodding. "So was that the Andrew you were with when you lived here?"

"What?" asked Anna.

"Liz said she made Andrew come. Then she said, 'I hope you don't mind'. To you. Then Marie acted all weird. Why would she think you would care?"

Anna stared at the road. "Yes, that's him, but it was a long time ago. I told you all about him. He doesn't matter to me anymore."

"Are you sure? Because that would be something I should know about."

"Yes, I'm sure. I told him about you right away."

"So you guys hang out and talk?" Raphael asked, his voice revealing a tinge of sarcastic anger.

Anna thought about their conversation, about the way Andrew had looked at her tonight. About their lunch date at his school. It weighed guiltily on her conscience for a moment, but there was no point in telling Raphael about that. It would make things worse. *Besides, it was in the past,* she told herself. And after he just stood there while she walked away tonight, she knew there was nothing more to say. "He was at Shaw's Wharf the day of my Uncle's funeral. We talked briefly. It's a really small town, Raphael."

"That's what I'm afraid of."

He turned on the radio, and found a recap of the baseball game. The Yankees had easily won against the Cardinals. Raphael sat quietly, chewing his fingernails down to stubs.

"Hon, you have nothing to worry about. He was there with his girlfriend. He's very old history. Let's forget it," she tried to backpedal and change the subject. "Listen, what do you think about buying some tickets to a Yankee game soon? Have something fun to look forward to when I get back?"

His hand relaxed, and in his fatigue, he nodded. "I would love that," he said, squeezing her hand. "If you're ever coming back." Something had drained out of him. She could feel it. She looked at him and squeezed his hand tighter.

"I'm coming back," she said softly.

The next morning, they both slept in. They woke up and showered, hurrying to catch Raphael's flight out of Portland at one p.m. They drank their coffee with eggs and bacon, then hurried to get dressed and leave by ten.

As the airport grew closer, they were at first polite. Then Raphael broke the ice. "Look, Anna, you know I love you. I am sorry that I talked to your father about your art. I am sorry for not being more sensitive. I – I trust you about Andrew. I would be lying if I said I wasn't concerned. But take the time you need here to figure out what you want. I think it is important for us – for our future – if you know what that is. So I want you to figure that out while you are here. Then come home to me. Please." His brown eyes seemed to plead with her of their own accord. He took her hand with one of his and stroked the back of her hair with the other.

I know," she said quietly. "You're right, and I think that's what I am trying to say to you; that is what I need to do here. I have to take this moment and breathe. It's what my heart is telling me to do. So I'm gonna listen. And I will let you know what it says as soon as I know." She smiled at him. "Thank you for being big enough to let me do this. And thank you for coming up here, it means a lot. I love you and I'll be home soon," she said, holding his hand in hers. They kissed, and held each other for a moment, and said goodbye.

"Vaya con Dios," he said, touching her cheek. "Go with God."

As she watched the planes taking off at the airport, she thought of birds migrating. She wondered if that was all she was doing, just going away from New York City for a season, then coming back. She longed to be guided by instincts like they were. To be relieved from all doubt and confusion. Then she realized that birds always migrated home, and knew that of course her instincts would take her back to Maine, and to the sea.

Chapter 17

After Raphael's visit, Anna threw herself into the work she was in Maine to do. Fixing up her uncle's house, finishing a few paintings, cataloging her mom's art. The only way she could know for sure what she wanted was to see how she felt after she saw these things through.

She scraped and painted the back screen door on a sunny morning. She cleaned up the yard, raking all the dead leaves and trimming back the dead heads. She edged the grass along the beds and laid down mulch. Putting Charlie's house in order started to put something inside her in order too.

One afternoon while she was edging the beds in the yard, she looked up at the clouds gathered over the ocean, making the view a study on shades of gray. She washed the dirt and mud and leaves off her hands and went down to the boathouse. She got out a new canvas and painted the background a milky gray. A wave of desire rose up in her, and she noticed it, but of what? Of painting? Of the ocean? She tried to work it out on the canvas. The haunting sky was translated into a bulbous and threatening white, black, and gray scene. As she worked, she noticed she was crying, and she wiped her nose and eyes on her sleeve. Then she started to laugh at herself for crying so hard. A great weight was lifting off her chest, her shoulders. All of her decisions, her pressures, were somewhere dissipating on the water. Inside her was fresh emotion, stripped of being charged, like she had issued her own lightning bolt while she painted, and now all the particles in her were balanced again.

She sat back and looked at the painting and realized the image was one of grief. All at once, she understood what she was trying to do here in Maine. She had to finally dive into the pool of grief that she had just locked behind a door since she had moved to New York. Losing her mother, and Andrew, and in a way her father all at once. She just moved on from it all without dealing with it. When she returned to grieve for Uncle Charlie, the door was budged open. That was what was calling her here. Her heart and her mind were trying to work it out now, after her years of strength, drawn from Raphael and her work and Genevieve. She had strength now. She needed to use it to face all she had lost.

Her first step was to pack her painting bag and travel easel. She hopped in her sister's truck and drove across town, through downtown Damariscotta, before ending up on a familiar winding dirt road. She went past a thick stone wall that led to a wrought-iron gate. Finally, she turned into the parking lot of St. Patrick's.

Instead of parking next to the church, she drove to the far corner of the lot. She stared into the cemetery. She thought of Uncle Charlie at a nearby cemetery. She wished that he was here, so she could visit both of them together. She got out and heard the echo of the heavy truck door close behind her. In her hand she carried a pot of tulips she had dug up from his garden. She figured he wouldn't mind.

She knew the spot like the back of her hand even though she had only been here four or five times. She went to the edge of the gravel parking lot and down a muddy path to a field outlined by a stone wall. To the northwest corner and up to a large slab of concrete, fifth from the right, that read:

Therese McAllister Goodrich, 1949–2004

Underneath her name it read:

There is a time for everything under the heavens.
A time to be born and a time to die.

She remembered when her father told them that her mother had asked for her headstone to say that. Before she went home and the hospice care started coming, before she was unable to think or speak. They had discussed many details, and that was one she had handed him on a little piece of paper. Anna thought of her mother thinking so finally about her own death. She must have gotten close to accepting it. It seemed that way to Anna. Still, her mother had been truly grieved to be leaving her children motherless. She had written them all letters—Anna had hers in her apartment safe, but she made a copy that she carried in her journal. She brought it with her and unfolded the creased, wrinkled pages.

My dearest Anna,

This is the hardest thing I have ever had to do, but the only thing worse than saying goodbye to your youngest daughter would be to not say goodbye. I don't want to leave you. I don't want you to ever have a single day where you feel the pain of needing your mother and not having her there, to comfort you, counsel you, love you, cherish you, tell you all the wonderful things inside you. But you will; I can't stop that. Instead I can ask you to remember every day that I love you so much and I wish I could be there.

I don't think dying means I am not there. I think it means I am there in a different way. Of course, we don't want it to be this way. We want it to be so that I can help you get dressed on your wedding day. That I can hold your children just like I held you.

But I believe that love is more powerful than death. It has to be. I hope you can picture, like I do, that way down deep inside your heart, in the very fabric of your soul, there is a connection to another world. Love is a thread. A river. It connects those two worlds between your heart and Heaven. Even though I am going to be somewhere else, our love will still bind us together.

After her mother died, Anna read the letter over and over again, and every night while she fell asleep she imagined a new way that their bond could look. One night, it was a piece of twine; the next night it was an electric cord; the next, a river with estuaries that looked like arteries, the earth's topography mirroring the heart's anatomy. She took great comfort from this, and always felt like somehow her mother could hear her, know what she was going through. She could always conjure up her mother's voice in her head trying to talk through any problem she was having.

Except when her father put enormous, unrealistic pressure on her. Then she couldn't hear her mother at all. She knew that no one loved her mother more than he did. Their pure devotion to each other made her feel even more confused and guilty when she was so angry at her father's behavior. The only thing she could figure out was that her grief made her so raw, and his made him so blind, and it was a combustible combination. It blew up one day, and that was the day she decided to leave. The day she asked Andrew to come with her to New York.

Anna looked out over the grave at the tops of the trees, the spring green leaves a vibrant color against a sky that was overcast and ominous.

Coming back and seeing Andrew had cast so much doubt over her. She felt both her hurt from all those years ago, and a new growing sense that she had hurt others, too. That she had been too angry. She had run from a lot of things she loved in her anger and hurt. *Did I make the right decision to leave here? If he loved me, he would have come with me, right?*

Suddenly a new thought washed over her.

If I'd loved him, I wouldn't have left.

She could see this easily now, how much hurt she must have caused him. In her grief, in her pain, she hadn't seen this clearly before. That explained the look on his face each time she had seen him here. He looked like he was in pain. She felt a sudden urge to comfort him, to say she was sorry. She had made so many mistakes, and she didn't know where to step next to avoid making more.

What should I do, Mom?

She heard herself ask with a small voice in her head. She looked over and could see the cross at the top of the church's steeple, the stained-glass windows of St. Patrick, another of Christ holding a sheep. She couldn't remember the last time she had prayed. She couldn't even remember the last time she didn't feel mad at God since her mom had died. But suddenly the depth of her heart unfolded a question, a prayer, without her even thinking it.

What do you want me to do, God?

A bird suddenly flew to the branches just over Anna's head. Its shrill cry pierced her heart, and she wept again. This time it was like a cleansing purge. She let every hurt, every painful thought flow through her head, ran over them like pearls, caressing them, feeling them fully. Her emotions swelled and burst, like the white caps of the ocean crashing on the rocks of the shore. She let the storm in her heart rage. It was so much easier to set it free then hold it in anymore. When she was done, she stood up, wiped her eyes and nose, and took a deep breath. A warmth on her face made her look up, and she saw a small stream of sunlight break through the clouds.

She knew what she needed to do. She needed to talk to her father. She set down the pot of tulips she had been gripping fiercely, walked back to the truck, and headed home.

Chapter 18

It was only a few minutes south of Uncle Charlie's house. Her childhood home sat on a large acre of green grass, with woods behind it. The brown barn stood out next to the white colonial, and a creek ran behind it that fed into a small pond. The hours her friends and siblings had spent in those woods, in that creek, were part of the canvas of her childhood.

When she pulled in, she noticed her dad had raked and mulched the beds since she had been there last, when she had stopped on the way to Marie's house to visit the barn. The yard was tidy and neatly edged, and the paint looked fresh. She saw her father's car and was glad he was home. She didn't know if she would have the guts to come here again to talk to him.

She walked up the brick path and noticed the purple hyacinths sprouting up like little happy children, next to tiny white forget-me-nots. Her mother had loved these flowers and had planted them all over the front of the house, along with a garden of lilies of the valley, under the shade of the living room picture window. Anna smiled; the flowers reminded her of her mother so much, she felt like they were blooming just for her.

Anna knocked twice before she swung open the thick green wooden door.

"Hey, Dad," she called out. "It's me, Anna." She realized how unexpected her visit would seem, since she hadn't once dropped in on him since she'd been home. The rooms were exactly as she remembered them. The whole scene looked familiar but aged, like a well-loved photo that had faded with time. The house was quiet and tidy, with a pile of newspapers neatly folded on the dining room table—the same table that had been filled with applications and brochures he was trying to push on her the last time she had been here. His slippers sat by the old armchair in the family room, next to an ash tray with a half-smoked cigar, the scent of it still lingering in the air. She heard the floor creak above her, then her father's voice. "Hello?" His strong voice seemed to echo through the hall.

"It's Anna," she said again. She shifted her weight awkwardly from one foot to another. She could feel her pulse racing. Her father came down the stairs, and in the poorly lit hall, he looked so old. Anna suddenly felt a pang of guilt. She had spent so long being mad at this old man. In her mind, he was a force of nature. In this room, he looked lonely and ancient. She noticed that he had a pained expression on his face as well, one of confusion and resignation. "Hi, Anna, good to see you," he said, in an even, deep voice. "It was wonderful to have you at the gala last Saturday. Thank you for coming. So, what brings you by?"

"I'm not sure exactly. I just felt like coming over to talk, I guess. D'you want some coffee? Mind if I make some?"

"Sure, I can make it." He walked into the kitchen, the movements of his long frame as familiar to Anna as her reflection in the mirror. She followed him into the kitchen, the wallpaper the same blue and white flower pattern her mother had picked out one summer. The white had turned yellow, but the tiny blue flowers still looked cheerful. Her dad busied himself with making a pot of coffee silently. As the machine started to gurgle and spit out the caramel-brown brew, Anna led right into her thoughts.

"Dad, I have been doing a lot of thinking over at Uncle Charlie's house, and when it comes right down to it, I don't understand. I don't understand why, after Mom died, you didn't let me take my time. With school. With art. With Andrew. I don't understand why you put all that pressure on me. I wasn't ready for it. I couldn't handle it. I needed time to heal. Was that so hard to see?" Anna felt the bricks falling off her chest as she laid down these words. It felt like the wall she had put up so securely for all these years suddenly had open doors and windows.

"Milk?" he asked. Anna nodded. He got down two mugs and poured milk into one of them. Anna remembered he always took his coffee black. They both stared at the coffee brewing. His hair was messy at the top like he had been running his hands through it, though his shirt was neatly pressed and his khakis had a crease down the middle.

"Anna, I've thought about this a lot since Charlie died, I don't know why. Maybe because you're here, in Maine, reminding me of how I've messed things up so much between us. Maybe it's because he died. I'm not even sure I know where to start. In case you didn't know it, your old man has some stubborn pride running through his veins." He chuckled, but the sadness around his eyes let Anna know he wasn't just kidding. "And I am sure I don't need to tell you that losing your mother was beyond my worst fears, beyond any pain I have ever known. If loving her saved me, losing her ruined me. I am sure you didn't get what you needed from me because I was incapable of giving anything other than what my blind grief drove me to do." He picked up the coffee pot and filled both mugs, then handed one to Anna.

"You asked the other day about the girl in the picture. Your Aunt Sheila. You don't remember hearing about her, do you?" he asked.

Anna thought for a minute while she took a sip of coffee. She remembered that name vaguely. "I remember the name but I don't remember connecting it as your sister."

"Yes, she was my sister," said her dad.

"Aunt Catherine said she died young, though, right?" She recalled the photo, remembering she looked a lot like Aunt Catherine. "You guys never talked about her," Anna said, leaning against the wall.

Her dad put one hand on the counter and with the other ran his fingers through his hair. "Right. There was a reason we didn't talk about her. I don't think I have told this story to anyone before except your mother," he said with a deep sigh. "Let's sit." He motioned to the round table in the kitchen, half surrounded by a built-in bench with cushions that matched the wallpaper. The chandelier reminded Anna of a game she had played with her brother and sister—who could push the chandelier highest without getting caught.

Her dad swallowed a sip of coffee and looked out the window, his eyes squinting from the sun breaking out from the clouds. "After my mother died, when I was about twenty, like you, my father just fell apart. He didn't do much but sit in his chair and drink. He died about five years later. Cirrhosis. That part you know. But I tried to keep Sheila's story from you and your brother, your sister. Mainly because I was ashamed." He took another sip of coffee and crossed his arms.

"When my mother died, Sheila was only fourteen. Growing up, she was very talented. She was an excellent student, loved to read and write, and was a virtuoso on the piano. She won all kinds of awards in school, and she had a teacher who took her under her wing and tried to get her to think about college. But after my mother died, my dad was horrible to Sheila. He refused to pay for her music lessons. In a drunken fit, he destroyed her piano. He told her to forget about college. He collapsed, and he brought her down with him. She bore the brunt of his anger at losing my mother, but he also let out a side of him from his own childhood, from his own violent father. I'm sure he must have hit her. I just steered clear of home when he turned into such a mess and I never saw the effects. Sheila met a boy a few years after I left home, and she married him when she was eighteen. They went out to California, joined some hippie commune, about a year before my father died. He introduced her to drugs. Sheila didn't make it to my dad's funeral, and I tried to track her down. Eventually, I found out she had overdosed when she was twenty-two. I was so torn up about her, I felt so much *guilt*." Her father paused, his voice thick and his eyes filled with pain. "Sheila really loved me. Even when we were little. She was so loyal, like a puppy. And I just ignored her after I left. After she died, I realized I should have done something. I should have given her money for her lessons, but I was a poor grad student at the time. I should have gone home to visit her, to invite her to visit me. I let her be destroyed by my father and I did nothing to stop it. I should have stood up to him. But I just wanted to run away from him. So I did."

Her dad's lower lip trembled. He gathered himself and continued talking.

"When your mother died, I held on to one solid thought in my grief. I had to help you, Anna. I had to make sure you didn't drift like my sister. You were so talented. You had your whole future wide open to you. But you wanted to waitress and go out with your boyfriend. I couldn't stand it. All I saw was you ending up like Sheila. I could see it. I know Andrew is different. I know that now." Her father sighed deeply. "But at the time, it felt like history was trying to repeat itself. And I couldn't let that happen. My guilt couldn't let that happen. I tried hard to get you to grab on to those chances, those things that would be sure to save you. A foundation that you could fall back on. Instead I pushed you away. I failed again."

Her father stopped talking. He twisted his mug around absentmindedly. He cleared his throat, then rubbed his eyes with the palm of his hands. Anna could see his shoulders shake with a sob. She had only seen her father cry when her mother died.

Her eyes filled for the third time that day. The ache of regret mingled with the peace of understanding and found their release in her tears. She went over to her father. She put her hand on his shoulder and tried to comfort him. He grabbed her, clutched her tightly. It was the embrace Anna had deeply wished for and didn't think possible.

A bird called loudly outside the kitchen window, as the coffee turned cold. At that moment, Anna knew that her prayer had actually been heard and answered.

"It's ok, dad. It's ok. I didn't understand before, and now I do," she said, holding him tight. "I'm sorry too. I was angry. I ran away, just like you did. I guess you passed down your stubborn streak," she said smiling. In the warmth of the sunlight, they both laughed, as forgiveness and understanding passed between them.

Later that afternoon, as she curled up on the guest bed at Uncle Charlie's, the picture with Aunt Sheila next to her bed, she stared out the window and watched the sea. She watched the water swell and fall, over and over, and the rhythm matched the two thoughts that wound around her mind, over and over, until she fell asleep. *Thank you. Thank you. I'm sorry. I'm so sorry.*

Chapter 19

The next week, Anna boarded a train for New York. It wasn't Raphael or Genevieve that made her decide to return. It was Georgia.

Her best friend had called mid-week with devastating news. Her boyfriend had left her. He decided to move to LA to pursuit his career in acting. Despite Anna's desire to stay in Maine, to spend time with her dad, to heal, the idea of her friend alone, coping with her sudden loss was more than Anna could bear. She knew all too well how that felt.

Marie drove her to Portland with Henry in tow, and they had lunch along the wharfs at Casco Bay before her train. They were early for her train, and the day was warm, like a prelude to summer. They ate lobster rolls and Henry had clam chowder with oyster crackers, and after they sat back, sunning themselves.

"Do you think going back to New York will make you want to stay?" Marie asked her as they sat on a bench watching Henry push his toy truck on the deck.

"I don't know," Anna answered. "I just know that Georgia needs me to be there for her. Coming back home has been amazing. To reconnect with Maine, with you and your family. That much I know. And I know that I don't want to sell Uncle Charlie's house. I realized that as I was sprucing it up and spring cleaning. So I know I'll be coming back up here a lot more. But I don't know how it will feel to be back in the city. I guess I'll have to see."

"It's been great to have you here. But I am sure Genevieve or Raphael will suck you back in," Marie said with a knowing smile. Anna hugged her sister and helped her corral Henry into the car. "And make sure you make it up to Stephen's restaurant. I talked to him yesterday, and he sounds a little on edge. I think he could use a visit. I'm going to try to make it down soon too but I'm not feeling that great right now. I'll try in a few weeks."

Anna hugged her sister. "I hope you feel better. You've been strait out with the funeral and the gala. And your annoying sister crashing at your house. Thanks, Marie, for everything. I love you."

"Hurry up before you make me cry," Marie said, blinking her eyes from under her bangs, her dimples punctuating her tender smile.

Her train was right on time, and when she boarded she put her head back on her seat and closed her eyes. As they rolled and lurched, she thought about everything the train was pulling away from. The rocking of the car lulled her to sleep, and in her dozing state, images of Andrew kept playing through her mind - walking up the ramp at Shaw's Wharf, teaching his class, in a tux standing next to a beautiful blonde.

How had she messed things up so badly? she thought. When she realized how much she must have hurt him, on that cold day at her mother's grave, she wanted to run right over to his house and apologize. Tell him she was sorry. Then Georgia called, and here she was on her way to New York. Would she ever get to tell him how sorry she was? That she understood how she had hurt him? She stared out the window, watching the East Coast weave past her, towns and cities and fields and rivers, the sunlight bouncing off the water.

Georgia met her at Penn Station. Her normally glamorous hair was pulled back into a ponytail and her eyes were red. "Hey," Anna said as she reached for a hug.

"Hi, I'm so glad you're back." Georgia sobbed into her friend's shoulder.

"Do you want to go somewhere and talk or just head back to the apartment..." Anna began.

"I just want to grab some wine and pizza and head home - is that ok?" Georgia said, her face like a little girl's, raw and honest.

"I think that sounds great," Anna said. They gathered up their favorite groceries at the corner market, and steaming pizza from their favorite place on the corner, and climbed the marble stairs to their apartment.

"Thank you so much for coming back to the city right away, hon. I couldn't bear to be alone right now and you know I think most of my other friends in the city are assholes." Anna laughed at her best friend's honest evaluation. "I know it's not fair to say that but really you knew Jake the best and you know how we were together. You know how I feel right now better than anyone."

Anna nodded and took off her boots, then sat back on their couch. "Start at the beginning, what happened?"

"Well, I knew after Christmas that he had sort of been looking into acting classes and auditions that were based out of LA. I talked to him about it, but then he got some commercials here and got promoted at the restaurant, and he said it was nothing, he was just trying to get a handle on what opportunities there were for him there. Then he went to visit a friend in LA a few weeks ago, and when he came back he said that his friend has a lot more opportunities there then he does here." Her face twisted in grief, and a sob caught in her throat. "He said that he decided to move, that he knew it was the right thing for him and that he wanted to go out there alone, single. That he wasn't ready for a big commitment when he was trying to launch his career. What kind of bullshit is that after being together for two years? I didn't see it coming at all. It was totally out of the blue. I even booked a weekend trip to come up to see you in Maine in a few weeks with him. He's such a selfish prick."

Anna couldn't believe her friend's relationship was over so fast. Jake had been a little selfish, or maybe vain was a better word, but not anything extraordinary. Keeping her waiting while he worked out or got a haircut was a frequent occurrence, but he acted as though Georgia was everything to him and he definitely threw out the signs that getting married, having a family, sharing his life with Georgia was what he wanted. Anna felt angry and blindsided for her friend.

"You know what, he's just having a mid-mid-life crisis," Anna said. "He's freaked out that he is almost thirty, his career is stalling, and he feels like he has to copy his friend to keep up. Men are so competitive. If they even begin to feel behind, their anxiety is through the roof. But I bet he will realize he made a huge mistake. After a few weeks of being out there and seeing how empty his life is without you, he'll be begging you to take him back.

"Well screw him," Georgia said. "I wouldn't want him back after this. He just seems like a flake to me now. I mean, you are either all in or you are all out as far as I'm concerned. Wanting different things will only tear you apart in the long run. It's better to realize it now in a way that he wants something so different then I do. I mean, could you imagine me in LA? Surrounded by fake boobs and plastic lips?"

Anna laughed at the thought of her sweet friend Georgia - who should have been born in the 50's just so she could have fully embraced the 70's minus the drugs with her hippy hair and clothes and love of all things Bohemian - surrounded by the LA scene. She felt confident that it would have fallen apart quickly if Jake had asked her to move out there with him. "It couldn't have worked," Anna agreed.

"It still hurts though," Georgia said, re-crossing her legs on the couch and picking at a bag of potato chips. "He was still my best friend, besides you I mean. We were just talking about going to France this summer. He was supposed to come out to my parent's house on Long Island for my little sister's birthday next week. It just is so sudden. It's not like we were even fighting at all. It's just like cardiac arrest or something."

Anna thought of her Uncle Charlie. His real cardiac arrest showed her how hard it is when someone is suddenly gone. The shock of the surprise has to be dealt with first before you can get to the other feelings.

"I'm sorry, Anna," Georgia looked up. "That was a crappy analogy. I'm such a jerk." She wiped her eyes with a sad looking tissue.

"Whatever, Georgia, I know what you meant. You're right. Jake was totally unfair to you. I hate him for you right now, if that's any consolation."

Georgia smiled at her friend through her tears. "I don't want you to hate him," she said as she dabbed her eyes with her wad of paper. "Ok, maybe just for a little while," she laughed. "I don't know. I guess I just wanted to believe in the fairy tale version of us. And, minus the crappy ending, we had that. He used to bring me home bagels after his run every Sunday morning, and he always brought me my favorite magazines home from the newsstand when he walked by and saw there was a new edition. I knew what he would order on a menu before he even got back from the bathroom and I could plan my meal around it like clockwork. I thought those things were what the old people on the couch being interviewed on their 75th wedding anniversary said made them last. The little intimacies that weave between each other and tie you together."

Anna listened, her head tilted on her fingers. "I know. You had a great relationship on many levels. This was unfortunately a structural issue – like a crack in the foundation. The right person will be someone whose foundation is so solid, who is loyal to himself and to you, so that you don't have to worry he will never ever be anything other than who he really is." As Anna said those words, her mind flashed a picture of Andrew, sitting at the dock, the sun in his eyes. *I belong in Maine. I thought you did too.*

Anna sat up right, and tried to take a deep breath. *This is not about Andrew*, she tried to remind herself. *This is about Georgia and she deserves your help right now.* "You know what you need? A giant slice of gooey New York Margherita pizza. I'm going to heat this up and you open the wine. I'll be right back."

She ducked into the kitchen and as she put slices of pizza on plates, she thought again about how much she wished she could have talked to Andrew before she left. How much she wanted to say sorry to him. As if he could hear her thoughts, at that moment Raphael rang on Anna's phone.

"Hey sweetie, you got in ok?"

"Yes, Georgia picked me up at Penn station and we are back at our place, having some heartbreak conversation and some comfort food. How are you doing?"

"I'm excellent now that you're back home," he sounded very happy. "I can't wait to see you, should I make reservations for dinner tomorrow?" "Sure," said Anna, "but you may want to make them for three. I'm not sure I'll want to leave Georgia home alone while we go out on a date."

"Alright, if you insist. But after dinner, you know, when she's asleep, maybe then it will be safe to leave her alone?" Raphael asked.

Anna laughed. "Sure, hon."

She hung up the phone and brought the pizza into the living room. The melted cheese spilled onto the plate, and Anna knew her friend's messy love affair would momentarily be forgotten with a bite of this pizza. She brought the hot slice over to the couch. "Want to eat out tomorrow with Raphael and me? You may have to shower first, though."

Georgia laughed as she sat up and reached for the pizza. "Alright, but there better be a bar."

Anna sat back and watched her beautiful friend. "You are too good for him you know."

Her friend sighed and met her eyes. "I know. That's why I plan on eating my weight in ice cream. To lower my standards."

They decided to meet at a new restaurant in Tribeca that had a great word of mouth buzz, and they had called a few friends to join them. Anna felt the slightest bit disoriented, having just sat in the quiet of her uncle's house, watching the sun set over the ocean and sitting by the fire reading a book about Mary Cassatt at this time two nights ago. In contrast to the quiet, the city felt so alive, practically buzzing with an energy, like it had a pulse, and she realized it felt exciting being back in it.

They settled into their table and as their friends arrived, one by one, they kissed on the cheek and began telling stories, laughing, and listening to Georgia's heartbreaking tale. They ordered Champagne to celebrate her freedom, and Raphael declared with a raised glass that it was good to have his Anna back, that he wouldn't have made it another day without her. Anna's heart felt warm with so many lovely people surrounding her, and she feasted on both food and friendship.

When she was stuffed and happy, Raphael turned to her and put his arm around her. "Did I tell you that Mike and Steve and I were all talking about getting a house in the Hamptons for a month this summer?" The news floated through her mind and immediately it pulled out the competing thought of Maine, of her uncle's house, of spending time with Henry, Marie, and her dad, of painting all the summer flowers like the lupines and the sea roses that grew everywhere.

"Well, it would be tough to be in the Hamptons when we're in Maine," she said. Raphael put down his glass and his smile fell.

"Well, the house is such a good deal and a lot of friends from work are going to be there at the same time. It is sort of a networking career move for me to spend time playing hard with the higher ups, you know." Anna wiped her mouth with her napkin even though she didn't need to; she needed something to cover her disappointment. After everything she showed him and everything she tried to explain to Raphael when he came to visit, he thought everything would go right back to being the same – he picked where they went, what they did, how they vacationed because Anna had become so numb inside she didn't have the energy to protest, and because outside of painting, she had been on autopilot. He didn't realize that had changed. When she went home for Uncle Charlie's funeral, she woke up. She knew what she wanted now. She knew just how short life really is, and what she wanted to be surrounded with. And it was very clear to her that she did not want to be surrounded by people she barely knew in the Hamptons.

"Maybe you should go to the Hamptons and I'll go to Maine," Anna said. The table got suddenly quiet, and their friends looked around uncomfortably.

"Honey, don' get like that," Raphael said, putting his arm around her. "We'll talk about it later – maybe we can do both," he said. And he raised his glass, "To the beautiful and newly single Georgia. Here's to the lucky man who'll get to find you now," he said. His charm to the rescue, yet again.

Chapter 20

The next day was Friday, and Anna had planned to meet with Genevieve in the morning. She was going to tell her whether or not she would show at Art Basel, and even as she woke up and brewed coffee in her own pot, which she decided tasted horrible compared to the one at Uncle Charlie's, she had not made up her mind. She was leaning toward yes, purely based on the fact that she loved Genevieve.

She decided to go for a run. Now that it was warm out, lacing up her sneakers felt like greeting an old friend. As she dodged pedestrians, her legs stretched out with ease in front of her, and she fell into a rhythm, loosening the muscles in her body and her mind. She replayed the scene from last night, and felt mad all over again at how Raphael completely ignored the house in Maine in his summer plans. She could barely talk to him after that. She was almost thankful when Georgia got weepy at the end of dinner, just so she could volunteer to take her home and wouldn't have to deal with Raphael. She would try to talk to him again about it, but she knew the topic of 'summer vacation' would be a sore spot between them now.

After she came back and showered, she stared at her closet, and if felt like it belonged to someone else. She hadn't seen these clothes in almost a month, and when she took a closer look, she tried to image wearing any of them in Maine. The fur, the leather, the silk blouses, but especially the heels. These items made sense for going to art openings and the opera and work cocktail parties for Raphael. To Shaw's Wharf, they did not. Even Portland would look twice at her in these fancy threads. She put on a navy silk blouse and white jeans, and found the lowest heel she could find in her closet. As she put them on she looked at the painting she had been working on before she left. It looked so different to her. She remembered her point of view when she was putting it down. She was attempting to be fresh and light with the colors and the brush, but very expressive with the use of black and blue in outlining things. She suddenly remembered she was stuck on the woman's face. She walked over and mixed a few colors together, found her brush, and finished it easily. When she was done, she put the brush down, stepped back and smiled. She was still smiling as the door shut behind her, the painting balanced under her arm, when she left for the gallery.

"Why are you wearing jeans?" Genevieve asked Anna when she walked through the door. She looked impeccable in a green and white DVF wrap dress and lots of gold jewelry.

"Good to see you too, Genevieve," Anna said, kissing her on both cheeks. The canvas she had just finished was still under her arm; Anna wanted to bring it in even though the face was still a bit wet. It was an excuse to take a cab, she told herself.

"Well, thank God you're back, that is all I can say. I was about to charter a plane to take me up to Maine to get a straight answer from you. How can you put a woman my age through something like this? Waiting and waiting while I have menopause to deal with on top of the stress. You're lucky there was a ton of sales this past month or I would be in the hospital and it would be your fault." She got up from her seat and grabbed the canvas from Anna. "Please tell me your answer is yes, because this painting is fabulous," she said.

"Yes, Genevieve. I will show at Art Basel. For you, I will do it." Genevieve gave her an enormous hug that was so tight it made Anna screamed, "Alright, I can't breathe!"

"I'm sorry, I don't hug very often so when I do, all my bottled-up hugs come out." Genevieve smiled at her happily, proudly. "You won't be sorry, I promise you. Please excuse me for a moment"- Genevieve strutted over to her desk and picked up her phone. - "I'm going to go gloat to Richard Turner over at the Turner Gallery. I have been wanting to tell him we'll be at Art Basel for two weeks now but you had to think it over, oy vey." She punched in a number and put her hand on her slim hip. "Hi, is Richard there? No, ok leave a message. Tell him Genevieve Keller called and I said to kiss my ass because I've been invited to Miami Basel. Yes, it's Keller, with a K."

Anna wandered around the gallery. Suddenly, one of the paintings stopped her in her tracks. It was one of her mother's. One that had hung in her gallery in Damariscotta before she died, Anna was sure of it. It should have been among the ones she and Marie and Stephen had inherited. She remembered her mother had painted it on Monhegan Island before she got sick. Anna had spent a day next to her painting as she was working on it. She remembered her mother talking about painting the ocean as they worked. *The secret to painting the ocean is to be a great observer. See how the waves today aren't really blue – they're more like yellow and brown? Just keep asking yourself what do you see? And then paint that.*

"I see you like the new McAllister," Genevieve called over her shoulder. "Isn't it great? I have a client who loves the Monhegan artists, I bet he'll grab it up in a second."

This was only the fourth painting the gallery had had of her mother's. But Anna had known her mother had sold the others herself, and they had floated through here after they were sold again. This one she felt sure had not been sold before. "We're lucky to get it. Chuck picked it up in Providence from some gallery."

Anna was puzzled and stood staring at it. How could it have gotten to a gallery in Providence? She stood there so long that Genevieve couldn't help but notice how strangely she was reacting to it. She walked over to the card and read about the painting. It was titled *Monhegan Waves*. Anna remembered it had been hanging in the window of her mother's gallery for a while, and she had held out a high price for it since it was large. It showed the rocky edge of the island, swirled with vibrant green grass, against the Atlantic in shades of blue – and yellow and brown too, Anna noticed - that made you want to dive into it. The brush strokes were masterful, as was her mother's use of color. But it was the three lobster boats, and the buoys that dotted the ocean, that made the painting so charming. Now it was probably worth ten times as much as she had been charging. The demand for most paintings from the 'The Artists' Island' as it was called had risen since then.

"Monhegan. Isn't that near where you have been hiding this past month? Where you're from? Do you know this painting?" Genevieve asked.

"Yes, I know it. It's my mother's painting," Anna said.

"Oh, did she know the artist?"

"She was the artist." Anna didn't flinch. Seven years of working for Genevieve and she had never told her. But today, she let it out. What did it matter now?

"Are you telling me that Therese McAllister is your mother?"

Anna didn't say anything at first. She stood with her arms crossed, staring at the painting. Then she turned to look at Genevieve. The look gave the answer away.

"Are you kidding me?" Genevieve whipped off her tortoiseshell glasses. She strode towards Anna until she stood right in front of her. "Why haven't you ever told me?"

"It's complicated," Anna finally managed.

"Complicated?" Genevieve said with her hand on her hip.

"I didn't mean to keep it from you, Gen. It was just really painful when my mom died and when I left I was desperately trying to find a fresh start. Everyone in Maine knows she's my mother. Everyone who saw me grow as an artist knew that I learned everything from her but mostly my father couldn't imagine me doing anything but trying to keep her memory alive. He got crazy and just wanted me to keep painting and go to these prestigious art programs when I was still reeling from her death. It was a pretty heavy burden then, being her artistic daughter, and I just wanted to lay it down. Now, I don't care. My dad knows I am painting again and we're...we're good. I don't know if it makes any sense, but I remembered who I am while I was in Maine. I don't have to worry about it anymore." Anna wandered over to Genevieve's chair and sat down. "Man I'm tired."

"You should be. Carrying around a secret like that can be exhausting. But do you know what I am thinking?"

"No, I couldn't possibly begin to know what you are thinking."

Genevieve put her glasses up on top of her head and sat down on the edge of her desk across from Anna. She crossed her arms and looked right at her. "I'm thinking Mother-Daughter show at Art Basel."

"Oh, come on, Gen. Don't be ridiculous." Anna threw her head back and looked at the ceiling. If she was tired before, now she was exhausted from even thinking about that idea.

"Of course, we'll have to find a supply of your mother's work, I don't suppose you know where we could find some do you? Any of her collectors that you are familiar with?

Anna thought of the enormous pile at Marie's and was thankful that Genevieve did not have telepathic powers. "Hmm, I'll have to think," Anna said, shrugging her shoulders. She was not excited at all about the idea of showing beside her mother's paintings. She had never thought about it before, but after the amount of work she had put in to creating a distance between her art and her mother's, it seemed crazy to close that distance in such an official capacity.

"Well I'll just have to get to work on it then. I'll start with Chuck and track down where he found this one. Then maybe the source can tell us if there are anymore."

Anna once again wondered where that painting had come from. Maybe Genevieve's search would help offer some kind of answer.

As she left the gallery, the streets were bathed in the kind of sunshine that warms every square inch of skin it touches, though it wasn't yet hot enough to start making the streets of the city ripe and sour smelling. Despite the mystery of the painting and the angst over Genevieve's suggestion of showing with her mother, Anna couldn't help but feel light and unencumbered. Being open about who her mother was with Genevieve was surprisingly freeing. It felt good to have it out in the open. To honor her as a mother and as an artist.

That reminded her – she wanted to talk to Miranda about going to the Foundation this summer. She picked up the phone to call her, and as she walked down the street listening to the phone ring, she watched a shop keeper tending to his fruit on the corner, carefully, almost tenderly. He was old and bent in a black wool sweater despite the warmth of the day, and he polished each apple on his white apron, despite the obvious stiffness of his arthritic fingers.

She picked up on the third ring. "Anna! Are you back?" Miranda said, her voice as bubbly as ever, her happiness filling her ears.

"I am," Anna smiled. "I was wondering if you wanted to reschedule that visit to the Met for this weekend?"

"Yes, I would love to! Does Sunday work?" she asked. "We have to go to church but I can meet you after that?"

An idea suddenly occurred to Anna. She remembered Miranda went to Mass with her mother and sister every weekend. "You know what, how about I meet you at church?" She was hoping to talk to her mother about the Foundation, and see if they could put the application in soon with her approval, if Miranda liked the idea.

"Really? Ok! That would be so much fun," Miranda said. "We go to the 10:00 mass at Epiphany. I'll text you the address."

"Ok. See you Sunday," Anna said, smiling as she hung up the phone and walked home, her heart feeling as bright and shiny as the apples on the corner.

Chapter 21

Later that evening, as she made her way up the steps to Raphael's apartment, she noticed her muscles feeling unusually strong since she had started running more. She had agreed to dinner there, and she was hoping they could finally resolve the issues they kept circling around every time they were together.

She thought about the first time she had come to this apartment, to help him hang some of the pieces he had bought from her. He was charming and fun then, and she hoped he would bring his charming and fun self tonight. Anna suddenly felt like she needed an old friend. She rang the buzzer, thinking of Georgia and how she had done the same thing at Jake's apartment so many times. She had promised her a day of shopping the following day, and she hoped the retail therapy would help her friend picture her new, Jake-free life. If that didn't work, they would retire once again to her living room, curled up with wine and chocolate.

Raphael opened the door looking handsome in a navy polo shirt. "Buenos dias, my beautiful girl," he said kissing her deeply and pulling her inside. Anna noticed he smelled good; he was wearing her favorite cologne. A total Raphael touch. "I'm so happy to finally have you back home." They walked into his apartment and Anna set down her bags, and he handed her a glass of Champagne. "I'm going to make you something special tonight, you won't believe it." Anna smiled as she surveyed the kitchen, filled with cutting boards and prep bowls and a salad in partial stages of assembly. "I may or may not have flown in Maine Lobster for Lobster Risotto. That is all I'll say."

"Raph, don't be ridiculous, you did not. It is, like, $5 a pound at home." Anna laughed as she sat down on his enormous sofa, and took in the beautiful skyline view of the city. Without warning her mind played an image of Andrew tossing his traps onto the dock at the co-op. Those lobsters would go to Round Pound and be the ones that sold for $5 a pound. The rest would be kept in stone basins the lobstermen created in the ocean waters, like little lobster jails where they could be pulled out during the winter months, keeping the supply steady. She instantly felt guilty for thinking of Andrew while she was with Raphael.

"I knew you would say that, and I was just kidding. I am making pasta primavera with fresh vegetables from the farmer's market near Central Park. But first, let's go sit outside, it's such a gorgeous day." He took her hand and stood her up to follow him out. She followed easily, and was glad for the distraction of such an amazing view – looking out at the other roof tops made her feel like she was floating high above the city. They sat at the small bistro table and chairs he had put out there, and Raphael took her hand and held up her glass. "I would like to say cheers to such a gorgeous day with such a gorgeous woman. I love you, Anna," he said, charm oozing from every pore. "And I am sorry we have been fighting lately. I think I was just so worried when you left, but you are back now and everything is fine." Raphael kissed her sweetly, and Anna returned the kiss and smiled, though something was pulling at her on the inside. Something about the perfection of this moment was not sitting right with her. She tried to brush it off and return Raphael's sentiments.

"I know, I love you too. And I am sorry we have been fighting, I think going home just made me figure out things that I should have figured out years ago. What is it they say? Youth is wasted on the young. And I was very, very young. But I can see myself balancing my time between Maine and New York now," Anna said smiling.

"Wait, whad'you mean? Balancing your time between here and Maine?" Raphael shook his head and looked confused. "You mean, you're thinking of something more permanent there? I thought you were just visiting your hometown, like millions of other people do without *moving* there."

"Well those people didn't get left a house in their hometown, I guess. Or have stellar painting views and happen to, I don't know, produce paintings," Anna said, her anger turning into sarcasm and making her sip her drink more quickly.

Raphael looked out at the skyline. He sighed deeply, and wandered inside, then came back out and sat down, holding Anna's hand. He looked up sweetly at her and said, "Close your eyes." Anna closed her eyes, and when she opened them, there on the table was a small black box, with a gorgeous diamond ring in the center.

"Anna," Raphael started as he got down on his knee. "I want you to be my wife. I want us to get married and live in New York and have a fabulous life. And if you want to go to Maine a few times a year, that is totally reasonable. But I want you to build a life with me here. Please, tell me yes, that you will marry me and build a life with me."

Anna stared in shock at the ring. She felt the pressure of Raphael's hand wrapped around hers, and she could feel the weight of the particles of sunlight bouncing off the diamond on her arm. The world seemed to stop spinning just for a moment, and in that moment Anna forgot to breathe. Everything was perfectly right about this, but everything was wrong. Anna couldn't deny it the second she saw the ring.

"Oh Raphael," she started.

"Say yes, please, make me the happiest man in New York, in the world!" he said.

Anna knew that in front of her was the most passionate, romantic man she had ever known, and simultaneously that she couldn't say yes. He had just been arguing with her about spending time in Maine, where her heart was pulling her. She knew that she couldn't marry him as sure and as strong as she knew she loved Henry, or Marie. *Or Andrew.* Her mind raced at the thought. What was happening right now? Was she crazily throwing away the luckiest thing that had ever happened to her on an old flame? *Andrew's not exactly waiting for you*, she chided herself. She was making a huge mistake. There was no way Raphael, king of loyalty and to-the-death passion would ever give her another chance. Her mind scrambled. What could she possible say? Her thoughts, her voice felt frozen in fear of ruining this moment.

"I..I can't," she said. She threw her face in her hands and felt her lip quiver. She looked up and her eyes welled up with tears. "I can't marry you Raphael. I love you, but I can't marry you."

A wave of sadness, then anger, then an empty stone-cold expression passed over Raphael's face. He held the box in his hand and looked out over the city. He sat silent for a long time. Anna didn't move. She didn't know what she could possibly say. Her heart beat loudly in her chest, and she tried to think of what she could do to make this moment better, to salvage the complete slashing she had just done to this relationship. She could feel the blood seeping out of it every second they sat there. She wanted a tourniquet, a compression to make it stop, make the hurting stop. For him, and for her. But there wasn't one.

"Ok," Raphael said. "Ok." He stood up and started toward the door.

"I'm so sorry, Raphael, I'm so sorry. I don't want to hurt you. Please! Tell me you don't hate me."

He turned around and looked at her, his eyes revealing a part of him that was closed off. "I don't hate you Anna. I don't. But I will never be able to love you as much as I did one minute ago."

Anna felt frozen, tied to the spot where she sat on an Earth that felt like it had stopped rotating.

Raphael snapped the box closed and picked up his Champagne glass. Anna watched him walk through the kitchen and pick up the Champagne bottle on the counter, then turn to his bedroom. She heard the door slam, and sat there, wondering what she should do. She walked into the kitchen and saw the pot of water boiling angrily on the stove. She turned the knob to the off position, killing the flame underneath, and left.

The next day she didn't leave her apartment. She sat on her couch in her robe, and stared out the window. She sat for hours, and replayed it all in her mind. Meeting Raphael in the gallery, their sweet, easy beginning, how it had opened up real happiness in her for the first time since her mother's death. Their rocky months before her uncle's death, and then her trip home to Maine. What did all this mean? What had she given up? Because that much she knew. She knew she had given up on them.

She had hardly moved when Georgia came in. It was late afternoon, and when she came in she stared at Anna wide-eyed. "What happened?" she said, in shock at her friend's appearance.

"I'll give you three guesses, and the first two don't count," Anna said.

"Raphael broke up with you? You look like I did when Jake stomped all over my heart. Did he – did Raphael stomp on your heart?" Georgia sat down next to her on the couch and grabbed her hand, ready to empathize with a likewise betrayed friend.

"No. Worse. There is worse than getting your heart stomped on I think. I am the heart stomper. I stomped all over his heart when it was wide open."

"What?" Georgia asked, confused.

"He asked me to marry him and I said no."

"You said no." Georgia didn't ask, she re-stated.

"I said no."

"Why?"

"That is what I have been trying to figure out here all day long. Why did I say no to a handsome, passionate, successful man who wanted to marry me?"

"I'm gonna go get the wine now, ok?" Georgia popped up and was back in a flash with a bottle and two glasses.

Anna sat with her head in her hands. "What kind of idiot am I?" she asked her friend. Her eyes sincerely pleaded for an answer.

"You're not an idiot. Confused, maybe, but Anna, you're not an idiot. I mean, there has to be a reason why you couldn't say yes. Do you know what that might be?" she poured the wine into the glasses and sat down next to her friend and crossed one leg under the other.

"Yes. No - I mean, I'm not sure. What is going on with me, please tell me!"

"Ok. Let's start with your first reaction. What was it? Gut reactions are very important," Georgia said, crossing her legs and settling in deeper on the couch.

Anna looked at her guiltily. She picked at the edge of her robe and tucked her feet underneath her. She looked back up and said, "That I couldn't say yes because of how I felt about Andrew."

"What?" Georgia looked at her with as much shock as if she had just announced she was moving to Brazil. "Are you serious?"

"Yup. I wish I wasn't, but I am."

"You still have feelings for Andrew? And just to be clear, you don't have any prospects of a relationship with Andrew, but you have feelings for him, and for that you threw away a pretty good lotto ticket for life?"

"Yup."

Georgia poured some wine in Anna's cup and handed it to her.

"So, are you planning on telling Andrew? Back up, wait, did you tell this to Raphael?"

"No, I didn't say that to Raphael, I just said I can't marry him. And I have zero plans, no plans at all, surrounding Andrew. Like you said, I went with my gut, and I am slightly afraid that my gut has led me horribly, horribly astray."

"Holy Crap." Georgia took it all in, picked up her wine and took a big sip, and sat thinking. After they had been quiet for a few moments she turned to Anna. "What was it you said to me a few nights ago? When Jake left? You said, sometimes, things are not right in the foundation, in the structure of a relationship itself. And it was better to find out about it before you built a life or a house or whatever analogy you used, I was too busy crying to remember all of it."

Anna sat back and thought about her own advice. It wasn't half bad. "You know, even though the moment he proposed was a perfect moment, we were fighting so much the past few months. I think...I think you might be right," Anna said. "I keep picturing the sunshine and the terrace and his cologne he wears for me and the way the diamond sparkled in the sunlight, and his crushed face when I said no. But you know, if I take the long view, I was pretty unhappy before I left for my uncle's funeral. Raphael is passionate, but his passion can sometimes, I don't know, swamp me. It was convenient when we first got together – I needed someone to jump start my life, and he did."

Anna took a sip of wine, and felt the weight of guilt and grief in her chest loosen a little. "But as I got stronger, as I healed and remembered the parts of me that are important, it was harder and harder to - I don't know - feel like he saw me, or heard me. It started to feel like he didn't even know me. I think...I think that's why it didn't feel right to say yes. I did the right thing. It's not just about Andrew. It was about us. Thank you, Georgia." She hugged her friend tightly and pulled back and looked at her with a smile. "Thank you."

"You're welcome." Her friend smiled at her, then laughed. "You know, I thought we were going to talk about me tonight and now I don't even feel like it. I am so sad for you I can't even be sorry for myself right now. Are you sure you aren't Jedi mind tricking me?" Georgia laughed again. "Did you really just end it with Raphael?"

Anna let out a small laugh and wandered over to get her phone. "No tricks here. But I do think that a double break up calls for some serious Chinese food. I haven't eaten anything and I'm starving." She started to make the call and saw that there was a message from Genevieve. She couldn't handle her strong-minded boss's persuasion right now. She'd call her tomorrow.

She placed their standard order of General Tao's Chicken extra spicy with broccoli and fried rice, and then sat down again, sighing heavily.

"What are you going to do about Andrew?" Georgia asked.

"I have no idea," Anna said. "I planned to go back up to Maine next weekend. I guess I'll just have to take it one day at a time. How about you? How is work going?"

"Ugg, I don't want to think about it. I am doing a photo shoot for a magazine of inspiring couples and it just makes me want to curl up on a ball."

"Want to come up to Maine?" Anna said. "I know a great house on the water we can stay at."

"I'll think about it," she said smiling.

Chapter 22

The next morning, as she watched people outside her kitchen window pass by with umbrellas every color of the rainbow, dodging the slow rain that had been falling all morning, Anna sat making a list of everything she needed to do before she went back to Maine. She sipped her coffee and wrote with gusto, freeing her brain from the weight of so much change happening. Georgia had fallen asleep while they watched a comedy, a welcome check-out they both needed but was still no match for the fatigue of heartbreak. She had moved her to her bed before she went to sleep and she hadn't woken up yet.

She replayed the evening at Raphael's in her head and still winced, although it felt less raw after talking and laughing with her friend. As each passing moment helped the memory of hurting him recede, she could see more clearly that she had been right. And whether or not she ever got to tell Andrew how she felt, she did the right thing. Raphael was not right for her.

After she wrote down everything she needed to do, she pulled out a new sheet of paper and tried to sketch a little, thinking it would clear her head, but she couldn't. Her mind felt too heavy. She dreamed of going back to the boathouse at her uncle's, feeling the violent wind off the ocean push against the weathered wooden shingles, and pouring out her heart through her fingers onto the canvas. She would wait until she was back to paint.

She took a shower and glanced at the clock. It was just after nine, and she was supposed to meet Miranda at church soon. Anna dressed and looked up directions to the church. She suddenly remembered her plans to go shopping with Georgia later that afternoon. She scribbled a quick note to see if they were still on, and if she could meet her on 5th Ave after the Met. She was glad her day was full, and that she was off the couch and out of her robe. With only five days left in the city and no boyfriend, and no ability to work in her current state of mind, what else was there to do but shop?

Anna walked up the steps to the church, and as she entered, shook off the rain from her umbrella. Her senses were bombarded. An organ was playing the entrance antiphon, and a group of choir voices were answering it in earnest. Light streamed in, rays of kaleidoscope color, through the stained-glass windows. The tall red brick walls made her feel solid and secure.

She saw Miranda wave at her, and took a seat by her side, squeezing her arm in greeting. Miranda's mother leaned forward and smiled at Anna. She sat back and listened to the voice of the priest echo against the brick walls, and in his reciting of prayers, Anna found herself draw inwards. She had gone to Mass a few times since the funeral, and she was amazed at how comforting it was. The familiar prayers, the feeling of being in a community. Her mind was on the conversation she wanted to have with Miranda's mother, but she found herself thinking of her mother. Of Sundays spent at church sitting next to her, just like Miranda was doing. As the readings of Genesis echoed against the walls, she thought of hours with her mother spent talking about God and nature and art. The Creator and creation. She did not expect to feel so peaceful here today.

Especially because she was still so upset about Raphael. As the days passed, the grief of ending her relationship with him seamed to expand, like bread rising. "It takes time," Georgia kept saying. She bent her head and said a prayer for him. And for herself. She could feel herself stronger, though, this time around. She knew a little more how grief worked. She had to feel all her feelings. The dreams that were gone, the memories that haunted. They all had to be counted and weighed and sorted in order for the knot in the center of her chest to loosen. She knew it would help to go to Maine, to let the sound of the ocean crashing in her ears drown out all of the memories she had of him here in the city.

After Mass, they streamed out, the rain finally ceasing. She smiled at Miranda and her family. Her mother Maria wore her long hair down, like her daughters, and she had added a little blush and mascara, and gloss on her lips, and looked pretty. Miranda's sister, Gabriella, looked just like Miranda, with the same long dark hair and dimples.

"Thank you so much for letting me go to church with you," Anna said.

Miranda's mother turned to Anna, "I didn't realize you went to church, Anna."

"I grew up going in Maine. I just came back from a family funeral there, and I guess it reminded me what I've been missing."

Maria looked at her. "Yes, you seem happier. I always thought you seemed just a little bit sad," she said.

Anna was taken by surprise at her honesty. How could she seem happier when she was so upset about Raphael? But perhaps it was true. Maybe she was happier after all. Stronger, definitely. "Well, my mom passed away a while ago, and I think I had a hard time getting over it. I probably did carry that sadness with me. But going home helped me, I think."

Maria nodded in understanding. "I'm sorry, I didn't know that. It's hard losing people we love." Anna saw a knowing look in her eyes, and she quickly realized it was the hard won kind of wisdom that you get when you lose your husband with two small daughters. She suddenly felt a wave of empathy and gratitude for the woman who stood before her. "So you two are off to the Met?" Maria asked.

Miranda brushed her long hair over her shoulder. "Yes - I am so excited!" She opened her eyes wide and grabbed Anna's arm. "Did you know they have a new exhibit on Georgia O'Keefe?" she asked, her voice bubbling over with excitement.

"Remember to be home in time to study for your big history test tomorrow, ok?" Marie interrupted.

"Si, mama," she answered smiling.

"Before we leave," Anna interrupted, "I just wanted to ask you a question Maria. When I went home, the foundation that my father runs – it's an art camp in my mother's name - they have some openings for art students to come up this summer for two weeks and paint. I thought it might be an amazing opportunity for Miranda. If you both think it is a good idea, I can fill out the application online with her."

Miranda's eyes got even wider, and she put her hands over her mouth to contain her excitement. Her mother looked distressed though. "Two weeks in Maine? Won't that be expensive?"

"There is no charge. The Foundation has benefactors and fund-raisers that pay for the tuition. And I will be there, teaching. So I will look out for her."

Miranda looked at her mother, and said, "Oh please mama? I would love to go!"

Maria looked at her daughter. She shifted her weight from side to side, and the look on her face was at first uncomfortable, until a softness passed over her and she sighed. "If Miss Anna will be there, I will think about it. Maine looks so pretty in pictures. Just let me think about it." Miranda hugged her so tight she groaned.

Anna smiled. She handed her a brochure about the Foundation from her purse. "Here's all the information you need. And I would love to have you both stay with me some weekend if you want to visit her."

Gabriella put her hand on her mother's arm. "That sounds so good, mama! I'll help you look it up when we get home on the com-puter, ok?"

Miranda hugged her sister and her mother, and smiled at her lit-tle family. "Gracias. Te amo Mami."

"Ok, ready for a little Georgia O'Keefe?" Anna said, as she hailed a taxi, the last notes of the music from the organ from the church fading behind them.

The next morning, Anna was just about to go for a run when she saw Genevieve had already called twice. She dialed her number as she rummaged around for socks and her running shoes. Now it wasn't just the warmer weather that made her want to run – it was her need for therapy after breaking up with Raphael.

"Hey Gen, it's me, Anna," she said. "I saw you called but you didn't leave a message."

"Yes, honey, I wanted to tell you about your mom's painting in the gallery. I asked Chuck to see if his source in Providence could get any more paintings, you know, to do a dual show, and when he followed up with him, he said a young man had given him that one and said he had more. He said there were several more up in Maine."

Anna sat at her kitchen table, picking dead leaves off of an almost dead house plant she had neglected while she was gone. "What? That is crazy...did he say who this guy was?"

"She said the man's name was Stephen something."

Anna sat silent, her mind struck numb at the mention of her brother's name.

"Anna, are you there?" Genevieve said. "Anna?"

"Yea, I'm here, Gen" she managed.

"Do you know who he is talking about?" Genevieve asked.

"I do. Stephen is my brother."

"Are you serious? How come he has all your mom's paintings?"

"He doesn't. We were all left her paintings in her will. My sister, my brother and myself."

"Oh, so if I happened to know the right people, I could end up finding some Therese McAllister originals is what you're saying? Even if they already told me *they didn't know if there were any other paintings,*" Genevieve sounded hopeful.

"No, what I am saying is my brother is going behind my back in violation of my uncle's will, and someone who I was previously proud of and who I thought wouldn't hurt a fly is in fact the same person who has totally hoodwinked me. I didn't volunteer those paintings because they don't just belong to me, they belong to all of us." Anna left out the fact that she would eventually own some of them herself. She had wanted to stall on Genevieve's idea of showing with her mother's work.

"So you're not happy about this news," Genevieve said.

"Not happy." Anna hung up the phone and paced in her kitchen. She couldn't believe Stephen would do something so underhanded. This wasn't like him. She had to call Marie. She couldn't think what to do next, how to confront him or hold him accountable. Maybe Marie had some idea.

"Marie, it's Anna, do you have a second?" she said after her sister picked up.

"Sure, what's going on?" she said.

"Well, I just found out some really upsetting news about Stephen and I wonder what you think we should do about it. A painting showed up in the gallery this week that was one of mom's later pieces. I remember it hanging in her gallery before she died. I know I was away at school, but I don't think it sold and all of the pieces from that summer were sent over to Uncle Charlie's. I feel like I saw it there but I wasn't sure. I asked Genevieve to check on where it was from, and she said that someone named Stephen in Providence had given it to her contact there. And he said he had more where it came from, that he could get them several more pieces from a house in Maine."

"Whoa," Marie said, letting out a breath of air. "That is crazy. Why would he act so independently, I mean that is the opposite of what the will told us to do. Why is he selling that one without consulting us? We said we would all vote to see if someone really wanted some of them. That's weird."

"I know," Anna agreed. "It seems like Stephen feels like he is the sole ambassador of mom's art."

"Do you want me to call him?"

"You could, although, do you think this is something we should talk about in person? I could try to drive up there this Friday."

"That's a good plan," Marie said. "Seems like face to face would get the truth out of him."

"Then that's what I'll do. I'll give you a call after I talk to him." Anna slide her feet into her unlaced running shoes. She needed to go for a quick, hard run with this stress added to her list of problems.

"Ok, yes call me right after. I'm kinda worried about him now,"

Marie said.

"I would be worried too if I crossed a McAllister woman. Word on the street is that we're tough as nails. Speaking of that, how are you feeling?"

"Good, good. Everything's fine. I'll fill you in on some stuff after we figure out what's going on with Stephen." she said. Anna thought she sounded a little strange, a little evasive in her tone, but she didn't press it. She said goodbye, and pictured Marie nestled in her house in Maine, and smiled at the thought.

Chapter 23

Anna adjusted the rear-view mirror for the third time before she slowly pulled out of the rental car lot, getting used to where the gears were, trying to follow the blue line highlighted on the GPS map. She had decided to rent a car to drive to Maine so that she could stop by Stephen's restaurant and talk to him. She had made plans to have lunch with him and see his restaurant, and Anna was glad she would finally get to see what he had been working so hard on this past year. Right before she tried to strangle him.

As she headed over the Triboro Bridge, she saw the tall city buildings recede in the mirror. She thought of her people – Georgia, Miranda, Genevieve – somewhere in the huge sea of gray and glass. She told Georgia she would keep paying half her rent, until she found a new roommate, and she would probably come down and visit now and then, but without Raphael to pull so hard at her, she was free to spend as much time as she wanted in Maine. As she thought of Raphael, she realized leaving the city was making it final that they were done. She kept wanting to call him, to check in on him, but she knew it would just make it worse. She had hurt his pride most of all, and the only thing to heal that was for her to leave him alone.

She looked down at the GPS as she merged on to 87 North. It would be two and half hours until she was in Providence. She had a bag of almonds and a pack of gum, along with an ice coffee that was so big it barely fit in the cup holder. She had filled her trunk with clothes and art supplies and books to bring to Uncle Charlie's house, keeping just her bedroom furniture and some clothes in her apartment for when she came to visit. She told Georgia she could keep everything else. She turned up the radio, and rolled down the windows, and felt a kind of freedom and peace seep into her bones.

It felt like no time had passed before she was taking the exit for Providence. As she pulled through the old city, flowers were blooming everywhere, and people were out walking their dogs and children in shorts and t-shirts. She finally pulled up to the curb a few doors down from Stephan's restaurant and attempted to parallel park, something she wasn't very good at, ever. She tried a few times before Stephen came out of the front door.

"Want me to do it?" he asked, laughing.

"No, I got it," Anna called out the window. It was infuriating that she had not gotten better at this then when they were teenagers. Just like her sister, her brother never let her forget that she was a bad driver.

"You've got parallel parking? Since when?" he teased.

Her third time was a charm and she grabbed her purse and locked the car. "I told you I had it," she said as she walked toward him, sticking out her tongue, then she smiled and hugged her tall brother. She pulled back and took a good look at him; he was pale, as if he hadn't been outside in the sun in months, which he probably hadn't, and he had dark circles under his eyes like he had been up late for months, which he probably had. But his eyes were still the same Irish blue eyes, smiling and warm. He seemed his jovial self as he smiled at her, but she sensed something tightly wound in him underneath his joking exterior. "Do you want to eat here, try some dishes we are working on?" he asked.

"Sure, that sounds great, unless you'd rather relax and go somewhere else."

"Nah, I'd love to show you around, c'mon, watch your step," he said as they walked in the front door, which was old, huge, and painted black. The inside was gorgeous, with tall windows, tables covered in white tablecloths and chairs and booths with luxurious fabrics. There were massive chandeliers in the four quarters of the ceiling. The walls were covered with large paintings with ornate gold frames. It also had an enormous bar made out of dark wood in the center, making all four sides of the bar easy to access. It had a classic old world feel. Anna loved it.

"Wow, Stephen, this place is amazing, how did you pull all this together?" Anna asked, turning around to take in the whole floor.

"We worked with a designer some friends put us in touch with. She was expensive, but worth it, I think" he said.

"I'm so glad I'm finally here to check it out. Let's go back to the kitchen and see what's cooking," Anna said, feeling like Dorothy about to see the man behind the curtain in Oz. "I've never been in a restaurant kitchen before, though it really should be Marie who gets to do this, she would love to see what you do every day."

"C'mon back," Stephen said leading the way. He took her to the open, clean work spaces and showed her the ingredients that had come in that morning and what the menu was going to look like that night based on those items. He was busy showing her a work station's mise-en-place for a dish when a tall, dark-haired man walked in. He looked up at Stephen and looked apologetic before he spoke. "Stephen, there's a problem with the meat order due in today," he said. "They said it's COD, they won't take a check or line of credit anymore. I don't know how you want me to handle it," he said.

"Ok, Rudy, I'll be right out," Stephen said wiping his hands on the white apron he was wearing. "Excuse me one sec, Anna. Gotta take care of this," he said. He looked so stressed; Anna could see the veins popping out of his forehead. He whipped around the corner, leaving Anna to stare at bowls of chopped shallots and capers and cherry tomatoes that she had no idea what to do with.

She heard some voices, and then Stephen was back in the kitchen, looking still stressed but taking a deep breath.

"Everything ok?" Anna asked. She hadn't seen much of her brother lately, and she suddenly had a wave of guilt that she hadn't checked in before this with him, seeing how much pressure he was under.

"For now, yea," Stephen said, trying to get back to the menu. "What are you hungry for?" he asked.

He showed her how to make a simple fish dish with Tuscan flavors, tossing butter and lemon juice over a swordfish steak in the pan expertly, swirling the wine with the chunky tomatoes together while they talked like he had done it a thousand times before. She watched him plate the fish with a perfect circle of warm vegetables on a bed of polenta, and her mouth drooled. While the food was still steaming they sat down to eat.

Anna took a bite and savored the amazing flavors; the fruity acidic tomatoes mixed with the rich butter and sour lemon, bright white wine, and the sharpness of briny capers. The fish tasted so fresh, too. "Mmm, Stephen, I wish you lived closer. You can cook at my house anytime. Or maybe we can get you up to Charlie's for a visit this summer. You can be the designated cook," Anna said in between bites.

Stephen laughed. "Yea, I don't know when I'll be able to take time off from this place. I can't really afford a sous chef right now, so it is just me and Pete running the show at the moment. He'll be here this afternoon, but it takes both of us to pull off a dinner."

"It's tough, isn't it?" Anna said as she put her fork down.

He let out a slow, deep breath. "Brutal," he said.

"Is that why you took one of mom's paintings and tried to sell it?" Anna asked, trying hard to be gentle.

Stephen froze and looked shocked, then remorseful. He ran his hands through his dark wavy hair with the salt and pepper temples. "How'd you find out?" he asked, looking guilty and sad.

"It sort of floated into my gallery. Of all the gin joints in all the world, right?"

"Are you kidding me?" He looked stunned. "I can't believe that. Maybe it's for the best. At least you know about it. Yes, I took the painting after we went to lunch the day we all read the will. I popped over there before I got on the highway and grabbed the biggest one I saw. It's a pretty crappy thing to do and I'm not proud of it. I felt like my back was up against the wall, and right now, I'm feeling it even more. I just gave the last $600 in the register to our meat supplier, so I'm not exactly sure how to pay my bills next month unless we have a killer weekend. I'm not saying this to excuse my behavior, I'm saying it so you'll understand and not hate me."

"I don't hate you Stephen. I wish I knew you were going through this stuff. Why didn't you ask Dad or me or Marie for the money?"

"I was too humiliated. We're Mainers, Anna. We're proud. We work hard even if we have to clean toilets and haul trash but we bust our butts and rely on ourselves. We don't ask for charity handouts." He finished his fish and sat back, pressing his fingers over the bridge of his nose. "I figured if I sold one of mom's paintings, no one would notice or I could buy it back down the road when the restaurant was finally making money. I'm so close, I just, we got in over our heads with our upfront costs, and people didn't eat out much over the winter. I'm sure - I know - if we can get through a summer season, we'll be a bit more established, we'll find our clientele. They just have to venture out of their homes and walk downtown. We've seen it start to pick up in the last two months, it's just that we were in the red already." He took a sip of water and sat back. Anna watched him cross his long legs. He looked defeated. "Plus, you know what dad's like about failing," he said quietly.

Anna breathed out a deep sigh. "Yes, yes I do. He doesn't take kindly to failure. But I think he would have lent you money – I think that's different then failing. That's helping you from failing."

"Maybe that's true. I guess I just thought I could handle it, not let anyone know how hard it's been."

"Now you're sounding like a Goodrich. That is our manual for existing. But you know what, Stephen? I hate our manual. I want to tear it up and start over, as a family that helps each other. A family that can be a net for each other. God knows we could all use one. And I think if you check in with dad, you'll find he feels that way too. He's changed a lot since Uncle Charlie died."

Anna reached into her purse, and pulled out a checkbook. She handed him a large check and asked, "Care to take on a silent partner for a little while? I mean really silent. And you can buy me out whenever you want. Or become fabulously successful and keep me on in gratitude. Either way is fine with me."

Stephen looked at the check and started to get choked up. "Are you kidding me? Are you serious?"

"I'm serious. I forgot to tell you that I sold a bunch of paintings to

New Yorkers for way too much money. And I have been sitting on it because I've been pretty busy."

"What? Are you kidding me Anna? Why the hell didn't you tell me?" he said.

"I'm telling you now," she said. "Remember, we're Mainers. We do everything the silent and hard way."

It felt so good to hug Stephen as she was leaving, and her belly felt full and warm and happy. As she drove back to Maine, she kept thinking hard about what had just happened with her brother. If only she could feel as peaceful about Raphael.

When she crossed the bridge at Bath Iron Works, the cranes rising up over the skyline like prehistoric creatures in the twilight sky, it started to dawn on her that her life was about to start over. Here in Maine. That she was coming back to stay.

She realized she was soon to be in the same place as Andrew. She still wanted to tell him that she was sorry, that she understood how much was her fault, and that she shouldn't have blamed him for not coming after her to New York. She had no idea if he even wanted to see her again, much less hear her explain herself after she had yelled at him at the gala. But she had to try. Just like Stephen had made mistakes and owned up to them, Anna had to try to explain to Andrew how sorry she was that she had pulled them apart. How she could see now how stubborn and wrong she had been to insist he become something he wasn't. That much she had to tell him, she decided. After that, she would have to let it be.

As the harbor where the *Christina Therese* was docked grew near, she could picture it. The boats and weathered docks, the rocky ledges with Maine pine trees surrounding the water like sentinels, the water spreading out at the mouth of the harbor into the wide ocean as far as the eye could see. It seemed to draw her. Perhaps it was the sea itself that pulled her. She was grateful to be home.

Chapter 24

She pulled into Marie's driveway in the late afternoon, realizing how great it was to be going to her house at this time of day, guessing her sister had made something delicious for dinner. She was so happy that she could feast off both her siblings today. With her windows down, she could smell the sea air, and she appreciated the quiet beauty of Pemaquid even more after her time in the city, where the noise and energy pulsed around her all the time.

When she walked inside, her sister was lying on the couch, and Henry was playing with his toy plastic hammer, bopping it on her head. "Hi guys," Anna said cheerfully. Her sister looked up at her with a pale face, messy hair and pajamas that were trying to pass for clothes.

"Hi," she said. "How was your visit?" she asked, her voice weak.

"Marie, what's wrong?" Anna asked, picking up blocks and trucks to make a path to the couch.

Marie smiled at her sheepishly. "Actually, I was waiting until you came back to tell you in person. I'm pregnant!"

Anna processed her words as she sat down at the kitchen island. "What, are you . . . oh my gosh!" She jumped up and hugged her sister. "I am so excited! I get to be an auntie again. How far along are you?"

"It is still early, I am only about eight weeks. But the wicked bad nausea just set in. I made peanut butter and jelly for lunch because I can't really cook right now." She set out the plate of triangle sandwiches.

"Oh no, I'm so sorry," Anna said, "What can I do? Do you want me to get dinner for Henry? Maybe something for you, like soup?"

"You don't have to Anna, it's ok," Marie tried to get up slowly. Henry ran toward Anna and shouted, "Auntie! Can I have some apple juice?"

"Sure buddy, your mom looks like she could use some too. And some crackers."

"I'll be fine after I eat something, I just had trouble getting up."

"You just stay there. I'll bring you something. Henry, come over here, let's do some play doh while Auntie makes you dinner."

"Play doh!" Henry said, pulling out his toddler-sized chair and sitting down at his small table in the kitchen.

"Wow, Anna, you sure picked a great time to come over. Thanks," Marie said smiling a sickly smile as Anna put Henry's cut up hot dog on a plate. "I can't even touch one of those right now and it's all he wants.

"I'm glad to be here too," Anna said. Her heart glowed at the happy news, and she set down the hot dogs next to Henry and reached out to hug him, imagining another person she would love as much as him. "Oh, I almost forgot to tell you about seeing Stephen today," she started, not sure if her sister could handle anything stressful.

"That's right, what happened with him and the painting?"

Anna poured a can of soup into a pot, then turned on the stove. "Poor guy, he did try to sell it. Didn't want any of us to know that his restaurant was under water and he thought that could help him get ahead. I gave him a loan, though. Or became a silent partner, not sure which. We're getting the painting back."

Marie nodded while she took in the news. "Oh Anna, how wonderful of you. I had no idea he was struggling. That makes me instantly forgive him, poor guy." Marie took a sip from a glass next to her and put her hand on her stomach in the universal way pregnant women do. She looked up and smiled at Anna. "She'd be proud of you, you know,"

"Who?"

"Mom. I don't like to feel sorry for myself too much when it comes to losing her. I like to think about how lucky we are to have had her as a mom. But I was thinking of her while I was lying on the couch, wishing she could have come in and played grandma to Henry and mom to me while I didn't feel good. I was really missing her. And then you came through the door. And she would be really proud of how you helped Stephen. It's nice to have you home." Marie said.

"It's good to be home," Anna said, squeezing her hand.

"So how is everything? How are you feeling about Raphael?"

"It's hard. I keep wanting to call him, to check in on him and see how he is doing. But I know that's a bad idea. I miss him, and at the same time I know I made the right choice." She took down a bowl and poured the soup into it, and set it on a plate with saltines.

Marie stood up from the couch and poured herself some ginger ale, then joined Anna at the table. Even in her state, she looked how Anna always pictured her at home – baggy sweatshirt, fur-lined slippers, messy ponytail. It was so good to be near her sister.

"I know, it seems odd to think of you guys not together, but at the same time, it always seemed like you were two puzzle pieces that almost fit, but not quite," Marie said as she sipped the hot broth.

"Really? That's a good way to put it. I would agree. Helps me know I'm not a total idiot for letting him go."

"No, you're not an idiot. You are following your heart. That's a good thing," she grabbed Anna's hand and squeezed it. "By the way, have you talked to dad lately?"

"I called him on the way up. He seems really good. I told him I was hoping to help teach this summer at the Foundation. I could tell it made him really happy. Oh, and I sent in Miranda's application, so let me know when you see it. I can't wait for her to come up her and see this light."

"I can't wait to meet her," Marie said.

"I can't wait to meet my new niece or nephew!" Anna gushed. "I'm so happy for you, Marie."

Just then, as if on cue, Henry screeched across the room, a horse on a stick between his legs, the pastel colors of the setting sun illuminating the sky in the window behind him like melted sherbert. "Guess what Auntie Anna! I'm gonna be a big brudder!"

Chapter 25

She woke up the next morning to the sound of her alarm. She had come back to Uncle Charlie's after she put Henry to bed, and as she sat outside listening to the harbor bell, letting it sink in that this was her new home, she had a thought. Maybe she could go out fishing on Andrew's boat, and have a chance to talk to him. It had been hanging over her head the whole time she was in New York that she had never apologized to him. She wanted to tell him how much she had realized was her fault since then. In her stubborn way, she wanted to do it as soon as possible. It would be easier then running in to him unexpectedly and fumbling an apology.

It was early; she could see the fog still thick around the harbor, net yet burned off by the sun, a white mist that wrapped around everything. The seagulls were screeching, which meant the lobstermen were filling their bait buckets, and they were fighting over the scraps that spilled onto the dock. She brewed some coffee and threw on her jeans, a T-shirt, and a thick navy sweater, and then pulled her hair in a ponytail. She tied a parka around her waist and drank her coffee quickly, then headed out the door.

It was a gorgeous morning, and the waves seemed to greet her as she looked out at the ocean. She walked the short walk to Shaw's Wharf. Right away, she saw Andrew loading his boat as soon as she turned the corner. He was wearing faded orange overalls and a gray parka, with a red baseball cap covering his messy hair. Chris was helping him coil rope into neat piles and stack lobster traps on the boat, and she heard them laughing about something as she got closer. Anna realized that they could fish for lobsters now. It was May and the lobster season had just begun.

Andrew glanced up briefly, then looked up again when he had processed who was walking toward him. Anna saw that his face first looked sweetly happy, then guarded. "Hey, Andrew. Do you have room for one more on the boat today?"

Andrew looked back toward the tower of traps he was stacking on the boat. She could see his mind thinking through the cost of bringing her on board. "I thought you were back in New York," he said, squinting.

Anna nodded. "I was. I just came back yesterday. I wondered if I could help you on the boat for a day – for old time's sake."

He readjusted his hat as he thought it over. "Alright. We have a lot of traps to put in and some to pull up from yesterday," he answered. "D'you mind, Chris?"

"It might help to have someone work the line and fill the bait our first time over by the fort," Chris said. "But just so you know, you only get paid on what we pull up tomorrow."

Anna laughed; she was relieved he was willing to take her on today. "Right," she said. "I remember. But you don't have to pay me."

Andrew threw her a pair of overalls, and she strapped them on. The bright orange made her feel like she was glowing, possibly even radioactive. They climbed aboard, Chris steadying the tower of traps, Andrew behind the wheel. They headed out of the harbor as Anna watched the pier at Shaw's disappear while they rounded the bend along the coast. The ocean waves, calm in the harbor, suddenly lifted the boat up and then sharply down. Anna remembered what it felt like to be out on open ocean and braced herself. The sun was warm on their faces but the ocean breeze and wind from their speed still chilled her enough to zip up her parka.

"We're going out around the fort, where we have a few lines to put down, then around the lighthouse where my dad's territory is,"

Andrew said. "Anna, do you want to help Chris fill about a hundred traps for the fort area?"

"Sure," said Anna. She sidestepped the huge pile of buoys, bright orange with a dark green strip around the middle. Anna remembered the day back in high school when Andrew had waited eagerly to find out from the fishing association what color buoys he would have when he headed out on his own boat with his own traps for the first time. But there were also white ones with a blue strip, and Anna knew those belonged to Andrew's dad. He had taken over for him as his MS had progressed, but still used his dad's stripe.

She found a seat next to a bucket filled with mackerel that was chopped into chunks. The bloody mess and stench were familiar to Anna; it took her right back to fishing with Andrew the summers they were home from school. As she scooped the chunks of fish into the traps, she thought about how much her father had discouraged her from going out fishing with him. She understood so much more now, and the familiar sting of her emotions was suddenly replaced with some new feeling. Peace? Absolution? Mostly it was understanding. She wanted to bring that understand to Andrew, to find peace with him too.

She also felt nervous. Last night she had thought being around Andrew on the boat would calm her nerves and be a good place to talk to him. Now she wasn't sure. She felt her legs quiver. She tried to focus on the task at hand. The work was messy and repetitive. They had just finished filling the last trap when Andrew slowed the boat down. They started a ritual of chucking traps over the edge, slowing down the coil to straighten the line so that the buoy floated just above where each trap rested on the ocean floor. Every buoy had two traps tied to it, so they drove the boat a few meters, then repeated the ritual. Chris was right. Three people made for a great rhythm and they were finished in no time.

They sped through the ocean water towards his dad's territory, the speed cutting the severity of the waves, and Anna took a moment to absorb what she was seeing. The expanse of the ocean on one side, and the familiar coastal town on the other, felt like a gift delivered to her heart. She could see why Andrew loved this life. It was amazing to think of spending one's days here, inside the beauty of nature. This perspective—the blue ocean, the shoreline—sharply elevated her deep longing for this place. The tide, the waves, the seasons, the people. It mirrored a rhythm deep in her heart.

She looked at him while he drove. His hat was off, and she saw the wind leveling his wild hair. She saw the calm strength in his hands, his eyes. He was a captain. There was something about him on the water. He was a person in his element, doing what he was born to do. Like God had called him to be a lobsterman. And behind him sat the wideness of the sea.

She was still looking at him when he glanced at her. He motioned her over to the wheel, and she rose and waited until she had steady footing before crossing the boat. Next to him, she could hear him ask her if she wanted to hold the wheel while he checked out the sonar. She nodded, and he stepped aside, his eyes glued to the multi-colored screen with shadowy outlines of the ocean floor.

After he studied the picture for a few minutes, he walked over to her. "So did you have a nice visit with your boyfriend in New York?" he asked casually, though he overdid the cold aloofness, trying too hard to mask any trace of emotion.

Anna was afraid to tell him that they broke up. She frowned just thinking about how guilty she felt hurting Raphael.

"What's the matter, he's not taking it too kindly that you're here?" he said.

Anna focused for a moment on the sound of his voice. Even with the wind, she noticed that his voice warmed something in her in a way nothing else could. It was the first thing she thought of when Raphael had asked her to marry him. Andrew's voice. She stared out at the water and tried to figure out how to tell Andrew all of this, how to share her decision. "I think he is not taking it too kindly that Maine is such a part of me. He would prefer that Manhattan was my only geographical relationship. He also isn't taking it too kindly that I told him I couldn't marry him when he asked."

She met his eyes then, directly, and the words she had been searching for weren't necessary now. He knew just from reading her eyes. But she still owed him something.

"Listen, I didn't come out here today just because I broke up with Raphael. I came out here to tell you that I realized something recently. I spent a long time being mad at your for not coming with me to New York. I blamed you for breaking us up. But..." she stepped aside as Andrew took over the wheel from her. "It finally dawned on me that it was my fault. I left. I broke us. What I asked you to do wasn't fair. I even yelled at you for it at the gala. But I realize now how wrong I was, and I wanted to tell you I am sorry, Andrew. For everything."

He stood silent for what felt like an eternity, his hands resting on the big silver wheel. He snapped out of his surprise when he saw the lighthouse looming large on their right. "Hang on a sec," he said as he turned the wheel and steered them around the tall white building and the jagged rocks that surrounded them. They got to the back-side and Anna saw there were already blue and white buoys in the water. "We threw these in yesterday, just to see where the bugs had reached. They get closer to the shore the warmer the water gets, but you might actually remember that," he said absentmindedly. He was clearly flustered, and the excuse to interrupt their conversation and focus on the traps was welcome.

He drove the boat right up next to one of his dad's buoys and Chris leaned over with his gaff and pulled up the line. The first trap was empty, the bait gone. The second one, though, held a beautiful large lobster. "They're here!" Andrew yelled. "Let's see if this is a keeper." He inspected the lobster for any V-notches in the tail, which would have been put there by another lobsterman indicating it was a breeding female. These were always thrown back. Then he flipped over the lobster to see if there were any eggs on the tail. There weren't; it was a male. He quickly held up the lobster to a ruler on the side of the boat to see if it was long enough, and it easily was. "It's a keeper. On the first buoy!" He tossed it into a large white bucket and Chris quickly put rubber bands on the claws.

They hauled the rest of the traps in no time, and the quick, fluid motions of checking of the tail, measuring the length, dumping the old bait, refilling the bait bag with new mackerel chunks over and over again became a rhythm. The work was going much faster with the addition of Anna as sternman. As they drove to each buoy, Anna was reminded of bees buzzing to each flower, pollinating them with a chunk of mackerel. She was glad Chris was doing the heavy work of pulling up the traps. She remembered how backbreaking that job was. Their first day was decent, about a hundred lobsters, which was great for only half the traps in the water. Tomorrow they should have well over two hundred with both locations. And it was only May, the lobsters just coming out of their rocky homes deep below the ocean toward warmer water.

As Andrew pulled the *Christina Therese* up to each buoy, he said nothing but his eyes were alert. Anna tried hard to quiet the butterflies that had erupted in her stomach. She tried not to think of what she had just done. She had hoped to find peace out here today with Andrew. But it turned out a lobster boat was a hard place to talk. She wanted to tell him more, tell him how she realized that she belonged here. Having dinner at her sister's house, playing with her nephew. Talking to her father, letting the new growth unfold between them after the forest fire she had let rage for so long. Painting at Uncle Charlie's boathouse. Shopping at Riley's, with Millie making her sandwiches. She hoped he would say something to her. Or maybe ask her to finish their conversation after they were done for the day. *Yes*, thought Anna. *I'll see if he can stay for lunch at Shaw's Wharf.*

Except Chris thought he should stay at Shaw's Wharf, too, next to Andrew, drinking a Smuttynose. They had to celebrate a great first catch, after all. After they had sold their catch and cleaned up the boat, it was only 1:30. And Anna didn't think it was fair to pour her heart out while this nice Maine boy was trying to enjoy his early happy hour. She had a haddock sandwich and a beer, though she could barely eat. Andrew also seemed distracted, but seemed like he was trying to celebrate with his right-hand man.

Of course, Anna thought. *Why should I expect him to drop everything just because I figured out what a huge mistake I made?*

"This was really fun, congrats on a great first day. Thanks for letting me tag along," she said as she drained her glass. "I should call it a day, though" she said. "Maybe I can bring Henry out sometime soon?"

Andrew's face pulled, like he wanted to say something. "Sure, you should definitely bring him out."

As she walked up the ramp, she turned around once. Andrew was watching her walk away. She waved, and he returned it with a nod of his head.

Alone, back at her uncle's, Anna curled up in a ball on the couch. She was cold down to her bones. The chill from the wind wasn't going anywhere, and she decided to build a fire. Her stomach felt like concrete one minute, and a leaky balloon the next. She had been so strong and peaceful yesterday, why did she have to go and mess it up by spilling her feelings out to Andrew? She lay the wood in the fire place, and crumpled up newspaper and struck a match on the stone mantel, watching the flame outline the paper, a jagged hot orange line that moved like it was alive then curled up like an enchanted snake. She opened the flue, and went into the kitchen to boil some water for tea. As the water boiled, she kept replaying the conversation. She couldn't believe he didn't say anything. Maybe he was so hurt he wasn't even going to acknowledge her apology. But the silence was deafening.

She let out a deep sigh just as the tea kettle whistled. She poured it in her cup and decided to run a hot bath while she sat in front of the fire. That would warm her chilly skin and even chillier nerves. She texted Marie, who said she was feeling better today, then turned to go upstairs when she heard a knock at the door. She could see from the window that it was Andrew standing outside, his hands in his pockets. She felt her muscles clench, but turned and forced herself to open the door. She hoped he couldn't hear her heart racing.

"Hey," she managed. She tried to sound casual, even though the sight of him had set adrenaline racing through her.

"Hey, Anna," he said, "do you think I could come in for a second?" His voice sounded so sincere, and she registered again the effect it had on her.

"Sure." She pushed open the screen to let him in. She couldn't believe she was watching him walk into the living room right now. The fire had warmed the room. "Do you want to sit down? Can I get you something to drink?" she offered, not sure if she sounded pathetic or like any good host.

"No, I think I'm fine. Unless you want one?" he said.

"I'm fine. I mean I have one," she said, putting her mug down. They both sat down on the couch, and next to him her heart pounded in her chest. The picture window behind their heads had a reflection of the fireplace perfectly centered between them. Andrew took off his coat, and Anna noticed he had taken off his overalls. His cargo pants and boots looked like the same ones he used to wear. She picked at the edges of her jeans at her ankles, which she had tucked underneath her.

She was surprised when he grabbed her hand. "Look, Anna, I'm sorry I didn't really respond to you today on the boat. I wasn't expecting to see you, and I definitely wasn't expecting an apology from you for breaking us up. I actually kept trying to say something back, but I had way too many thoughts about everything. And, well, here's the thing," he said, running his hands through his thick hair. "I'm not sure I agree with you. I don't think it was all your fault." He got up and walked over to the fire, and used the poker to adjust one of the logs that had fallen, he sleeves rolled up revealing his strong arms. He came back and sat down, and it seemed to Anna that his closeness set off something in every molecule in her body.

He let out a sigh. "Yesterday, I was at my parents' house, and I watched my mom help my dad get out of the house before we all went out to dinner. He was having a really bad day, and she got him in his wheelchair, and got on his shoes, and brushed his hair, and put on his sweater, and then," Andrew stopped, and took Anna's hand. "She leaned down to kiss him. And they smiled at each other. And when I think…when I think about how she pours herself out, unselfishly, for that love, and how happy they are, I doubt every decision I've ever made. My choices just seem so…selfish."

Anna looked up at him. "No, Andrew, you're not selfish. You were right, you belong in Maine. I'm the one who was selfish. I expected you to drop your whole life and follow me because I was mad at my dad. And then I left you, when you had shown me nothing but love.

It's my fault. I should never have hurt you like that."

Andrew shook his head. "I can't stop thinking about you Anna. I belong wherever you are. I know that now. I need you."

Her heart thumped in her chest, and deep down, Anna knew she needed this strong, brave, honest person too. She was silent as she tried to think of everything she wanted to say to him. She didn't dare hope that he would still feel this way for her.

But he did.

"I need you too." Anna looked straight into his eyes. "I'm so sorry, Andrew. I didn't know I was ending us," she said quietly. Anna's eyes filled with tears, and she wiped them away as they spilled on her cheek. She felt so relieved to get it all out, to tell Andrew how much she understood, and how she regretted her choice.

Andrew reached over and wiped a tear on her cheek. "It's okay. You don't need to be sorry." And he kissed her.

In that kiss was all the healing they both could have ever hoped for. It wasn't cautious or tender, it was the language of their pure need and love for each other, made stronger through time, translated through something more powerful than words. She couldn't believe what release, what relief, this kiss held. She could barely think. He held her head between his hands tenderly. Finally, he pulled away carefully and was quiet for a moment. He looked at her said, "I love you. I have always loved you. I realized a few years ago how much I needed you. When I did my research trips, I used to go into every museum or gallery I could find. Anyplace that had paintings on their walls, really. Every port, every town. I felt like I was looking for something, and I couldn't put my finger on what it was. After a few trips, I realized what I was looking for was you. The paintings or galleries were the closest thing I had to you, to remind me of you. Now, I have you here, in my arms." He looked into her eyes. "Is it really you?" Anna nodded and kissed him again, her heart overflowing with joy. Andrew did care. All these years, he had still loved her. She was not prepared for this gift.

Chapter 26

They fell asleep talking, catching up on almost seven years' worth of their separate lives, and woke up the next morning to a high beeping noise, their necks stiff from sleeping on the couch. "Sorry to wake you," he whispered. "My phone goes off at this time every morning." Threw the slits of her eyes, Anna looked outside. It was still so dark out, she wasn't sure she believed him that it was even morning. He held her close and kissed her neck from her shoulder to her ear, then whispered, "So are you going to crash my work today?"

She laughed and playfully shrugged. "I think I have sufficiently embarrassed myself doing that," she said, her smile lighting up her eyes. Andrew bent down and kissed her.

He was a few minutes late to the boat.

Anna put on a sweatshirt and yoga pants and went downstairs to make coffee. It was strange going through a normal routine when her whole world had changed. Her love for Andrew was so strong and pure. Now she got to feel it, let it fill every part of her. It didn't have to be buried or covered up or ignored. And the amazing thing was he loved her back. She thought of Raphael suddenly, and how hurt he must feel, how painful it was that she couldn't love him back this way. She felt guilty to suddenly be this happy while realizing he was heartbroken. She told herself that he was probably already dating some pretty young girl who loved living in the city.

Anna worked down at the boathouse all morning, settling the art supplies she had brought, and sketching a little. She was right – something about the weathered walls of the boathouse let her ideas flow freely, and she did three rough sketches that she would try to turn into paintings for Miami. Around lunchtime, she made her way to Marie's house. She couldn't wait to tell her about Andrew. And Marie said she had news too when she had texted her. She wondered what it could be. In the middle of her thoughts, her phone rang. It was Georgia.

"Hey, Anna," she said. "I'm taking a quick minute for lunch but wanted to see if I could catch you." Anna could hear the voices shouting inside the sandwich shop she must have been in. "You will never believe what happened."

"What?" Anna asked.

"Jake asked if we could get back together."

"No way," Anna said, stunned. "I totally called that, remember? He would get out there and get lonely. Do you want to?"

"Are you kidding? And dump this cute new guy I'm seeing tonight? Not a chance."

Anna laughed. "So glad you are on the mend. Can't wait to meet him."

"I know, just had to tell you the news. How's Maine?"

"About as amazing as possible," Anna answered smiling.

"Well don't you sound happy! What happened?"

"Andrew came over last night. We talked and realized we still had a lot between us," Anna said.

"Oh my gosh! I can't believe it. Good thing you listened to that voice, Anna."

"Thanks, Georgia. I am just thankful he'll take me back."

"Oh, I think fate is somewhere in all of it, don't you think?"

"Yes, that's what we call it when you end up with the person you are supposed to end up with, isn't it?"

"Yes. Well, I guess I have fate to thank for not having to put up with Jake's vanity sessions in the bathroom and chronic lateness. We'll save that for some other lucky lady." Anna couldn't help laughing at her friend as they said goodbye and she hung up the phone.

When she walked into Marie's house, she found Henry playing with blocks on the floor while he watched Elmo. She snuck up quietly until she got her hands right under his armpits; then she tickled him until his shrieking got so loud her ears were practically bleeding.

"How's my little munchkin doing?" she said, covering him with kisses. He laughed so hard, his pure joy overflowing her heart.

Marie walked in with a slight smile. "Auntie Anna is here, and she is much better entertainment than red furry puppets" she said, laughing.

"It's true," Anna said. "That's because I know how to tickle!" She tickled him some more, followed by more kisses, then let him return to his show. She got up and turned to her sister. "Are you feeling any better?"

"A little. Trying to eat something every hour or so and I think it helps. So what was the big news you had to tell me about?" Anna let herself think back to her amazing night with Andrew for just a moment. A huge smile formed on her face, and Marie was looking bewildered. "What is it?" she pleaded.

"Andrew," Anna said, smiling.

"What! You are kidding me. What happened? Tell me everything, every detail . . . wait, not every detail."

"Well, I went out lobstering with him yesterday, and I told him what I had been thinking. That I was sorry for everything that had happened between us. I had blamed him for so long, and that I realized it was my fault too. He didn't say too much because Chris was there. But he came over to Uncle Charlie's house later, and I don't know. We just righted everything between us, I guess. We still have so many feelings for each other. It just feels very right." Anna couldn't stop smiling. "Actually, it feels more than right. It feels like Champagne on Christmas."

"Oh my gosh. That is amazing. I am so happy for you. Wow, you've had a lot going on for being home for two days. Oh, speaking of having a lot going on, you'll never believe who Dad just asked to bring to dinner here."

"Who?"

"The woman from the new gallery over by Riley's."

Anna sat dumbfounded on the stool at her sister's island. "Abigail?"

"Yes, that is exactly who."

Anna tried to picture her father and Abigail together. Her dad was dating? The thought had never occurred to her. Of course he was free to date, but Anna had always assumed he was still not over her mother. Which was probably true.

"Wow, how long has that been going on?" Anna asked Marie. She thought of what she had told Abigail about her father, and wondered if she'd said anything to him.

"I'm not sure, but I think before Uncle Charlie died. I think it was so new at the funeral he wasn't ready to tell anyone, but apparently now he is. I guess we know why he started to act so different."

"Well, did he tell you about Aunt Sheila?" Anna asked. So much had happened she hadn't even updated Marie on this piece of their history.

"He did, actually. He said he understood a lot better about why he treated you the way he did after Mom died. He said he tried to explain it all to you?"

"Yes," Anna said. The relief of laying down the burden between her and her father swept over her again.

"He said that Abigail helped him a lot. To see it all more clearly."

So she had Abigail in part to thank for her reconciliation with her dad, she thought. Love has such an amazing way of healing. She couldn't picture her father with anyone else before, which was unfair. He deserved to be happy too.

"Wow. I am so happy for him. How are you feeling about it?"

"The same. Just happy, and relieved. I didn't ever think about Dad dating someone. But based on the change in him, I would say it is just what the doctor ordered."

Anna laughed. She just had a funny picture of everyone at Marie's house for dinner. "So should I bring Andrew over too? Let Dad have another shock?"

"Why not?" Marie answered. "But get ready. You may have to cook. My nausea won't let me near the stove."

"No problem," said Anna. "We'll just have lobster."

Chapter 27

Summer seemed to settle in New Harbor as soon as Anna decided to stay. Genevieve was so thrilled Anna agreed to show alongside her mother's paintings in December she told her to paint every day. She had already hired a new gallery girl. The tourists started to trickle into New Harbor and Damariscotta. Anna worked every day and had completed a series of paintings she was calling *Pemaquid*. And every night, Andrew came over for dinner, and they sat outside, sometimes with a glass of wine, enjoying the quiet beauty of a Maine summer evening.

Anna worked on a few changes to her uncle's house. She got rid of the linoleum. Andrew and Chris helped her put down some wide pine boards and she loved it. She also repainted the room she was sleeping in to a light blue that matched the color of the sky on most mornings. But her favorite addition was hanging the picture she had painted of St. Patrick's over the mantel. She credited her moment of grace at her mother's grave with her current happiness and all the healing that had gone into her relationships. That, and Abigail's relationship with her dad.

She couldn't believe the way her dad was around Abigail. So protective. A little like he had been with her mother. He was his best self. Gracious, loving, kind. And Abigail could share his love of art, and her sense of humor had them all laughing constantly. She couldn't imagine anything better than finding love again with Andrew. Then life went and surprised her. Turns out her father finding love again made her pretty happy too.

She said lots of prayers these days. All in gratitude.

One night, as she and Andrew sat outside under the stars, his arms wrapped around her, they looked up at the North Star. He told her stories about fishermen who survived using the star to navigate home long ago. "You know, I used it too."

"What do you mean?" Anna asked. She knew Andrew relied on his navigation equipment.

"I used to talk to the North Star when I was out doing research. I just pretended it was you. It always helped me stay on the path I needed to be. I actually should tell you about the last trip I took."

Anna turned and looked at his face. "What happened?"

"That girl I brought to the gala. Her name is Elaine. She was on that trip with me. She lives in Oregon. We got serious, but we were alone, out on the water every day. It felt easy. As it got toward the end of the trip, it seemed like we might keep our relationship going after we were done. But that night as we sat under the stars, I looked at the North Star and knew. I still loved you. And I beat myself up plenty for not getting over you, for not grabbing this chance at happiness with this woman. When I got back from that trip, suddenly you were here. Like it was meant to be. But then, you had a boyfriend, and I was totally confused. I flew her out for that weekend to see if I could maybe just get over it, when I knew you were with Raphael. But it didn't work. When she left, we said goodbye. Now I know the stars were just making sure they led me back to you."

Anna sat quietly for a minute. She wasn't shocked or hurt by Andrew's confession. She once again felt gratitude. And relief. Relief that Andrew waited for her.

She cuddled in closer. He held her tighter. She looked up at the stars again.

"I have something I should tell you too," she said.

"What's that?" Andrew said. He put his chin on her shoulder.

"You know that I worked in a gallery in the city, right?"

"Right," he said.

"Well, it grew into something more. I had been painting all along, and a few years ago, my boss held an opening for me. It went really well. I sold out. Then she held another one and I sold all of it too. We were invited to Art Basel Miami, this big art show in December. She wants me to show with my mom's stuff too. When I found out we were invited, I wasn't sure I wanted to stop being just Anna Goodrich, to tell the world I was Therese McAllister's daughter. But when my dad and I healed so much, I wasn't afraid anymore. So I am showing there, in December, with my mom's paintings." She looked up to try to read his face.

"So can I come crash the show?" he said, smiling. "I have a great baseball cap and hoodie; I am sure you would never even know I was there." Anna started laughing, and they couldn't stop, remembering her in Andrew's classroom.

"You can come if you want to, as my guest, of course."

"I wouldn't miss it for the world," he said as he kissed her. Anna's phone started to ring next to them.

"Hold on one sec," Anna said, raising her eyebrows apologetically at Andrew. "Hey Marie, what's up?" she said.

"Hi Anna. I am sorry to call so late but I just put Henry down. I'm calling to see if you have some time in the morning. I wanted to talk to you and wondered if I could come over for coffee around 9:30?"

"Sure," Anna said to Marie. She noticed Marie sounded strange. Not stressed exactly…scared. Marie sounded afraid. Anna grew anxious but tried to sound casual. "That time works great for me, are you bringing the little guy?"

"No, Mike has a day off and he is planning to go fishing with him. I'll see you tomorrow morning?"

"Yes, see you then," Anna said. She hung up her phone and looked at Andrew.

"Everything ok?" he asked.

"I'm not sure," Anna answered as she grabbed Andrews hand in hers. "I'll know more tomorrow, when Marie is coming over for coffee to talk."

She looked out at the ocean, and thought of the happiness she had just found again with Andrew, the happiness that sat with them here, outside under the stars, like it was its own separate being. It seemed to look over at her with a calm, wise expression. *You knew this couldn't last, right?*

The next morning, Anna woke up early to a beautiful sunny day, but despite the weather she had a knot in her stomach. She scowled at the clock that said 5:30, wishing she could hurry up and talk to Marie and find out what was going on. What couldn't just be said over the phone? Maybe something was wrong with the pregnancy? With Mike? She tried to go out to the boat house and paint to keep her mind occupied, but after a little while she gave up, and went for a run instead. By the time she was toweling off she was starting to feel better, and the doorbell rang just as she finished getting dressed.

Marie smiled and gave her a hug as she came in. She looked tired and pale. Probably the nausea, Anna thought.

"I was just going to make more coffee; do you want some?"

Marie laughed a little nervously. "I don't know what I was thinking when I said that, I haven't been able to drink coffee in weeks. Wishful thinking, I guess. Do you have any tea? I can drink that for some reason."

"Sure," Anna said as she turned the pot on to boil. "So what's up?" she asked with her hand on her hip, looking at her big sister.

Marie put down her keys and her sunglasses and sat down, letting out a deep sigh. She wore jeans and her favorite striped t-shirt, and Anna saw dots of yogurt on her sleeve from Henry's breakfast. Her brown hair was just starting to show a few strands of gray around her face, but Anna noticed it looked healthy and strong, which almost overshadowed her pale face and made her sister look healthy. "Well, it's not great news." Marie sat back and put her feet up on the chair next to her and sighed deeply. She crossed her arms. "Before I became pregnant, I started seeing a new OB/GYN doctor - a new one to me since I had Henry in Upstate New York. At my first visit, a few months ago I gave him our family's medical history, and he paused when he heard about mom and grandma dying so young from ovarian cancer. He suggested I have some genetic tests done. I really didn't think anything of it since I've been so out of it with the pregnancy and morning sickness and Henry, but...the tests just came back." Marie's voice cracked, and like a break in a damn, that crack let all of the waters she had been holding back rush forward. She closed her eyes tightly as tears streamed down her face. "They're not good, Anna. They show that I have the faulty BRCA gene. A gene that's mutated and will very likely give me breast or ovarian cancer. It mutated somewhere down our DNA line, and because of that mom and grandma developed cancer so young. Which sucks even more. Because it means that they didn't just get cancer, they were born with a death sentence, but didn't know it. How unfair is that?"

Anna sat there, stunned. She could barely process all the information Marie was giving her. Such a rush of emotions went off in her, and she felt foggy-headed as she tried to make sense of what she was saying.

"So what do we do next?" Anna asked.

"The best options are surgery to remove the parts affected, and I talked it over with Mike. I'm going to have a hysterectomy soon after this baby, and a double mastectomy too, after I am done nursing." Marie broke down again. She began sobbing and leaned over and reached for her sister. She gripped her tightly as the depth of her fears came bubbling up through her tears. Anna held her and let her cry for a few minutes. Finally she pulled away and reached for a tissue on the table. "I really wanted more kids. But I don't want to risk that for Henry and Mike and this baby. I can't believe this is it for our family. But Anna," she said as she tried to recover herself as she dabbed the tissue under her eyes, "you should get tested too."

Anna sat silently with her arms crossed. She closed her eyes and pictured her mother in her bed, right before she died. Her bird-like arms, her bald head, and her big beautiful eyes tinged with pain as she lay under a pile of blankets because she was so cold. It felt like someone was playing over her feelings like a keyboard; grief and worry for Marie, the briefest moment of worry for herself, then two notes started to play rhythmically in her head: anger and regret. That her mother could still be alive if they had this test fifteen years ago. Maybe even ten years ago. What a waste her pain and death may have been. Watching someone you love suffer is beyond difficult. To think that any of the suffering could have been avoided felt like torture.

"Anna, say something," Marie said.

"I'm just thinking. Of mom." Anna said, her eyes starting to fill with tears. "I can't believe it." The whistle started to blow on the stove, and she wiped the tears as they hit her cheeks and got up to make the tea. It took a lot of energy just to stand up, she noticed.

"I know." Marie said. "That was the first thing I thought of too. And my next thought was that it felt like a ticking bomb in my genes, waiting to go off. I just want to get the bomb out. Thank God - for Henry's sake - that I have that choice. Mom never did. But Henry only gets this sibling. That's it. It sucks. I know we could adopt, and maybe we will, I just loved the idea of more."

Anna carried the cups over, sat down and grabbed Marie's hand, and looked at her. A moment ago she had seen her healthy hair and thought Marie looked strong. Now the news changed her perception of her sister ever so slightly, and she thought she could see shadows under her eyes and her shoulders sag. "You won't be alone. Henry and this baby won't just have each other. You all have us. I am so glad I'm home now. And whatever happens with my test, I can only hope I will be as strong as you are."

"Thanks Anna. I'm glad your home now too. I don't know how I would be able to get through this without you." They hugged for a long time, while the skies turned from blue to overcast, a New England storm coming in, changing the day without warning.

That night, Andrew had asked Anna to go out on a proper date. He was taking her to a nearby inn that had an amazing restaurant, with a great wine list and a stone fireplace. He knew from their brief phone call after he got off the boat the news from Marie wasn't good, but he told her to wait to tell him after their second sip of Champagne. The first sip was a toast to their one month anniversary.

As Anna got dressed for their evening, rifling through the drawers she had finally put her clothes in, she couldn't stop thinking of Marie. She grieved for her sister. But she noticed her own detachment about the fact that she might one day get the same news. It was sort of like being told 'you might get cancer', she decided. There's no cancer yet, so it's hard to pinpoint the fear, yet it was there. It made it hard to process.

But if she got the news - she had booked the first appointment she could to get tested in a few weeks, and the results took a month or two - what would it feel like to know that you needed to make yourself infertile to survive? That put the whole dilemma into a new light. It wasn't just chemo and radiation as an action plan. It was no babies. For Marie, there was some mercy finding out while carrying her second baby, but still a loss of a dream for her. For Anna, getting back Andrew while putting their ability to have kids in jeopardy felt like the universe was playing a cruel joke on her. Come on, you're going out for your one month anniversary, you don't need to figure out your whole life, she chided herself as she buttoned the keyhole closure of her blouse behind her neck. But that was what this news did. It made her think about her whole life. What risks to take? What choices? Anna still didn't know.

When Andrew came to the door, he looked so handsome in a white button down, tweed jacket and jeans. He had a bouquet of daisies for her. She smiled from ear to ear; he remembered her favorite flower from so long ago. They were one month in, but they had another lifetime of memories to draw from, she realized. *I am in deep*, she thought as she smiled up at him and took the flowers.

The whole way to the restaurant they talked about memories from when they were very young and teased each other about who had said I love you first. They settled into their corner of the restaurant with a bottle of Champagne between them and, as he promised, Andrew toasted to their one month anniversary. They clinked their glasses and took a sip, and after the warmth from the bubbles had settled down into them, he turned to look at her. He shook his head from side to side and smiled.

"What?" Anna asked.

"I just can't believe we're here. Together, right now in this restaurant. In Maine. Life is so strange. We're so unbelievably lucky. I love you, Anna. And I just wanted to tell you that before you tell me what's going on with Marie."

Anna smiled and put both of her hands in his hand and squeezed them tight. Falling in love a second time with the same man – with Andrew - was indeed unbelievably lucky. But she couldn't resist setting the record straight.

"So you're saying I love you. First again, huh?" she let herself laugh for a moment, and take in the joy of laughing with him again. "I love you too, Andrew. I can't believe we are together either, but I'm so thankful I found my way back to you." Then her smile faded, and she tried to face up to the news she had to share. She didn't know why but she was so afraid to tell Andrew.

"Marie told me that she had some tests done, and she has a gene, a faulty gene, that will make her predisposed to cancer. It was passed down from my grandmother and my mom, who both had cancer so early, and died so young, because of this genetic mutation. So, she is going to get a hysterectomy after the baby, and a double mastectomy after this baby is weaned. Her focus is Henry, and Mike, which is really good. She wants to do everything she can to be there for them." Anna took one of her hands out of his and took a big sip of her Champagne.

Andrew looked down for a while without speaking, brushing his thumb over the back of her other hand. Finally he looked up and asked, "What about you? Doesn't that mean that you could have the same gene?"

"Yes. I hate for you to think about it and to worry at all. But I made an appointment to get tested and will know in three months or so. But I would be lying if I said I didn't make me worry about us. How far does our luck run, do you think?"

Andrew took his hand and brushed the side of her face. He looked in her eyes. "Anna, there is nothing, nothing that could change how I feel about you. You know that right?"

Anna felt her stubborn streak rise up, and she felt like she had to know the answer to the question that weighed on her the most. "But what if I couldn't have any kids, Andrew? What if the risks end up so high that I shouldn't wait until after I have kids to do the same surgery Marie is doing?"

Andrew laughed. "Then we are going to be the best adoptive parents in Maine. We'll figure out a way to share our love, and our incredible luck, with little ones somehow. It would just be a different path that I would get to walk with you. You next to me on any path, for as long as possible, is what I care the most about."

Anna felt her face fall more deeply into his hand. He had, with those words, removed all of her concern, all of her worry. She smiled at him as she leaned toward him. "Thank you for saying that. I love you, Andrew," and she kissed him softly.

The next day, Anna sat with her father and Abigail and Marie on the back deck at Marie's, drinking lemonade. The air was moist and sticky. Even after a short storm the humidity was so thick you could cut it with a knife, but Anna didn't mind. The pressure of the air against her skin made her feel like some force was holding her up, giving her support in this moment. Anna knew they would eventually talk about Marie's test results. That same crushing anger came back and sat on her chest when she thought about her mother, how if they had known about all this just a few years earlier, she might have been here today.

She worried about her father's reaction to the news. Based on how long and hard he struggled to get to higher ground after her death, Anna was worried the news could easily shatter his new happiness too, but he needed to know. She called her Dad and Abigail and told them to come over to Marie's for dinner. He said they would bring dinner, since he wanted Marie to rest and not have to do anything. When they came in, Abigail looked beautiful in a green blouse that set off her dark hair and hazel eyes. She came in carrying a casserole dish that was filled with pasta, chicken, spinach and bacon that smelled amazing. The top was smothered in caramelized onions and more bacon, and Anna was equal parts thankful and hungry. Abigail could make delicious food. Marie had someone else now who could be there with a meal. Everyone but Marie devoured it in minutes, and Abigail promised her to make it again when she felt better. Henry kept yelling 'more pasta!' It was so comforting to lose herself in the delicious flavors of the creamy cheese – Abigail said it was Asiago – that Anna almost forgot why Marie had invited them all over.

After they had all settled on the deck and laughed at Henry's performance of The Itsy Bitsy Spider, Marie settled him to play in the yard while they all sipped lemonade. Anna noticed her Dad's leg bounced up and down, a nervous twitch she remembered from sitting next to him for hours in the hospital, after surgeries and treatments and pain medications administered to her mother.

"Dad, I have something to tell you that might not be easy to hear," Marie started, Mike sitting next to her holding her hand. Anna stared at Henry playing in the sandbox, shoveling the sand into the back of a dump truck happily over and over. "My doctor just gave me some test results. They say that I inherited the BRCA gene, which causes breast or ovarian cancer in 45 to 90% of the people who carry it. It's likely the reason that mom and grandma got cancer. They just didn't know about it back then." Marie said it slowly, all the while she keeping her hand on her belly.

They sat quietly for a few moments, the sound of Henry talking to himself mingling with the rise and fall of the chirping from the birds in the trees and the sound of crickets at the edge of the yard.

Their father stared at Henry, then up at the clouds. He breathed in deeply. "Do you mean…are you saying you have…" he began.

"I don't have cancer yet," Marie said. "But I will have to have surgery – a double mastectomy and hysterectomy – to lower my risk of getting it. Because right now that risk is really high. And if I have an option not to live with that high of a risk, for Henry's sake, and for this baby's sake, and for Michael, then I need to do that."

Mike squeezed her hand. "We're incredibly thankful we get to keep you."

Anna's father was silent for a moment, thinking and shaking the ice cubes in his glass of lemonade. Then he said, "You mean, if we had known, if these tests had been around, your mother might have had a chance?"

"You could look at it that way," Anna chimed in. "What-ifs are a recipe for misery, but theoretically, yes." They were silent for a while. Then she spoke again. "There is a chance I carry it too, but I'm getting tested soon. We'll see in a few months."

"Both of you girls might have it?" he asked.

Abigail came over and put her arm around Marie. "What about Stephen?" she asked.

"If he carries it, Stephen could develop some cancers later on too, but his risk is much lower, closer to the chances of the normal population," Marie said. "I already called him and he was super supportive, but laughed at the idea of getting tested himself. We'll see if he still feels that way when he's a dad. But there is nothing he would need to do."

Anna's father stood up and looked down at Henry. "I can't even begin to think about losing you girls," her dad said. "Thank God for your doctor, Marie. For telling you to get tested."

"Yes, I am so thankful to him. And don't worry, we're not going anywhere, Dad," Marie said, taking a deep breath and starting to smile. "But you are."

"What do you mean?"

"Well, right before this baby is due, in December, your daughter Anna has been invited to show at Art Basel Miami. And you're invited. So you have to get on a plane and fly down to Florida and be her special guest." Marie switched back into her role as supportive older sister with relief.

He turned to Marie with a quizzical look on his face. "What?"

"You're invited to my art show at Art Basel Miami," Anna said.

She and Marie had decided to announce this right after the test results to help him with the news.

"Wait, Anna," he said, pointing his finger at her. "First you have to promise me something. You have to promise me that whatever Marie does, whatever surgery or care she gets, you do it too, if you need to."

Anna nodded. "I promise, Dad."

"Good. Now, how in the world are you are showing at Miami Basel?"

"It's a long story, Dad."

"We've got time," he said. "Thank God."

The next day, Andrew made good on his promise to take Henry out on the boat. He was trying to distract everyone and have fun, which Anna was so thankful for. The harbor was busy, even at midday, with boats coming in and dropping off their lobsters at the Co-op and tourists climbing aboard the Hardy Boat cruise that headed out to Monhegan Island. Anna smiled as they pulled into the harbor, and held up her hand to shield the sun as he pulled up to the dock to meet her, Marie, Mike, and Henry. She thought back to Marie asking for this trip when they all bumped into each other at Shaw's Wharf the weekend of Uncle Charlie's funeral. She remembered thinking how strange that would feel. She couldn't believe they were here now, boarding his boat, or that just a few months ago her life was in New York City, and now her family going on Andrew's boat was totally normal.

Andrew smiled at Henry, his hair as messy as usual, his eyes crinkling on the sides as he smiled at the little boy and helped him on board. "Here you go, squirt," he said as put on a tiny life jacket and a captain's hat on his head. "You ready to go on a boat ride?"

Henry squealed and shouted, "Yes, I am!" before he ran to the wheel of the boat and pretended to steer. They pulled out of the harbor, the waves hitting the boat as they sped up across the water toward the Pemaquid Lighthouse. "Whoa," said Henry. "Are we gonna go fast?"

"You bet we are, Henry. You ready to go get some lobster? You want to help me drive?" Henry shouted yes loud enough to be heard in Canada, and helped Andrew steer. Anna and Marie sat down across from a pile of traps.

"How are you feeling?" Anna asked her.

"Okay," Marie said. "I am super nauseous but if I sleep enough and eat crackers around the clock, I'll survive. I hopefully only have a few more weeks of it."

Anna thought about being on a boat at sea when you were already nauseous and felt pity for her sister. "It doesn't sound fun."

"No, it's not. But when I realize what a miracle it is that we found out about everything, I can't really complain about anything. I'll take a little nausea instead of what could have been." Anna stared out at the water. Silently, she wondered what her test results would be. What if she couldn't have kids? She tried hard not to wrap her head around it because it hurt too much. And she tried instead to be grateful, like Marie was doing, that she was together with Andrew. The fact that he had already declared they would make it through whatever news they got, and adoption was always an option, made Anna's heart skip a beat. She was in love with such a good man.

They pulled up to the blue and white buoys in front of the lighthouse, and he asked Henry if he wanted to help him pull them up. "Oh boy, I'm going to catch a lobster!" Henry shouted.

"Yes you are," said Andrew. They pulled the trap up, and there, sitting in the trap, was a blue lobster.

"What the…." Andrew gasped. "No way!"

"What is it?" asked Henry. "Is it a lobster?"

"Yes, it's a lobster, all right." Andrew said in awe. "A very special one, that is very rare." Anna stared at the blue shell on the squirming creature. "Think it's a good luck charm, Anna?" Andrew said laughing, the wind blowing his hair.

Anna stared in disbelief at the trap. "A blue lobster. I can't believe it," Anna said, laughing. She hoped it was an answer from the universe about what she had been silently thinking about. Good luck does happen.

"Do you think a genetic mutation makes our luck?" Marie said. "I hope not."

It took Anna a minute to realize what she meant. She put her arms around her sister. "I'm sorry hon."

Marie sighed. "I don't mean to be a downer. I guess it does get to you after a while. Plus I'm pregnant. I'm overly emotional about everything. But I'm especially touchy about mutant genes." She laughed and hugged Anna back, then looked at the lobster with Henry.

"What do you think, bud?" she asked.

"More lobsters!" said Henry.

"The kid is right," said Andrew. "Let's get some more lobsters! We'll get some pictures when we get back to the dock." Andrew pointed out the buoys with his father's blue and white marking to Henry and told him to count how many of those he could see. Marie helped him as they trolled up to each. Andrew turned to Anna and put his arm around her. "Remember the first time we met?"

"Of course I do," she answered smiling.

"I thought you were the most beautiful girl in the world looking over that lobster that summer." Anna smiled at his bright red cheeks, twinkling blue eyes, and rubbed the reddish-brown stubble he let grow during the summer, and put her head on his shoulder. Suddenly, she knew what her next painting would be for her collection.

Chapter 28

Five Months Later

"Darling, come over here, I want you to meet someone," Genevieve called over to Anna. It was only the hundredth time she had done this in the last hour. They were at an outside party next to the gallery where the official Art Basel paintings were on display, letting people wander through the show in between drinking cocktails and eating canapés. Anna was waiting for the young, inebriated crowd to wind up in the pools they were surrounded by, but on the whole the art show was a big fun party.

"Wait here," Anna said to Andrew, "and if anyone walks by with meat on a stick, grab it for me please. I'll be right back." She was smiling as she made her way around the pool to Genevieve.

"This is the artist, Anna Goodrich," Genevieve said as she put her arm around Anna. "Anna, this is Steven Bennington and Mort Shapiro, and they love what you've done. They are building a few new hotels and they are hoping you might be able to provide them with some statement pieces for their lobbies." Genevieve loved this part. Anna, not so much. But she loved Genevieve.

"Thank you, gentleman. I'm just happy to be here. This is my first time in Miami, and I love it." Anna smiled. After all of her worries, she was genuinely thrilled to be here. Especially since she came here with Andrew.

"You must have had an amazing childhood, painting with your mother. It's a lovely story," the one named Mort said.

Anna smiled. Feeling like her life was boiled down to a great PR pitch stung a little, but she was too happy right now to let it bother her completely. "It was, she was a lovely mother and we miss her so. But it feels great to celebrate her in this way."

"You're a natural at this schmoozing part," Genevieve gushed in her ear as she was pulled away by a group of people. "Thank you for not hating me." Anna smiled at her friend.

Andrew strolled up to them. He looked so handsome after getting plenty of sun on his face fishing in the Everglades all day yesterday while Anna hung her works with Genevieve. "Sorry to interrupt, but guess who's here?" Anna looked around and saw from the other side of the pool; her father was strolling towards them.

"Excuse me, gentleman. So glad to have met you both," Anna said, shaking their hands.

She walked over and hugged him. "I can't believe you actually made it! How was the flight?"

"It was great - Miami is so easy from Portland. Not sure why I haven't done this more often."

"That's great dad," Anna said. She couldn't believe how much he had changed in the last few months. He looked so relaxed and happy.

"Enough about me, though. Anna, I just looked over your collection. I am blown away," he said. "And seeing your collection with your mother's pieces," he said, choking up. "You were right about finding your path. You did it your way, and I couldn't be more proud of you." He held up his glass to hers, and toasted her.

Anna blushed. It was so amazing to her that her father was here, supporting her. She was thrilled he liked the show with her mom's art. When she had first looked at their exhibit, with her mom's paintings side by side with hers, it had been surreal. It was almost like a dream, like she was right back where she had started, painting in the barn, with her canvas next to her mother's. Now that her dad had seen it too, it felt even sweeter. The night couldn't be more perfect. The one exception was missing Marie and Stephen, but they had excellent excuses. Marie was due in a few weeks and couldn't fly, and

Stephen had declared that missing her show was the last straw – he was training his sous chef to step up more so he could be around for things like this. They could afford it now that his restaurant had taken off this past summer. And he promised by next summer he would spend a whole week with them on vacation in Maine.

"I know, I don't know why I was so against this before," Anna said. "Sunshine in December with lots of good food and wine? This feels pretty perfect to me right now. Of course, it could be because I live in Maine. It's different to have a taste of all the glamour every once in a while when I know I am going to be in the peace and quiet of a New England winter next week."

"Well, maybe you can join us next month for a bit of glamour in Boston," her father said. "We are invited to a fundraiser at the Berkley School of Music, and I would love for you to be there."

"Sure," Anna said. "But why are you invited there?"

"Because we started a scholarship there. The Sheila M. Goodrich piano scholarship. With Charlie's money," said her father.

Anna sighed and smiled. "Wow, dad, what a perfect idea. What did Aunt Catherine say about it?"

"Oh, it was my idea but we both went in on it," he smiled. "It's never too late to do the right thing, right?" He winked at Anna. "Now, where is Genevieve? I want to meet the woman who is responsible for all of this."

As if on cue, Genevieve strolled over to where they were standing.

"Don't tell me, Anna," she said, taking a sip of Champagne. "This must be your father. Delighted to meet you."

"Likewise. I can't thank you enough for giving my daughter this opportunity," he said. Anna couldn't believe how positive he was. Such a change in their relationship from six months ago.

"I can't thank you enough for raising such an artist," Genevieve said. "So when am I going to visit you all in Maine? I have a week in August I was hoping you could leave open for me, dear."

"August is perfect," Anna said. "Just in time for the nice weather and the tourists. Maybe my brother will be there then too."

"Oh, hold on darling, Julian Schnabel's over there and I have been dying to talk to him. Be right back," Genevieve said as she crossed to the other side of the pool. Anna couldn't help but smile seeing her friend so happy.

"I am dying to see a few of the other exhibits," her father said, holding up a brochure about the show. "Although I can tell you a few that I am going to be more than happy to skip. I do have to question some of their choices of artists. Garbage bags and spray paint just sounds horrible. But I'm going to run and see a few other artists. Can I meet you two later for dinner?" her father said. No matter how much he changed this year, he wasn't going to change his attitude on the art world.

Anna laughed. "Sure thing Dad, we'll meet you by the pool in an hour?"

They waved him off, and she turned to Andrew and kissed his cheek. "Thank you for being here too. It means everything, having you with me. I couldn't have imagined doing this alone." He smiled at her and kissed her

Genevieve came up next to them. "Ok, love birds. How do you feel about coming with me to a big party later with Heidi Klum and Leo DiCaprio?"

Anna and Andrew looked at each other. "No thanks," Anna said. "We're good."

"What? What do you mean? It's Leo Friging DiCaprio?"

"We're Mainers, Genevieve. We can't keep up with New York or Hollywood. At least I came to the show!" Anna laughed at her friend as she rolled her eyes and walked away.

The rest of the weekend was a blur. Anna was exhausted by the time they got to the airport, but Andrew seemed to be buzzing with excitement to return home. He was extremely cheerful as they packed up their hotel room and cabbed over to the airport. As they waited to board their plane, they sat by a Christmas tree studded with red and silver ornaments. Anna started at the reflection of people walking past in the ornaments while she sipped her coffee. "What do you want for Christmas, Andrew?" she asked.

"You," he said as he kissed the top of her head.

Anna slept the whole flight home, Andrew stroking her dark hair.

When they got back to Portland, it was snowing. They pulled out their winter coats from their suitcases and set out to explore the city, grabbing clam chowder and coffee and strolling through snowy streets and Christmas shoppers to look at the art galleries and shops there. Spending the afternoon together, unfettered, walking aimlessly, without hurry, after such an intense busy period felt sweetly peaceful. Anna felt like she could reach out and touch her happiness, like the snow.

They finally got back to Pemaquid late afternoon, just before the sun was setting. Andrew drove up to Uncle Charlie's house, which had a snowy dusting covering the driveway and a lone wreath on the door that Anna had put up before they left. Even though it was freezing out and a shock to their sun-warmed bodies, he asked Anna to come down to the dock with him for a minute. The late sunlight slanted across the frozen dock as they walked down to the wooden bench next to the boat house at the end of the dock. As they sat looking out at the ocean, the peace of being back home lapping at their hearts like the waves against the rocks below, Anna sighed a deeply happy sigh.

"You know what would be great?" he asked, looking out at the water.

"What's that?" Her hands were wrapped around his, her head resting on his chest.

"Well, since everyone is coming up next summer, why don't we just give them a wedding to attend?" he said, his face serious.

Anna stopped and looked up at Andrew. "What?"

"That is, if you will marry me?" he asked, his eyes shining, a smile turning up the corners of his mouth. Anna looked down. He was holding open a mussel shell, and in it was the most beautiful ring she had ever seen. "I asked your dad in Miami, and he gives his full blessing."

So many thoughts flashed through her mind jumbled together, but they all merged into one thought. Him. As her husband. "Oh, my gosh, Andrew. Yes, of course I will!" Anna cried, kissing him repeatedly, then looking down at her hand where he had placed the ring on her finger, and then kissing him again.

"I wanted to ask you for months but you were so busy getting ready for the show and I was finishing up my semester. I wanted to wait until all of it was completely over and we were back right here, where we belong. I am so proud of you, Anna. I can't believe I will be lucky enough to spend the rest of my life with you, as my wife." He kissed her just as tears sprang to her eyes.

"I am the lucky one, Andrew." She smiled. "You gave me another chance. And brought in the best, truest happiness I could have ever hoped to find in my life. Thank you. Thank you for loving me." She kissed him until their breath hung in clouds all around them, and they laughed as the cold air started to freeze their hands and noses. They went inside to light a fire, even though they were already lit from within.

The next day, as they ate a celebratory brunch at a cafe in Damariscotta, Mike called to say that Marie was in labor. She was a week early, but Anna was so glad she had waited until they returned from Miami to have the baby. They came over quickly to watch Henry, and then distracted him by taking him out to lunch at the coffee shop and playing at the train table at the bookstore downtown. Anna glancing at her phone eagerly. Finally, she got the call. Baby girl Therese Marie – Tessie for short - was here and they were all healthy. Marie would take a quick nap, and they could come see her after dinner.

When they reached the hospital, Henry ran ahead of them down the corridor carrying a pink balloon and teddy bear for his new sister. Anna held Andrew's hand with one hand and roses with the other, her heart bursting with joy at this moment in time. They walked into the room, and Anna kissed Marie hello and looked down at the beautiful little baby in the bassinet. Her charms were endless, her long eyelashes looked like caterpillars, and her thin coating of fuzzy black hair made her look like a princess. She was beautiful.

Anna stared at her face for what seemed like an eternity. Just then, Mike walked in the room. "Hey Anna! Andrew! Thanks so much for taking care of Henry," Mike said, every ounce the proud papa, kissing their cheeks, beaming. "Hey buddy! Want to meet your new sister?"

"Hold on, let me get some pictures," Anna said as Mike sat Henry next to Marie on the bed. Henry reached out and touched her tiny

nose and eyes. "Gentle, buddy, we can't touch her eyes," Marie said.
"Congratulations, she's so beautiful you guys." Anna gushed.
"Thanks. We feel so unbelievably lucky right now," Mike said
sweetly. Her sister's test results had brought out a compassionate side
of Mike that made Anna so happy for her to have him.
"Her nose is so tiny!" Henry shrieked, making them all laugh.
"Did you tell them the great news?" Andrew asked, taking the
baby out of Anna's hands. He looked so sweet with her, Anna had to
take deep breaths.
"We got engaged!" she said, holding up her ring.
"Oh, Anna that is fantastic," Marie smiled. The winter sunlight
streamed into the room as the sun was setting and the fragrance
from the roses filled the air. The baby started to fuss and Andrew
started to bounce the baby on his shoulder, which soothed her immediately.
Anna sat down next to her sister on the side of the bed to show her
the ring, and then took her hand. "So how was it? Having a baby?"
Marie looked back up at her, and put her head back on the pillow.
"It's absolutely amazing. Hurt like hell when we got here, but thank
God for epidurals. And then, seeing her face, and having her nurse
right away, I just can't even describe it. I feel like my heart exists outside my chest, for the second time." She glanced up from the baby,
and looked Anna in the eye. "I am so glad it's still possible for you
one day, Anna."
Anna smiled and nodded. "I still can't help but feel sort of guilty
that my test results came back negative for the gene."
Marie smiled at her. "Don't feel guilty, I am so happy for you! For
the test results and the engagement," she added laughing.
"You just had a baby and you're still worrying about me," she
laughed. "If you're trying for the big sister of the year award I think
you've got it," Anna smiled.
Marie reached out as Andrew handed her Therese back just as
she began to start fussing. "I know it is so morbid, and it is probably
just crazy hormones, but last night as I stared at her, I started to worry for her that she might, you know... that Therese might face this
horrible thing in her future. But then I realized, we McAllister wom-

an are tough as nails. She'll get through it just fine if she does have the faulty gene. She has all of us to help her. And thanks to modern medicine, she will have a very alive mother with a great boob job. She'll be fine."

Anna's eyes filled with tears. She thought of her mother's letter to her. *I don't think dying means I am not there. I think it means I am there in a different way. Of course, we don't want it to be this way. We want it to be so that I can help you get dressed on your wedding day. That I can hold your children just like I held you.* She suddenly felt such an ache for her mother it was palpable, like a punch to the gut. How much would Tessie miss not knowing her grandmother? How much would Marie miss not sharing her daughter and son with her mother? Some losses were not quantifiable; they stretched out like time, or space, and were infinite. Then she remembered the rest of her letter -

But I believe that love is more powerful than death. It has to be. I hope you can picture, like I do, that way down deep inside your heart, in the very fabric of your soul, there is a connection to another world. Love is a thread. A river. It connects those two worlds between your heart and Heaven. Even though I am going to be somewhere else, our love will still bind us together.

Anna smelled the roses in the room, and smiled. Her mother was right. Of course she was there. She would always be there.

Author's Note

Dear Reader,

Food has been such a big part of helping me tell this story, and of sharing the world that Anna and Andrew inhabit. No doubt this was because it has always played such a big role in my relationships, having grown up in a large family with a mother who was an amazing cook. Because it has been such a passion for me, I started a food blog, www.thehumbleonion.com to share the everyday art of food with others, and it has been so much fun. I wanted to share a few recipes that were the dishes I imagined them making in this story, some I created and some of which are family favorites.

Thank you for reading, and I hope you enjoy these dishes as much as I do.

Katie Curtis
March 2017

Tuscan Butter Basted Swordfish with Onions, Tomatoes and Capers

This recipe is one I created at home based on the dish that I imagined Stephen making for Anna when she goes to visit his restaurant. I can picture him showing Anna the butter basted fish technique (which I learned from reading Rick Moonen's book, Fish*), swirling the brown butter in the industrial pan with a white towel, while the simple Tuscan flavors of tomato, capers, wine and lemon reflect his clean style of cooking. Tuscan cooking leans more heavily on olive oil then butter, but the end result of butter basting fish is so flavorful I think they would make an exception. You can substitute any white fish for the swordfish and cook it the same way, adjusting the time for thickness of the filet.*

Ingredients:

2 tablespoons olive oil
1 medium onion, thinly sliced
2 garlic cloves, minced
2 ripe tomatoes, diced
Salt & pepper
½ cup white wine
Juice from 1 lemon
2 tablespoons of capers
2 swordfish steaks
8 tablespoons unsalted butter, divided (this is for the butter basting; don't worry, you leave most of it in pan)

Directions:

To make the Onion, Tomato & Caper Sauce: Heat olive oil in pan on medium heat. Add sliced onions and a small pinch of salt and cook until soft, about 5 minutes. Add garlic and cook for 1 minute. Add tomatoes and another 1 teaspoon salt and ½ teaspoon pepper. Cook for 5 minutes, then add wine and lemon juice. Cook for 10 minutes, then add capers and stir. Keep warm in pan to until ready to serve under fish.

To make Butter Basted Swordfish: Have a large spoon, spatula, and paper towels next to pan. Melt 4 tablespoons of the butter in a pan on medium-high heat (watch closely so butter doesn't burn, but you are looking for a nutty browned butter flavor so browning is good). Pat dry swordfish and season with salt and pepper. When the butter has melted, place in the far side of the pan and, using a spatula, press down on fish for the first 30 seconds, which helps the fish start to brown. Cut the other 4 tablespoons of butter into pieces and add to the pan. Tip pan toward you and using large spoon, continuously spoon butter on top of fish. Continuously tip, baste and set down pan again over heat, so that butter becomes nutty brown and top of fish is cooked, for 6 minutes. Then turn fish over, turn off heat, and let it sit in butter for 1 minute. Set on paper towels and use another to blot the top. Serve on a bed of the onion-tomato sauce, and sprinkle lemon and salt, if desired, on top of fish.

Chicken & Spinach Casserole with Bacon and Caramelized Onions:

This next dish I imagined Abigail bringing over to Marie's house when she gets the genetic test results back. Comfort food at its best. I wrote the recipe for my husband, whose love language is bacon, but it reminds me of the casseroles my mom would create for us growing up.

Ingredients:

3 cooked chicken breasts, cubed
2 tablespoons olive oil
2 onions, sliced
2 tablespoons thyme
1 pound of penne
4 tablespoons of butter
4 tablespoons flour
3 1/2 cups milk
1 cup shredded mozzarella
1 cup shredded asiago cheese
4 cups fresh spinach
6 bacon strips, crumbled

Directions:

1. Preheat oven to 350. Place chicken on tin-foil lined cookie sheet with salt, pepper and olive oil on top, then put tin foil over the pan (this keeps the chicken moist). Cook for 30 minutes, let cool 5 minutes before cubing.

2. Meanwhile, heat olive oil in pan over medium heat. Placed sliced onions, ¼ teaspoon salt and thyme in pan and stir until caramelized, about 15-20 minutes.

3. Bring large pot of salted water to a boil. Cook penne for 2 minutes less than package directions (since it will be cooked again in oven)

4. In large frying pan, cook 6 strips of bacon. Remove when cooked and lay on paper towel, reserving 2 tablespoons of the bacon drippings in the pan

5. Add spinach to bacon drippings with a ¼ teaspoon salt. Cook until wilted, about 4-5 minutes.

6. In the same pot used to cook pasta, melt 4 tablespoons butter. Add flour and whisk together to make a roux, cooking for 1 minute. Then add milk, stirring constantly until sauce starts to thicken and there are no lumps. Add 1 teaspoon salt, ½ teaspoon pepper, then add mozzarella and asiago and stir until cheese is melted.

7. Combine the pasta, chicken and spinach to the cheese sauce. Divide caramelized onions and bacon into two piles. Chop up half the onions and bacon and mix into pasta.

8. Spray a casserole pan with cooking spray and spoon mixture into pan. Put remaining caramelized onions and bacon crumbs on top and cook at 350 for 20-25 minutes or until golden and bubbly.

Jacques Pépin's Red Wine Beef Stew:

This is the dish Marie makes for dinner at her house. It is the most delicious beef stew I have ever had and I make it for special occasions. I felt her pain when Anna and her dad had ruined the meal because of their fight. It is truly memorable.

Ingredients:

tablespoon unsalted butter
2 tablespoons olive oil
2 pounds trimmed beef flatiron steak or chuck, cut into 8 pieces
Salt
Freshly ground black pepper
1 cup finely chopped onion
1 tablespoon finely chopped garlic
1 tablespoon all-purpose flour
One 750-milliliter bottle dry red wine
2 bay leaves
1 thyme sprig
One 5-ounce piece of pancetta
15 pearl or small Cipollini onions, peeled
15 cremini mushrooms
15 baby carrots, peeled
Sugar
Chopped fresh parsley, for garnish

Directions:

1. Preheat the oven to 350°. In a large enameled cast-iron casserole, melt the butter in 1 tablespoon of the olive oil. Arrange the meat in the casserole in a single layer and season with salt and pepper. Cook over moderately high heat, turning occasionally, until browned on all sides, 8 minutes. Add the chopped onion and garlic and cook over moderate heat, stirring occasionally, until the onion is softened, 5 minutes. Add the flour and stir to coat the meat with it. Add the wine, bay leaves and thyme, season with salt and pepper and bring to a boil, stirring to dissolve any brown bits stuck to the bottom of the pot.

2. Cover the casserole and transfer it to the oven. Cook the stew for 1 1/2 hours, until the meat is very tender and the sauce is flavorful.

3. Meanwhile, in a saucepan, cover the pancetta with 2 cups of water and bring to a boil. Reduce the heat and simmer for 30 minutes. Drain the pancetta and slice it 1/2-inch-thick, then cut the slices into 1-inch-wide lardons.

4. In a large skillet, combine the pancetta, pearl onions, mushrooms and carrots. Add the remaining 1 tablespoon of olive oil, 1/4 cup of water and a large pinch each of sugar, salt and pepper. Bring to a boil, cover and simmer until almost all of the water has evaporated, 15 minutes. Uncover and cook over high heat, tossing, until the vegetables are tender and nicely browned, about 4 minutes.

5. To serve, stir some of the vegetables and lardons into the stew and scatter the rest on top as a garnish. Top with a little chopped parsley and serve.

Adapted from *www.food&wine.com*

Indian Lamb and Spinach Curry (from Williams Sonoma):

This is such a foodie dish. I first saw it in my Williams-Sonoma Slow Cooker cook book, then it was reproduced in Oprah magazine after it has already become a favorite of mine. The perfume of flavors created between the lamb juices, garlic, ginger, cumin and turmeric are simply heaven.

Ingredients:

1/3 cup canola oil
3 yellow onions, chopped
4 garlic cloves, minced
2-inch piece fresh ginger, peeled and grated
2 tsp. ground cumin
1 1/2 tsp. Cayenne pepper
1 1/2 tsp. ground turmeric
2 cups beef broth
3 lb. boneless leg of lamb, cut into 1-inch cubes
1 Tbs. salt, plus more, to taste
6 cups baby spinach
2 cups plain yogurt

Directions:

Sauté the vegetables and spices

In a large fry pan over medium-high heat, warm the oil. Add the onions and garlic and sauté until golden, about 5 minutes. Stir in the ginger, cumin, cayenne and turmeric and sauté until fragrant, about 30 seconds more. Pour in the broth, increase the heat to high and deglaze the pan, stirring to scrape up the browned bits from the pan bottom. When the broth comes to a boil, remove the pan from the heat.

Cook the curry

Put the lamb in a slow cooker and sprinkle with the 1 Tbs. salt. Pour in the contents of the fry pan. Cover and cook on high for 4 hours or on low for 8 hours according to the manufacturer's instructions.

Finish the curry

Add spinach to the slow cooker and cook, stirring occasionally, until the spinach is wilted, about 5 minutes. Just before serving, stir 1 1/3 cups of the yogurt into the curry. Adjust the seasonings with salt. Spoon the curry into shallow bowls and serve immediately, passing the remaining 2/3 cup yogurt at the table. Serves 6 to 8.

Adapted from Williams-Sonoma Food Made Fast Series, *Slow Cooker,* by Norman Kolpas (Oxmoor House, 2007).

CPSIA information can be obtained
at www.ICGtesting.com
Printed in the USA
BVOW10s1501130717
489174BV00001B/17/P